The Further Adventu Cruso

Daniel Defoe

Published: 1719
Categorie(s): Fiction, Action & Adventure

About Defoe:

English novelist, pamphleteer and journalist Daniel Defoe is best known for his novels Robinson Crusoe and Moll Flanders.

Daniel Defoe was born in 1660 in London, England. He became a merchant and participated in several failing businesses, facing bankruptcy and aggressive creditors. He was also a prolific political pamphleteer which landed him in prison for slander. Late in life he turned his pen to fiction and wrote Robinson Crusoe, one of the most widely read and influential novels of all time. Defoe died in 1731.Daniel Foe, born circa 1660, was the son of James Foe, a London butcher. Daniel later changed his name to Daniel Defoe, wanting to sound more gentlemanly.

Defoe graduated from an academy at Newington Green, run by the Reverend Charles Morton. Not long after, in 1683, he went into business, having given up an earlier intent on becoming a dissenting minister. He traveled often, selling such goods as wine and wool, but was rarely out of debt. He went bankrupt in 1692 (paying his debts for nearly a decade thereafter), and by 1703, decided to leave the business industry altogether.

Having always been interested in politics, Defoe published his first literary piece, a political pamphlet, in 1683. He continued to write political works, working as a journalist, until the early 1700s. Many of Defoe's works during this period targeted support for King William III, also known as "William Henry of Orange." Some of his most popular works include The True-Born Englishman, which shed light on racial prejudice in

England following attacks on William for being a foreigner; and the Review, a periodical that was published from 1704 to 1713, during the reign of Queen Anne, King William II's successor. Political opponents of Defoe's repeatedly had him imprisoned for his writing in 1713.

Defoe took a new literary path in 1719, around the age of 59, when he published Robinson Crusoe, a fiction novel based on several short essays that he had composed over the years. A handful of novels followed soon after—often with rogues and criminals as lead characters—including Moll Flanders, Colonel Jack, Captain Singleton, Journal of the Plague Year and his last major fiction piece, Roxana (1724).

In the mid-1720s, Defoe returned to writing editorial pieces, focusing on such subjects as morality, politics and the breakdown of social order in England. Some of his later works include Everybody's Business is Nobody's Business (1725); the nonfiction essay "Conjugal Lewdness: or, Matrimonial Whoredom" (1727); and a follow-up piece to the "Conjugal Lewdness" essay, entitled "A Treatise Concerning the Use and Abuse of the Marriage Bed."

While little is known about Daniel Defoe's personal life—largely due to a lack of documentation—Defoe is remembered today as a prolific journalist and author, and has been lauded for his hundreds of fiction and nonfiction works, from political pamphlets to other journalistic pieces, to fantasy-filled novels. The characters that Defoe created in his fiction books have been brought to life countless times over the years, in editorial works, as well as stage and screen productions.

With Defoe's interest in trade went an interest in politics. The first of many political pamphlets by him appeared in 1683. When the Roman Catholic James II ascended the throne in 1685, Defoe—as a staunch Dissenter and with characteristic impetuosity—joined the ill-fated rebellion of the Duke of Monmouth, managing to escape after the disastrous Battle of Sedgemoor. Three years later James had fled to France, and Defoe rode to welcome the army of William of Orange—"William, the Glorious, Great, and Good, and Kind," as Defoe was to call him. Throughout William III's reign, Defoe supported him loyally, becoming his leading pamphleteer. In 1701, in reply to attacks on the "foreign" king, Defoe published his vigorous and witty poem The True-Born Englishman, an enormously popular work that is still very readable and relevant in its exposure of the fallacies of racial prejudice. Defoe was clearly proud of this work, because he sometimes designated himself "Author of 'The True-Born Englishman'" in later works.

Foreign politics also engaged Defoe's attention. Since the Treaty of Rijswijk (1697), it had become increasingly probable that what would, in effect, be a European war would break out as soon as the childless king of Spain died. In 1701 five gentlemen of Kent presented a petition, demanding greater defense preparations, to the House of Commons (then Tory-controlled) and were illegally imprisoned. Next morning Defoe, "guarded with about 16 gentlemen of quality," presented the speaker, Robert Harley, with his famous document "Legion's Memorial," which reminded the Commons in outspoken terms that "Englishmen are no more to be slaves to Parliaments than to a King." It was effective: the Kentishmen were released, and Defoe was feted by the citizens of London. It had been a courageous gesture and one of which Defoe was ever afterward proud, but it undoubtedly branded him in Tory eyes as a dangerous man who must be brought down.

What did bring him down, only a year or so later, and consequently led to a new phase in his career, was a religious question—though it is difficult to separate religion from politics in this period. Both Dissenters and "Low Churchmen" were mainly Whigs, and the "highfliers"—the High-Church Tories—were determined to undermine this working alliance by stopping the practice of "occasional conformity" (by which Dissenters of flexible conscience could qualify for public office by occasionally taking the sacraments according to the established church). Pressure on the Dissenters increased when the Tories came to power, and violent attacks were made on them by such rabble-rousing extremists as Dr. Henry Sacheverell. In reply, Defoe wrote perhaps the most famous and skillful of all his pamphlets, "The Shortest-Way With The Dissenters" (1702), published anonymously. His method was ironic: to discredit the highfliers by writing as if from their viewpoint but reducing their arguments to absurdity. The pamphlet had a huge sale, but the irony blew up in Defoe's face: Dissenters and High Churchmen alike took it seriously, and—though for different reasons—were furious when the hoax was exposed. Defoe was prosecuted for seditious libel and was arrested in May 1703. The advertisement offering a reward for his capture gives the only extant personal description of Defoe—an unflattering one, which annoyed him considerably: "a middle-size spare man, about 40 years old, of a brown complexion, and dark-brown coloured hair, but wears a wig, a hooked nose, a sharp chin, grey eyes, and a large mole near his mouth." Defoe was advised to plead guilty and rely on the court's mercy, but he received harsh treatment, and, in addition to being fined, was sentenced to stand three times in the pillory. It is likely that the prosecution was primarily political, an attempt to force him into betraying certain Whig leaders; but the attempt was evidently unsuccessful. Although miserably apprehensive of his punishment, Defoe had spirit enough, while awaiting his ordeal, to write the audacious "Hymn To The Pillory" (1703); and this helped to turn the occasion into something of a triumph, with the pillory garlanded, the mob drinking his health, and the poem on sale in the streets. In An Appeal to Honour and Justice (1715), he gave his own, self-justifying account of these events and of other controversies in his life as a writer.

Triumph or not, Defoe was led back to Newgate, and there he remained while his Tilbury business collapsed and he became ever more desperately concerned for the welfare of his already numerous family. He appealed to Robert Harley, who, after many delays, finally secured his release—Harley's part of the bargain being to obtain Defoe's services as a pamphleteer and intelligence agent.

Defoe certainly served his masters with zeal and energy, traveling extensively, writing reports, minutes of advice, and pamphlets. He paid several visits to Scotland, especially at the time of the Act of Union in 1707, keeping Harley closely in touch with public opinion. Some of Defoe's letters to Harley from this period have survived. These trips bore fruit in a different way two decades later: in 1724–26 the three volumes of Defoe's animated and informative Tour Through the Whole Island of Great Britain were published, in preparing which he drew on many of his earlier observations.

Perhaps Defoe's most remarkable achievement during Queen Anne's reign, however, was his periodical, the Review. He wrote this serious, forceful, and long-lived paper practically single-handedly from 1704 to 1713. At first a weekly, it became a thrice-weekly publication in 1705, and Defoe continued to produce it even when, for short periods in 1713, his political enemies managed to have him imprisoned again on various pretexts. It was, effectively, the main government organ, its political line corresponding with that of the moderate Tories (though Defoe sometimes took an independent stand); but, in addition to politics as such, Defoe discussed current affairs in general, religion, trade, manners, morals, and so on, and his work undoubtedly had a considerable influence on the development of later essay periodicals (such as Richard Steele and Joseph Addison's The Tatler and The Spectator) and of the newspaper press.

.With George I's accession (1714), the Tories fell. The Whigs in their turn recognized Defoe's value, and he continued to write for the government of the day and to carry out intelligence work. At about this time, too (perhaps prompted by a severe illness), he wrote the best known and most popular of his many didactic works, The Family Instructor (1715). The writings so far mentioned, however, would not necessarily have procured literary immortality for Defoe; this he achieved when in 1719 he turned his talents to an extended work of prose fiction and (drawing partly on the memoirs of voyagers and castaways such as Alexander Selkirk) produced Robinson Crusoe. A German critic has called it a "world-book," a label justified not only by the enormous number of translations, imitations, and adaptations that have appeared but by the almost mythic power with which Defoe creates a hero and a situation with which every reader can in some sense identify.

Here (as in his works of the remarkable year 1722, which saw the publication of Moll Flanders, A Journal of the Plague Year, and Colonel Jack) Defoe displays his finest gift as a novelist—his insight into human nature. The men and women he writes about are all, it is true, placed in unusual circumstances; they are all, in one sense or another, solitaries; they all struggle, in their different ways, through a life that is a constant scene of jungle warfare; they all become, to some extent, obsessive. They are also ordinary human beings, however, and Defoe, writing always in the first person, enters into their minds and analyzes their motives. His novels are given verisimilitude by their matter-of-fact style and their vivid concreteness of detail; the latter may seem unselective, but it effectively helps to evoke a particular, circumscribed world. Their main defects are shapelessness, an overinsistent moralizing, occasional gaucheness, and naiveté. Defoe's range is narrow, but within that range he is a novelist of considerable power, and his plain, direct style, as in almost all of his writing, holds the reader's interest.

In 1724 he published his last major work of fiction, Roxana, though in the closing years of his life, despite failing health, he remained active and enterprising as a writer.

A man of many talents and author of an extraordinary range and number of works, Defoe remains in many ways an enigmatic figure. A man who made many enemies, he has been accused of double-dealing, of dishonest or equivocal conduct, of venality. Certainly in politics he served in turn both Tory and Whig; he acted as a secret agent for the Tories and later served the Whigs by "infiltrating" extremist Tory journals and toning them down. But Defoe always claimed that the end justified the means, and a more sympathetic view may see him as what he always professed to be, an unswerving champion of moderation. At the age of 59 Defoe embarked on what was virtually a new career, producing in Robinson Crusoe the first of a remarkable series of novels and other fictional writings that resulted in his being called the father of the English novel.

Summary:

The book starts with the statement about Crusoe's marriage in England. He bought a little farm in Bedford and had three children: two sons and one daughter. Our hero suffered a distemper and a desire to see "his island." He could talk of nothing else, and one can imagine that no one took his stories seriously, except his wife. She told him, in tears, "I will go with you, but I won't leave you." But in the middle of this felicity, Providence unhinged him at once, with the loss of his wife.

Crusoe's return to his island

At the beginning of 1693, Crusoe made his nephew the commander of a ship. Around the beginning of January 1694, Crusoe and Friday went on board this ship in the Downs on the 8th, then arrived at Crusoe's Island via Ireland. They discovered that the English mutineers left on the island by Crusoe a decade earlier had been making trouble, but that when the island fell under attack by cannibals the various parties on the island were forced to work together under truce to meet the threat. Crusoe takes various steps to consolidate leadership on the island and assure the civility of the inhabitants, including leaving a quantity of needed supplies, setting up a sort of rule of law under an honour system and ensuring cohabitating couples are married. He also leaves additional residents with necessary skills. On the way to the mainland once again from Crusoe's island, the ship is attacked by the cannibals. Friday dies from three arrow shots during an attempt to negotiate, but the crew eventually wins the encounter without further serious casualty.

Crusoe's adventures in Madagascar

After having buried Friday in the ocean, the same evening they set sail for Brazil. They stayed for a long period there, then went directly over to the Cape of Good Hope. They landed on Madagascar where their nine men were pursued by three hundred natives, because one of his mariners had carried off a young native girl among the trees. The natives hanged this person, so the crew massacred 32 persons and burned the houses of the native town. Crusoe opposed all these, therefore he was marooned, and settled at the Bay of Bengal for a long time.

Crusoe's travels in Southeast Asia and China

Finally, he bought a ship that later turned out to be stolen. Therefore, they went to the river of Cambodia and Cochinchina or the Bay of Tonquin, until they came to the latitude of 22 degrees and 30 minutes, and anchored at the island of Formosa (Taiwan). Then they arrived on the coast of China. They visited Nanking near the river of Kilam, and sailed southwards to a port called Quinchang. An old Portuguese pilot suggested that they go to Ningpo by the mouth of a river. This Ningpo was a canal that passed through the heart of that vast empire of China, crossed all the rivers and some hills by the help of sluices and gates, and went up to Peking, being near 270 leagues long. So they did, then it was the beginning of February, in the Old Style calendar, when they set out from Peking.

Then they travelled through the following places: Changu, Naum (or Naun, a fortified city), Argun(a) on the Chinese-Russian border (13 April 1703).

Crusoe's travels in Siberia

Argun was the first town on the Russian border; then they went through Nertzinskoi (Nerchinsk), Plotbus, touched a lake called Schaks Ozer, Jerawena, the river Udda, Yeniseysk, and Tobolsk (from September 1703 to beginning of June 1704). They arrived in Europe around the source of the river Wirtska, south of the river Petrou, in a village called Kermazinskoy near Soloy Kamskoy (Solikamsk). They passed a little river called Kirtza, near Ozomoys (or Gzomoys), came to Veuslima (?) on the river Witzogda (Vychegda), running into the Dwina, then they stayed in Lawrenskoy (3–7 July 1704; possibly Yarensk, known as Yerenskoy Gorodok at that time). Finally Crusoe arrived at the White Sea port town Arch-Angel (Archangelsk) on 18 August, sailed into Hamburg (18 September), and Hague. He arrived at London on 10 January 1705, having been gone from England ten years and nine months.

Chapter 1

Revisits Island

That homely proverb, used on so many occasions in England, viz. "That what is bred in the bone will not go out of the flesh," was never more verified than in the story of my Life. Any one would think that after thirty-five years' affliction, and a variety of unhappy circumstances, which few men, if any, ever went through before, and after near seven years of peace and enjoyment in the fulness of all things; grown old, and when, if ever, it might be allowed me to have had experience of every state of middle life, and to know which was most adapted to make a man completely happy; I say, after all this, any one would have thought that the native propensity to rambling which I gave an account of in my first setting out in the world to have been so predominant in my thoughts, should be worn out, and I might, at sixty one years of age, have been a little inclined to stay at home, and have done venturing life and fortune any more.

Nay, farther, the common motive of foreign adventures was taken away in me, for I had no fortune to make; I had nothing to seek: if I had gained ten thousand pounds I had been no richer; for I had already sufficient for me, and for those I had to leave it to; and what I had was visibly increasing; for, having no great family, I could not spend the income of what I had unless I would set up for an expensive way of living, such as a great family, servants, equipage, gaiety, and the like, which were things I had no notion of, or inclination to; so that I had nothing, indeed, to do but to sit still, and fully enjoy what I had got, and see it increase daily upon my hands. Yet all these things had no effect upon me, or at least not enough to resist the strong inclination I had to go abroad again, which hung about me like a chronic distemper. In particular, the desire of seeing my new plantation in the island, and the colony I left there, ran in my head continually. I dreamed of it all night, and my imagination ran upon it all day: it was uppermost in all my thoughts, and my fancy worked so steadily and strongly upon it that I talked of it in my sleep; in short, nothing could remove it out of my mind: it even broke so violently into all my discourses that it made my conversation tiresome, for I could talk of nothing else; all my discourse ran into it, even to impertinence; and I saw it myself.

I have often heard persons of good judgment say that all the stir that people make in the world about ghosts and apparitions is owing to the strength of imagination, and the powerful operation of fancy in their minds; that there is no such thing as a spirit appearing, or a ghost walking; that people's poring affectionately upon the past conversation of their deceased friends so realises it to them that they are capable of fancying, upon some extraordinary circumstances, that they see them, talk to them, and are answered by them, when, in truth, there is nothing but shadow and vapour in the thing, and they really know nothing of the matter.

For my part, I know not to this hour whether there are any such things as real apparitions, spectres, or walking of people after they are dead; or whether there is anything in the stories they tell us of that kind more than the product of vapours, sick minds, and wandering fancies: but this I know, that my imagination worked up

14

to such a height, and brought me into such excess of vapours, or what else I may call it, that I actually supposed myself often upon the spot, at my old castle, behind the trees; saw my old Spaniard, Friday's father, and the reprobate sailors I left upon the island; nay, I fancied I talked with them, and looked at them steadily, though I was broad awake, as at persons just before me; and this I did till I often frightened myself with the images my fancy represented to me. One time, in my sleep, I had the villainy of the three pirate sailors so lively related to me by the first Spaniard, and Friday's father, that it was surprising: they told me how they barbarously attempted to murder all the Spaniards, and that they set fire to the provisions they had laid up, on purpose to distress and starve them; things that I had never heard of, and that, indeed, were never all of them true in fact: but it was so warm in my imagination, and so realised to me, that, to the hour I saw them, I could not be persuaded but that it was or would be true; also how I resented it, when the Spaniard complained to me; and how I brought them to justice, tried them, and ordered them all three to be hanged. What there was really in this shall be seen in its place; for however I came to form such things in my dream, and what secret converse of spirits injected it, yet there was, I say, much of it true. I own that this dream had nothing in it literally and specifically true; but the general part was so true— the base; villainous behaviour of these three hardened rogues was such, and had been so much worse than all I can describe, that the dream had too much similitude of the fact; and as I would afterwards have punished them severely, so, if I had hanged them all, I had been much in the right, and even should have been justified both by the laws of God and man.

But to return to my story. In this kind of temper I lived some years; I had no enjoyment of my life, no pleasant hours, no agreeable diversion but what had something or other of this in it; so that my wife, who saw my mind wholly bent upon it, told me very seriously one night that she believed there was some secret, powerful impulse of Providence upon me, which had determined me to go thither again; and that she found nothing hindered me going but my being engaged to a wife and children. She told me that it was true she could not think of parting with me: but as she was assured that if she was dead it would be the first thing I would do, so, as it seemed to her that the thing was determined above, she would not be the only obstruction; for, if I thought fit and resolved to go— [Here she found me very intent upon her words, and that I looked very earnestly at her, so that it a little disordered her, and she stopped. I asked her why she did not go on, and say out what she was going to say? But I perceived that her heart was too full, and some tears stood in her eyes.] "Speak out, my dear," said I; "are you willing I should go?"—"No," says she, very affectionately, "I am far from willing; but if you are resolved to go," says she, "rather than I would be the only hindrance, I will go with you: for though I think it a most preposterous thing for one of your years, and in your condition, yet, if it must be," said she, again weeping, "I would not leave you; for if it be of Heaven you must do it, there is no resisting it; and if Heaven make it your duty to go, He will also make it mine to go with you, or otherwise dispose of me, that I may not obstruct it."

This affectionate behaviour of my wife's brought me a little out of the vapours, and I began to consider what I was doing; I corrected my wandering fancy, and began to argue with myself sedately what business I had after threescore years, and after such a life of tedious sufferings and disasters, and closed in so happy and easy a manner; I, say, what business had I to rush into new hazards, and put myself upon adventures fit only for youth and poverty to run into?

With those thoughts I considered my new engagement; that I had a wife, one child born, and my wife then great with child of another; that I had all the world could give me, and had no need to seek hazard for gain; that I was declining in years, and ought to think rather of leaving what I had gained than of seeking to increase it; that as to what my wife had said of its being an impulse from Heaven, and that it should be my duty to go, I had no notion of that; so, after many of these cogitations, I struggled with the power of my imagination, reasoned myself out of it, as I believe people may always do in like cases if they will: in a word, I conquered it, composed myself with such arguments as occurred to my thoughts, and which my present condition furnished me plentifully with; and particularly, as the most effectual method, I resolved to divert myself with other things, and to engage in some business that might effectually tie me up from any more excursions of this kind; for I found that thing return upon me chiefly when I was idle, and had nothing to do, nor anything of moment immediately before me. To this purpose, I bought a little farm in the county of Bedford, and resolved to remove myself thither. I had a little convenient house upon it, and the land about it, I found, was capable of great improvement; and it was many ways suited to my inclination, which delighted in cultivating, managing, planting, and improving of land; and particularly, being an inland country, I was removed from conversing among sailors and things relating to the remote parts of the world. I went down to my farm, settled my family, bought ploughs, harrows, a cart, waggon-horses, cows, and sheep, and, setting seriously to work, became in one half-year a mere country gentleman. My thoughts were entirely taken up in managing my servants, cultivating the ground, enclosing, planting, &c.; and I lived, as I thought, the most agreeable life that nature was capable of directing, or that a man always bred to misfortunes was capable of retreating to.

I farmed upon my own land; I had no rent to pay, was limited by no articles; I could pull up or cut down as I pleased; what I planted was for myself, and what I improved was for my family; and having thus left off the thoughts of wandering, I had not the least discomfort in any part of life as to this world. Now I thought, indeed, that I enjoyed the middle state of life which my father so earnestly recommended to me, and lived a kind of heavenly life, something like what is described by the poet, upon the subject of a country life:-

"Free from vices, free from care, Age has no pain, and youth no snare."

But in the middle of all this felicity, one blow from unseen Providence unhinged me at once; and not only made a breach upon me inevitable and incurable, but drove me, by its consequences, into a deep relapse of the wandering disposition, which, as I may say, being born in my very blood, soon recovered its hold of me; and, like the returns of a violent distemper, came on with an irresistible force upon me. This blow was the loss of my wife. It is not my business here to write an elegy upon my wife, give a character of her particular virtues, and make my court to the sex by the flattery of a funeral sermon. She was, in a few words, the stay of all my affairs; the centre of all my enterprises; the engine that, by her prudence, reduced me to that happy compass I was in, from the most extravagant and ruinous project that filled my head, and did more to guide my rambling genius than a mother's tears, a father's instructions, a friend's counsel, or all my own reasoning powers could do. I was happy in listening to her, and in being moved by her entreaties; and to the last degree desolate and dislocated in the world by the loss of her.

When she was gone, the world looked awkwardly round me. I was as much a stranger in it, in my thoughts, as I was in the Brazils, when I first went on shore there; and as much alone, except for the assistance of servants, as I was in my island. I knew neither what to think nor what to do. I saw the world busy around me: one part labouring for bread, another part squandering in vile excesses or empty pleasures, but equally miserable because the end they proposed still fled from them; for the men of pleasure every day surfeited of their vice, and heaped up work for sorrow and repentance; and the men of labour spent their strength in daily struggling for bread to maintain the vital strength they laboured with: so living in a daily circulation of sorrow, living but to work, and working but to live, as if daily bread were the only end of wearisome life, and a wearisome life the only occasion of daily bread.

This put me in mind of the life I lived in my kingdom, the island; where I suffered no more corn to grow, because I did not want it; and bred no more goats, because I had no more use for them; where the money lay in the drawer till it grew mouldy, and had scarce the favour to be looked upon in twenty years. All these things, had I improved them as I ought to have done, and as reason and religion had dictated to me, would have taught me to search farther than human enjoyments for a full felicity; and that there was something which certainly was the reason and end of life superior to all these things, and which was either to be possessed, or at least hoped for, on this side of the grave.

But my sage counsellor was gone; I was like a ship without a pilot, that could only run afore the wind. My thoughts ran all away again into the old affair; my head was quite turned with the whimsies of foreign adventures; and all the pleasant, innocent amusements of my farm, my garden, my cattle, and my family, which before entirely possessed me, were nothing to me, had no relish, and were like music to one that has no ear, or food to one that has no taste. In a word, I resolved to leave off housekeeping, let my farm, and return to London; and in a few months after I did so.

When I came to London, I was still as uneasy as I was before; I had no relish for the place, no employment in it, nothing to do but to saunter about like an idle person, of whom it may be said he is perfectly useless in God's creation, and it is not one farthing's matter to the rest of his kind whether he be dead or alive. This also was the thing which, of all circumstances of life, was the most my aversion, who had been all my days used to an active life; and I would often say to myself, "A state of idleness is the very dregs of life;" and, indeed, I thought I was much more suitably employed when I was twenty-six days making a deal board.

It was now the beginning of the year 1693, when my nephew, whom, as I have observed before, I had brought up to the sea, and had made him commander of a ship, was come home from a short voyage to Bilbao, being the first he had made. He came to me, and told me that some merchants of his acquaintance had been proposing to him to go a voyage for them to the East Indies, and to China, as private traders. "And now, uncle," says he, "if you will go to sea with me, I will engage to land you upon your old habitation in the island; for we are to touch at the Brazils."

Nothing can be a greater demonstration of a future state, and of the existence of an invisible world, than the concurrence of second causes with the idea of things which we form in our minds, perfectly reserved, and not communicated to any in the world.

My nephew knew nothing how far my distemper of wandering was returned upon me, and I knew nothing of what he had in his thought to say, when that very morning, before he came to me, I had, in a great deal of confusion of thought, and revolving every part of my circumstances in my mind, come to this resolution, that I would go to Lisbon, and consult with my old sea-captain; and if it was rational and practicable, I would go and see the island again, and what was become of my people there. I had pleased myself with the thoughts of peopling the place, and carrying inhabitants from hence, getting a patent for the possession and I know not what; when, in the middle of all this, in comes my nephew, as I have said, with his project of carrying me thither in his way to the East Indies.

I paused a while at his words, and looking steadily at him, "What devil," said I, "sent you on this unlucky errand?" My nephew stared as if he had been frightened at first; but perceiving that I was not much displeased at the proposal, he recovered himself. "I hope it may not be an unlucky proposal, sir," says he. "I daresay you would be pleased to see your new colony there, where you once reigned with more felicity than most of your brother monarchs in the world." In a word, the scheme hit so exactly with my temper, that is to say, the prepossession I was under, and of which I have said so much, that I told him, in a few words, if he agreed with the merchants, I would go with him; but I told him I would not promise to go any further than my own island. "Why, sir," says he, "you don't want to be left there again, I hope?" "But," said I, "can you not take me up again on your return?" He told me it would not be possible to do so; that the merchants would never allow him to come that way with a laden ship of such value, it being a month's sail out of his way, and might be three or four. "Besides, sir, if I should miscarry," said he, "and not return at all, then you would be just reduced to the condition you were in before."

This was very rational; but we both found out a remedy for it, which was to carry a framed sloop on board the ship, which, being taken in pieces, might, by the help of some carpenters, whom we agreed to carry with us, be set up again in the island, and finished fit to go to sea in a few days. I was not long resolving, for indeed the importunities of my nephew joined so effectually with my inclination that nothing could oppose me; on the other hand, my wife being dead, none concerned themselves so much for me as to persuade me one way or the other, except my ancient good friend the widow, who earnestly struggled with me to consider my years, my easy circumstances, and the needless hazards of a long voyage; and above all, my young children. But it was all to no purpose, I had an irresistible desire for the voyage; and I told her I thought there was something so uncommon in the impressions I had upon my mind, that it would be a kind of resisting Providence if I should attempt to stay at home; after which she ceased her expostulations, and joined with me, not only in making provision for my voyage, but also in settling my family affairs for my absence, and providing for the education of my children. In order to do this, I made my will, and settled the estate I had in such a manner for my children, and placed in such hands, that I was perfectly easy and satisfied they would have justice done them, whatever might befall me; and for their education, I left it wholly to the widow, with a sufficient maintenance to herself for her care: all which she richly deserved; for no mother could have taken more care in their education, or understood it better; and as she lived till I came home, I also lived to thank her for it.

My nephew was ready to sail about the beginning of January 1694-5; and I, with my man Friday, went on board, in the Downs, the 8th; having, besides that sloop which I mentioned above, a very considerable cargo of all kinds of necessary things for my colony, which, if I did not find in good condition, I resolved to leave so.

First, I carried with me some servants whom I purposed to place there as inhabitants, or at least to set on work there upon my account while I stayed, and either to leave them there or carry them forward, as they should appear willing; particularly, I carried two carpenters, a smith, and a very handy, ingenious fellow, who was a cooper by trade, and was also a general mechanic; for he was dexterous at making wheels and hand-mills to grind corn, was a good turner and a good pot-maker; he also made anything that was proper to make of earth or of wood: in a word, we called him our Jack-of-all-trades. With these I carried a tailor, who had offered himself to go a passenger to the East Indies with my nephew, but afterwards consented to stay on our new plantation, and who proved a most necessary handy fellow as could be desired in many other businesses besides that of his trade; for, as I observed formerly, necessity arms us for all employments.

My cargo, as near as I can recollect, for I have not kept account of the particulars, consisted of a sufficient quantity of linen, and some English thin stuffs, for clothing the Spaniards that I expected to find there; and enough of them, as by my calculation might comfortably supply them for seven years; if I remember right, the materials I carried for clothing them, with gloves, hats, shoes, stockings, and all such things as they could want for wearing, amounted to about two hundred pounds, including some beds, bedding, and household stuff, particularly kitchen utensils, with pots, kettles, pewter, brass, &c.; and near a hundred pounds more in ironwork, nails, tools of every kind, staples, hooks, hinges, and every necessary thing I could think of.

I carried also a hundred spare arms, muskets, and fusees; besides some pistols, a considerable quantity of shot of all sizes, three or four tons of lead, and two pieces of brass cannon; and, because I knew not what time and what extremities I was providing for, I carried a hundred barrels of powder, besides swords, cutlasses, and the iron part of some pikes and halberds. In short, we had a large magazine of all sorts of store; and I made my nephew carry two small quarter-deck guns more than he wanted for his ship, to leave behind if there was occasion; so that when we came there we might build a fort and man it against all sorts of enemies. Indeed, I at first thought there would be need enough for all, and much more, if we hoped to maintain our possession of the island, as shall be seen in the course of that story.

I had not such bad luck in this voyage as I had been used to meet with, and therefore shall have the less occasion to interrupt the reader, who perhaps may be impatient to hear how matters went with my colony; yet some odd accidents, cross winds and bad weather happened on this first setting out, which made the voyage longer than I expected it at first; and I, who had never made but one voyage, my first voyage to Guinea, in which I might be said to come back again, as the voyage was at first designed, began to think the same ill fate attended me, and that I was born to be never contented with being on shore, and yet to be always unfortunate at sea. Contrary winds first put us to the northward, and we were obliged to put in at Galway, in Ireland, where we lay wind-bound two-and-twenty days; but we had this satisfaction with the disaster, that provisions were here exceeding cheap, and in the utmost plenty; so that while we lay here we never touched the ship's stores, but rather added to them. Here, also, I took in several live hogs, and two cows with their calves, which I resolved, if I had a good passage, to put on shore in my island; but we found occasion to dispose otherwise of them.

We set out on the 5th of February from Ireland, and had a very fair gale of wind for some days. As I remember, it might be about the 20th of February in the evening late, when the mate, having the watch, came into the round-house and told us he saw a flash of fire, and heard a gun fired; and while he was telling us of it, a boy came in and told us the boatswain heard another. This made us all run out upon the quarter-deck, where for a while we heard nothing; but in a few minutes we saw a very great light, and found that there was some very terrible fire at a distance; immediately we had recourse to our reckonings, in which we all agreed that there could be no land that way in which the fire showed itself, no, not for five hundred leagues, for it appeared at WNW. Upon this, we concluded it must be some ship on fire at sea; and as, by our hearing the noise of guns just before, we concluded that it could not be far off, we stood directly towards it, and were presently satisfied we should discover it, because the further we sailed, the greater the light appeared; though, the weather being hazy, we could not perceive anything but the light for a while. In about half-an-hour's sailing, the wind being fair for us, though not much of it, and the weather clearing up a little, we could plainly discern that it was a great ship on fire in the middle of the sea.

I was most sensibly touched with this disaster, though not at all acquainted with the persons engaged in it; I presently recollected my former circumstances, and what condition I was in when taken up by the Portuguese captain; and how much more deplorable the circumstances of the poor creatures belonging to that ship must be, if they had no other ship in company with them. Upon this I immediately ordered that five guns should be fired, one soon after another, that, if possible, we might give notice to them that there was help for them at hand and that they might endeavour to save themselves in their boat; for though we could see the flames of the ship, yet they, it being night, could see nothing of us.

We lay by some time upon this, only driving as the burning ship drove, waiting for daylight; when, on a sudden, to our great terror, though we had reason to expect it, the ship blew up in the air; and in a few minutes all the fire was out, that is to say, the rest of the ship sunk. This was a terrible, and indeed an afflicting sight, for the sake of the poor men, who, I concluded, must be either all destroyed in the ship, or be in the utmost distress in their boat, in the middle of the ocean; which, at present, as it was dark, I could not see. However, to direct them as well as I could, I caused lights to be hung out in all parts of the ship where we could, and which we had lanterns for, and kept firing guns all the night long, letting them know by this that there was a ship not far off.

About eight o'clock in the morning we discovered the ship's boats by the help of our perspective glasses, and found there were two of them, both thronged with people, and deep in the water. We perceived they rowed, the wind being against them; that they saw our ship, and did their utmost to make us see them. We immediately spread our ancient, to let them know we saw them, and hung a waft out, as a signal for them to come on board, and then made more sail, standing directly to them. In little more than half-an-hour we came up with them; and took them all in, being no less than sixty-four men, women, and children; for there were a great many passengers.

Upon inquiry we found it was a French merchant ship of three- hundred tons, home-bound from Quebec. The master gave us a long account of the distress of his ship; how the fire began in the steerage by the negligence of the steersman, which, on his crying out for help, was, as everybody thought, entirely put out; but they soon found that some sparks of the first fire had got into some part of the ship so difficult to come at that they could not effectually quench it; and afterwards getting in between the timbers, and within the ceiling of the ship, it proceeded into the hold, and mastered all the skill and all the application they were able to exert.

They had no more to do then but to get into their boats, which, to their great comfort, were pretty large; being their long-boat, and a great shallop, besides a small skiff, which was of no great service to them, other than to get some fresh water and provisions into her, after they had secured their lives from the fire. They had, indeed, small hopes of their lives by getting into these boats at that distance from any land; only, as they said, that they thus escaped from the fire, and there was a possibility that some ship might happen to be at sea, and might take them in. They had sails, oars, and a compass; and had as much provision and water as, with sparing it so as to be next door to starving, might support them about twelve days, in which, if they had no bad weather and no contrary winds, the captain said he hoped he might get to the banks of Newfoundland, and might perhaps take some fish, to sustain them till they might go on shore. But there were so many chances against them in all these cases, such as storms, to overset and founder them; rains and cold, to benumb and perish their limbs; contrary winds, to keep them out and starve them; that it must have been next to miraculous if they had escaped.

In the midst of their consternation, every one being hopeless and ready to despair, the captain, with tears in his eyes, told me they were on a sudden surprised with the joy of hearing a gun fire, and after that four more: these were the five guns which I caused to be fired at first seeing the light. This revived their hearts, and gave them the notice, which, as above, I desired it should, that there was a ship at hand for their help. It was upon the hearing of these guns that they took down their masts and sails: the sound coming from the windward, they resolved to lie by till morning. Some time after this, hearing no more guns, they fired three muskets, one a considerable while after another; but these, the wind being contrary, we never heard. Some time after that again they were still more agreeably surprised with seeing our lights, and hearing the guns, which, as I have said, I caused to be fired all the rest of the night. This set them to work with their oars, to keep their boats ahead, at least that we might the sooner come up with them; and at last, to their inexpressible joy, they found we saw them.

It is impossible for me to express the several gestures, the strange ecstasies, the variety of postures which these poor delivered people ran into, to express the joy of their souls at so unexpected a deliverance. Grief and fear are easily described: sighs, tears, groans, and a very few motions of the head and hands, make up the sum of its variety; but an excess of joy, a surprise of joy, has a thousand extravagances in it. There were some in tears; some raging and tearing themselves, as if they had been in the greatest agonies of sorrow; some stark raving and downright lunatic; some ran about the ship stamping with their feet, others wringing their hands; some were dancing, some singing, some laughing, more crying, many quite dumb, not able to speak a word; others sick and vomiting; several swooning and ready to faint; and a few were crossing themselves and giving God thanks.

I would not wrong them either; there might be many that were thankful afterwards; but the passion was too strong for them at first, and they were not able to master it: then were thrown into ecstasies, and a kind of frenzy, and it was but a very few that were composed and serious in their joy. Perhaps also, the case may have some addition to it from the particular circumstance of that nation they belonged to: I mean the French, whose temper is allowed to be more volatile, more passionate, and more sprightly, and their spirits more fluid than in other nations. I am not philosopher enough to determine the cause; but nothing I had ever seen before came up to it. The ecstasies poor Friday, my trusty savage, was in when he found his father in the boat came the nearest to it; and the surprise of the master and his two companions, whom I delivered from the villains that set them on shore in the island, came a little way towards it; but nothing was to compare to this, either that I saw in Friday, or anywhere else in my life.

It is further observable, that these extravagances did not show themselves in that different manner I have mentioned, in different persons only; but all the variety would appear, in a short succession of moments, in one and the same person. A man that we saw this minute dumb, and, as it were, stupid and confounded, would the next minute be dancing and hallooing like an antic; and the next moment be tearing his hair, or pulling his clothes to pieces, and stamping them under his feet like a madman; in a few moments after that we would have him all in tears, then sick, swooning, and, had not immediate help been had, he would in a few moments have been dead. Thus it was, not with one or two, or ten or twenty, but with the greatest part of them; and, if I remember right, our surgeon was obliged to let blood of about thirty persons.

There were two priests among them: one an old man, and the other a young man; and that which was strangest was, the oldest man was the worst. As soon as he set his foot on board our ship, and saw himself safe, he dropped down stone dead to all appearance. Not the least sign of life could be perceived in him; our surgeon immediately applied proper remedies to recover him, and was the only man in the ship that believed he was not dead. At length he opened a vein in his arm, having first chafed and rubbed the part, so as to warm it as much as possible. Upon this the blood, which only dropped at first, flowing freely, in three minutes after the man opened his eyes; a quarter of an hour after that he spoke, grew better, and after the blood was stopped, he walked about, told us he was perfectly well, and took a dram of cordial which the surgeon gave him. About a quarter of an hour after this they came running into the cabin to the surgeon, who was bleeding a Frenchwoman that had fainted, and told him the priest was gone stark mad. It seems he had begun to revolve the change of his circumstances in his mind, and again this put him into an ecstasy of joy. His spirits whirled about faster than the vessels could convey them, the blood grew hot and feverish, and the man was as fit for Bedlam as any creature that ever was in it. The surgeon would not bleed him again in that condition, but gave him something to doze and put him to sleep; which, after some time, operated upon him, and he awoke next morning perfectly composed and well. The younger priest behaved with great command of his passions, and was really an example of a serious, well-governed mind. At his first coming on board the ship he threw himself flat on his face, prostrating himself in thankfulness for his deliverance, in which I unhappily and unseasonably disturbed him, really thinking he had been in a swoon; but he spoke calmly, thanked me, told me he was giving God thanks for his deliverance, begged me to leave him a few moments, and that, next to his Maker, he would give me thanks also. I was heartily sorry that I disturbed him, and not only left him, but kept others from interrupting him also. He continued in that posture about three minutes, or little more, after I left him, then came to me, as he had said he would, and with a great deal of seriousness and affection, but with tears in his eyes, thanked me, that had, under God, given him and so many miserable creatures their lives. I told him I had no need to tell him to thank God for it, rather than me, for I had seen that he had done that already; but I added that it was nothing but what reason and humanity dictated to all men, and that we had as much reason as he to give thanks to God, who had blessed us so far as to make us the instruments of His mercy to so many of His creatures. After this the young priest applied himself to his countrymen, and laboured to compose them: he persuaded, entreated, argued, reasoned with them, and did his utmost to keep them within the exercise of their reason; and with some he had success, though others were for a time out of all government of themselves.

I cannot help committing this to writing, as perhaps it may be useful to those into whose hands it may fall, for guiding themselves in the extravagances of their passions; for if an excess of joy can carry men out to such a length beyond the reach of their reason, what will not the extravagances of anger, rage, and a provoked mind carry us to? And, indeed, here I saw reason for keeping an exceeding watch over our passions of every kind, as well those of joy and satisfaction as those of sorrow and anger.

We were somewhat disordered by these extravagances among our new guests for the first day;

but after they had retired to lodgings provided for them as well as our ship would allow, and had slept heartily— as most of them did, being fatigued and frightened— they were quite another sort of people the next day. Nothing of good manners, or civil acknowledgments for the kindness shown them, was wanting; the French, it is known, are naturally apt enough to exceed that way. The captain and one of the priests came to me the next day, and desired to speak with me and my nephew; the commander began to consult with us what should be done with them; and first, they told us we had saved their lives, so all they had was little enough for a return to us for that kindness received. The captain said they had saved some money and some things of value in their boats, caught hastily out of the flames, and if we would accept it they were ordered to make an offer of it all to us; they only desired to be set on shore somewhere in our way, where, if possible, they might get a passage to France. My nephew wished to accept their money at first word, and to consider what to do with them afterwards; but I overruled him in that part, for I knew what it was to be set on shore in a strange country; and if the Portuguese captain that took me up at sea had served me so, and taken all I had for my deliverance, I must have been starved, or have been as much a slave at the Brazils as I had been at Barbary, the mere being sold to a Mahometan excepted; and perhaps a Portuguese is not a much better master than a Turk, if not in some cases much worse.

I therefore told the French captain that we had taken them up in their distress, it was true, but that it was our duty to do so, as we were fellow-creatures; and we would desire to be so delivered if we were in the like or any other extremity; that we had done nothing for them but what we believed they would have done for us if we had been in their case and they in ours; but that we took them up to save them, not to plunder them; and it would be a most barbarous thing to take that little from them which they had saved out of the fire, and then set them on shore and leave them; that this would be first to save them from death, and then kill them ourselves: save them from drowning, and abandon them to starving; and therefore I would not let the least thing be taken from them. As to setting them on shore, I told them indeed that was an exceeding difficulty to us, for that the ship was bound to the East Indies; and though we were driven out of our course to the westward a very great way, and perhaps were directed by Heaven on purpose for their deliverance, yet it was impossible for us wilfully to change our voyage on their particular account; nor could my nephew, the captain, answer it to the freighters, with whom he was under charter to pursue his voyage by way of Brazil; and all I knew we could do for them was to put ourselves in the way of meeting with other ships homeward bound from the West Indies, and get them a passage, if possible, to England or France.

The first part of the proposal was so generous and kind they could not but be very thankful for it; but they were in very great consternation, especially the passengers, at the notion of being carried away to the East Indies; they then entreated me that as I was driven so far to the westward before I met with them, I would at least keep on the same course to the banks of Newfoundland, where it was probable I might meet with some ship or sloop that they might hire to carry them back to Canada.

I thought this was but a reasonable request on their part, and therefore I inclined to agree to it; for indeed I considered that to carry this whole company to the East Indies would not only be an intolerable severity upon the poor people, but would be ruining our whole voyage by devouring all our provisions; so I thought it no breach of charter-party, but what an unforeseen accident made absolutely necessary to us, and in which no one could say we were to blame; for the laws of God and nature would have forbid that we should refuse to take up two boats full of people in such a distressed condition; and the nature of the thing, as well respecting ourselves as the poor people, obliged us to set them on shore somewhere or other for their deliverance. So I consented that we would carry them to Newfoundland, if wind and weather would permit: and if not, I would carry them to Martinico, in the West Indies.

The wind continued fresh easterly, but the weather pretty good; and as the winds had continued in the points between NE. and SE. a long time, we missed several opportunities of sending them to France; for we met several ships bound to Europe, whereof two were French, from St. Christopher's, but they had been so long beating up against the wind that they durst take in no passengers, for fear of wanting provisions for the voyage, as well for themselves as for those they should take in; so we were obliged to go on. It was about a week after this that we made the banks of Newfoundland; where, to shorten my story, we put all our French people on board a bark, which they hired at sea there, to put them on shore, and afterwards to carry them to France, if they could get provisions to victual themselves with. When I say all the French went on shore, I should remember that the young priest I spoke of, hearing we were bound to the East Indies, desired to go the voyage with us, and to be set on shore on the coast of Coromandel; which I readily agreed to, for I wonderfully liked the man, and had very good reason, as will appear afterwards; also four of the seamen entered themselves on our ship, and proved very useful fellows.

From hence we directed our course for the West Indies, steering away S. and S. by E. for about twenty days together, sometimes little or no wind at all; when we met with another subject for our humanity to work upon, almost as deplorable as that before.

Chapter 2

Intervening History of Colony

It was in the latitude of 27 degrees 5 minutes N., on the 19th day of March 1694-95, when we spied a sail, our course SE. and by S. We soon perceived it was a large vessel, and that she bore up to us, but could not at first know what to make of her, till, after coming a little nearer, we found she had lost her main-topmast, fore-mast, and bowsprit; and presently she fired a gun as a signal of distress. The weather was pretty good, wind at NNW. a fresh gale, and we soon came to speak with her. We found her a ship of Bristol, bound home from Barbadoes, but had been blown out of the road at Barbadoes a few days before she was ready to sail, by a terrible hurricane, while the captain and chief mate were both gone on shore; so that, besides the terror of the storm, they were in an indifferent case for good mariners to bring the ship home. They had been already nine weeks at sea, and had met with another terrible storm, after the hurricane was over, which had blown them quite out of their knowledge to the westward, and in which they lost their masts. They told us they expected to have seen the Bahama Islands, but were then driven away again to the south-east, by a strong gale of wind at NNW., the same that blew now: and having no sails to work the ship with but a main course, and a kind of square sail upon a jury fore-mast, which they had set up, they could not lie near the wind, but were endeavouring to stand away for the Canaries.

But that which was worst of all was, that they were almost starved for want of provisions, besides the fatigues they had undergone; their bread and flesh were quite gone—they had not one ounce left in the ship, and had had none for eleven days. The only relief they had was, their water was not all spent, and they had about half a barrel of flour left; they had sugar enough; some succades, or sweetmeats, they had at first, but these were all devoured; and they had seven casks of rum. There was a youth and his mother and a maid-servant on board, who were passengers, and thinking the ship was ready to sail, unhappily came on board the evening before the hurricane began; and having no provisions of their own left, they were in a more deplorable condition than the rest: for the seamen being reduced to such an extreme necessity themselves, had no compassion, we may be sure, for the poor passengers; and they were, indeed, in such a condition that their misery is very hard to describe.

I had perhaps not known this part, if my curiosity had not led me, the weather being fair and the wind abated, to go on board the ship. The second mate, who upon this occasion commanded the ship, had been on board our ship, and he told me they had three passengers in the great cabin that were in a deplorable condition. "Nay," says he, "I believe they are dead, for I have heard nothing of them for above two days; and I was afraid to inquire after them," said he, "for I had nothing to relieve them with." We immediately applied ourselves to give them what relief we could spare; and indeed I had so far overruled things with my nephew, that I would have victualled them though we had gone away to Virginia, or any other part of the coast of America, to have supplied ourselves; but there was no necessity for that.

37

But now they were in a new danger; for they were afraid of eating too much, even of that little we gave them. The mate, or commander, brought six men with him in his boat; but these poor wretches looked like skeletons, and were so weak that they could hardly sit to their oars. The mate himself was very ill, and half starved; for he declared he had reserved nothing from the men, and went share and share alike with them in every bit they ate. I cautioned him to eat sparingly, and set meat before him immediately, but he had not eaten three mouthfuls before he began to be sick and out of order; so he stopped a while, and our surgeon mixed him up something with some broth, which he said would be to him both food and physic; and after he had taken it he grew better. In the meantime I forgot not the men. I ordered victuals to be given them, and the poor creatures rather devoured than ate it: they were so exceedingly hungry that they were in a manner ravenous, and had no command of themselves; and two of them ate with so much greediness that they were in danger of their lives the next morning. The sight of these people's distress was very moving to me, and brought to mind what I had a terrible prospect of at my first coming on shore in my island, where I had not the least mouthful of food, or any prospect of procuring any; besides the hourly apprehensions I had of being made the food of other creatures. But all the while the mate was thus relating to me the miserable condition of the ship's company, I could not put out of my thought the story he had told me of the three poor creatures in the great cabin, viz. the mother, her son, and the maid-servant, whom he had heard nothing of for two or three days, and whom, he seemed to confess, they had wholly neglected, their own extremities being so great; by which I understood that they had really given them no food at all, and that therefore they must be perished, and be all lying dead, perhaps, on the floor or deck of the cabin.

As I therefore kept the mate, whom we then called captain, on board with his men, to refresh them, so I also forgot not the starving crew that were left on board, but ordered my own boat to go on board the ship, and, with my mate and twelve men, to carry them a sack of bread, and four or five pieces of beef to boil. Our surgeon charged the men to cause the meat to be boiled while they stayed, and to keep guard in the cook-room, to prevent the men taking it to eat raw, or taking it out of the pot before it was well boiled, and then to give every man but a very little at a time: and by this caution he preserved the men, who would otherwise have killed themselves with that very food that was given them on purpose to save their lives.

At the same time I ordered the mate to go into the great cabin, and see what condition the poor passengers were in; and if they were alive, to comfort them, and give them what refreshment was proper: and the surgeon gave him a large pitcher, with some of the prepared broth which he had given the mate that was on board, and which he did not question would restore them gradually. I was not satisfied with this; but, as I said above, having a great mind to see the scene of misery which I knew the ship itself would present me with, in a more lively manner than I could have it by report, I took the captain of the ship, as we now called him, with me, and went myself, a little after, in their boat.

I found the poor men on board almost in a tumult to get the victuals out of the boiler before it was ready; but my mate observed his orders, and kept a good guard at the cook-room door, and the man he placed there, after using all possible persuasion to have patience, kept them off by force; however, he caused some biscuit-cakes to be dipped in the pot, and softened with the liquor of the meat, which they called brewis, and gave them every one some to stay their stomachs, and told them it was for their own safety that he was obliged to give them but little at a time. But it was all in vain; and had I not come on board, and their own commander and officers with me, and with good words, and some threats also of giving them no more, I believe they would have broken into the cook-room by force, and torn the meat out of the furnace—for words are indeed of very small force to a hungry belly; however, we pacified them, and fed them gradually and cautiously at first, and the next time gave them more, and at last filled their bellies, and the men did well enough.

But the misery of the poor passengers in the cabin was of another nature, and far beyond the rest; for as, first, the ship's company had so little for themselves, it was but too true that they had at first kept them very low, and at last totally neglected them: so that for six or seven days it might be said they had really no food at all, and for several days before very little. The poor mother, who, as the men reported, was a woman of sense and good breeding, had spared all she could so affectionately for her son, that at last she entirely sank under it; and when the mate of our ship went in, she sat upon the floor on deck, with her back up against the sides, between two chairs, which were lashed fast, and her head sunk between her shoulders like a corpse, though not quite dead. My mate said all he could to revive and encourage her, and with a spoon put some broth into her mouth. She opened her lips, and lifted up one hand, but could not speak: yet she understood what he said, and made signs to him, intimating, that it was too late for her, but pointed to her child, as if she would have said they should take care of him. However, the mate, who was exceedingly moved at the sight, endeavoured to get some of the broth into her mouth, and, as he said, got two or three spoonfuls down—though I question whether he could be sure of it or not; but it was too late, and she died the same night.

The youth, who was preserved at the price of his most affectionate mother's life, was not so far gone; yet he lay in a cabin bed, as one stretched out, with hardly any life left in him. He had a piece of an old glove in his mouth, having eaten up the rest of it; however, being young, and having more strength than his mother, the mate got something down his throat, and he began sensibly to revive; though by giving him, some time after, but two or three spoonfuls extraordinary, he was very sick, and brought it up again.

But the next care was the poor maid: she lay all along upon the deck, hard by her mistress, and just like one that had fallen down in a fit of apoplexy, and struggled for life. Her limbs were distorted; one of her hands was clasped round the frame of the chair, and she gripped it so hard that we could not easily make her let it go; her other arm lay over her head, and her feet lay both together, set fast against the frame of the cabin table: in short, she lay just like one in the agonies of death, and yet she was alive too. The poor creature was not only starved with hunger, and terrified with the thoughts of death, but, as the men told us afterwards, was broken-hearted for her mistress, whom she saw dying for two or three days before, and whom she loved most tenderly. We knew not what to do with this poor girl; for when our surgeon, who was a man of very great knowledge and experience, had, with great application, recovered her as to life, he had her upon his hands still; for she was little less than distracted for a considerable time after.

Whoever shall read these memorandums must be desired to consider that visits at sea are not like a journey into the country, where sometimes people stay a week or a fortnight at a place. Our business was to relieve this distressed ship's crew, but not lie by for them; and though they were willing to steer the same course with us for some days, yet we could carry no sail to keep pace with a ship that had no masts. However, as their captain begged of us to help him to set up a main-topmast, and a kind of a topmast to his jury fore-mast, we did, as it were, lie by him for three or four days; and then, having given him five barrels of beef, a barrel of pork, two hogsheads of biscuit, and a proportion of peas, flour, and what other things we could spare; and taking three casks of sugar, some rum, and some pieces of eight from them for satisfaction, we left them, taking on board with us, at their own earnest request, the youth and the maid, and all their goods.

The young lad was about seventeen years of age, a pretty, well- bred, modest, and sensible youth, greatly dejected with the loss of his mother, and also at having lost his father but a few months before, at Barbadoes. He begged of the surgeon to speak to me to take him out of the ship; for he said the cruel fellows had murdered his mother: and indeed so they had, that is to say, passively; for they might have spared a small sustenance to the poor helpless widow, though it had been but just enough to keep her alive; but hunger knows no friend, no relation, no justice, no right, and therefore is remorseless, and capable of no compassion.

The surgeon told him how far we were going, and that it would carry him away from all his friends, and put him, perhaps, in as bad circumstances almost as those we found him in, that is to say, starving in the world. He said it mattered not whither he went, if he was but delivered from the terrible crew that he was among; that the captain (by which he meant me, for he could know nothing of my nephew) had saved his life, and he was sure would not hurt him; and as for the maid, he was sure, if she came to herself, she would be very thankful for it, let us carry them where we would. The surgeon represented the case so affectionately to me that I yielded, and we took them both on board, with all their goods, except eleven hogsheads of sugar, which could not be removed or come at; and as the youth had a bill of lading for them, I made his commander sign a writing, obliging himself to go, as soon as he came to Bristol, to one Mr. Rogers, a merchant there, to whom the youth said he was related, and to deliver a letter which I wrote to him, and all the goods he had belonging to the deceased widow; which, I suppose, was not done, for I could never learn that the ship came to Bristol, but was, as is most probable, lost at sea, being in so disabled a condition, and so far from any land, that I am of opinion the first storm she met with afterwards she might founder, for she was leaky, and had damage in her hold when we met with her.

I was now in the latitude of 19 degrees 32 minutes, and had hitherto a tolerable voyage as to weather, though at first the winds had been contrary. I shall trouble nobody with the little incidents of wind, weather, currents, &c., on the rest of our voyage; but to shorten my story, shall observe that I came to my old habitation, the island, on the 10th of April 1695. It was with no small difficulty that I found the place; for as I came to it and went to it before on the south and east side of the island, coming from the Brazils, so now, coming in between the main and the island, and having no chart for the coast, nor any landmark, I did not know it when I saw it, or, know whether I saw it or not. We beat about a great while, and went on shore on several islands in the mouth of the great river Orinoco, but none for my purpose; only this I learned by my coasting the shore, that I was under one great mistake before, viz. that the continent which I thought I saw from the island I lived in was really no continent, but a long island, or rather a ridge of islands, reaching from one to the other side of the extended mouth of that great river; and that the savages who came to my island were not properly those which we call Caribbees, but islanders, and other barbarians of the same kind, who inhabited nearer to our side than the rest.

In short, I visited several of these islands to no purpose; some I found were inhabited, and some were not; on one of them I found some Spaniards, and thought they had lived there; but speaking with them, found they had a sloop lying in a small creek hard by, and came thither to make salt, and to catch some pearl-mussels if they could; but that they belonged to the Isle de Trinidad, which lay farther north, in the latitude of 10 and 11 degrees.

Thus coasting from one island to another, sometimes with the ship, sometimes with the Frenchman's shallop, which we had found a convenient boat, and therefore kept her with their very good will, at length I came fair on the south side of my island, and presently knew the very countenance of the place: so I brought the ship safe to an anchor, broadside with the little creek where my old habitation was. As soon as I saw the place I called for Friday, and asked him if he knew where he was? He looked about a little, and presently clapping his hands, cried, "Oh yes, Oh there, Oh yes, Oh there!" pointing to our old habitation, and fell dancing and capering like a mad fellow; and I had much ado to keep him from jumping into the sea to swim ashore to the place.

"Well, Friday," says I, "do you think we shall find anybody here or no? and do you think we shall see your father?" The fellow stood mute as a stock a good while; but when I named his father, the poor affectionate creature looked dejected, and I could see the tears run down his face very plentifully. "What is the matter, Friday? are you troubled because you may see your father?" "No, no," says he, shaking his head, "no see him more: no, never more see him again." "Why so, Friday? how do you know that?" "Oh no, Oh no," says Friday, "he long ago die, long ago; he much old man." "Well, well, Friday, you don't know; but shall we see any one else, then?" The fellow, it seems, had better eyes than I, and he points to the hill just above my old house; and though we lay half a league off, he cries out, "We see! we see! yes, we see much man there, and there, and there." I looked, but I saw nobody, no, not with a perspective glass, which was, I suppose, because I could not hit the place: for the fellow was right, as I found upon inquiry the next day; and there were five or six men all together, who stood to look at the ship, not knowing what to think of us.

As soon as Friday told me he saw people, I caused the English ancient to be spread, and fired three guns, to give them notice we were friends; and in about a quarter of an hour after we perceived a smoke arise from the side of the creek; so I immediately ordered the boat out, taking Friday with me, and hanging out a white flag, I went directly on shore, taking with me the young friar I mentioned, to whom I had told the story of my living there, and the manner of it, and every particular both of myself and those I left there, and who was on that account extremely desirous to go with me. We had, besides, about sixteen men well armed, if we had found any new guests there which we did not know of; but we had no need of weapons.

As we went on shore upon the tide of flood, near high water, we rowed directly into the creek; and the first man I fixed my eye upon was the Spaniard whose life I had saved, and whom I knew by his face perfectly well: as to his habit, I shall describe it afterwards. I ordered nobody to go on shore at first but myself; but there was no keeping Friday in the boat, for the affectionate creature had spied his father at a distance, a good way off the Spaniards, where, indeed, I saw nothing of him; and if they had not let him go ashore, he would have jumped into the sea. He was no sooner on shore, but he flew away to his father like an arrow out of a bow. It would have made any man shed tears, in spite of the firmest resolution, to have seen the first transports of this poor fellow's joy when he came to his father: how he embraced him, kissed him, stroked his face, took him up in his arms, set him down upon a tree, and lay down by him; then stood and looked at him, as any one would look at a strange picture, for a quarter of an hour together; then lay down on the ground, and stroked his legs, and kissed them, and then got up again and stared at him; one would have thought the fellow bewitched. But it would have made a dog laugh the next day to see how his passion ran out another way: in the morning he walked along the shore with his father several hours, always leading him by the hand, as if he had been a lady; and every now and then he would come to the boat to fetch something or other for him, either a lump of sugar, a dram, a biscuit, or something or other that was good. In the afternoon his frolics ran another way; for then he would set the old man down upon the ground, and dance about him, and make a thousand antic gestures; and all the while he did this he would be talking to him, and telling him one story or another of his travels, and of what had happened to him abroad to divert him. In short, if the same filial affection was to be found in Christians to their parents in our part of the world, one would be tempted to say there would hardly have been any need of the fifth commandment.

But this is a digression: I return to my landing. It would be needless to take notice of all the ceremonies and civilities that the Spaniards received me with. The first Spaniard, whom, as I said, I knew very well, was he whose life I had saved. He came towards the boat, attended by one more, carrying a flag of truce also; and he not only did not know me at first, but he had no thoughts, no notion of its being me that was come, till I spoke to him. "Seignior," said I, in Portuguese, "do you not know me?" At which he spoke not a word, but giving his musket to the man that was with him, threw his arms abroad, saying something in Spanish that I did not perfectly hear, came forward and embraced me, telling me he was inexcusable not to know that face again that he had once seen, as of an angel from heaven sent to save his life; he said abundance of very handsome things, as a well-bred Spaniard always knows how, and then, beckoning to the person that attended him, bade him go and call out his comrades. He then asked me if I would walk to my old habitation, where he would give me possession of my own house again, and where I should see they had made but mean improvements. I walked along with him, but, alas! I could no more find the place than if I had never been there; for they had planted so many trees, and placed them in such a position, so thick and close to one another, and in ten years' time they were grown so big, that the place was inaccessible, except by such windings and blind ways as they themselves only, who made them, could find.

I asked them what put them upon all these fortifications; he told me I would say there was need enough of it when they had given me an account how they had passed their time since their arriving in the island, especially after they had the misfortune to find that I was gone. He told me he could not but have some pleasure in my good fortune, when he heard that I was gone in a good ship, and to my satisfaction; and that he had oftentimes a strong persuasion that one time or other he should see me again, but nothing that ever befell him in his life, he said, was so surprising and afflicting to him at first as the disappointment he was under when he came back to the island and found I was not there.

As to the three barbarians (so he called them) that were left behind, and of whom, he said, he had a long story to tell me, the Spaniards all thought themselves much better among the savages, only that their number was so small: "And," says he, "had they been strong enough, we had been all long ago in purgatory;" and with that he crossed himself on the breast. "But, sir," says he, "I hope you will not be displeased when I shall tell you how, forced by necessity, we were obliged for our own preservation to disarm them, and make them our subjects, as they would not be content with being moderately our masters, but would be our murderers." I answered I was afraid of it when I left them there, and nothing troubled me at my parting from the island but that they were not come back, that I might have put them in possession of everything first, and left the others in a state of subjection, as they deserved; but if they had reduced them to it I was very glad, and should be very far from finding any fault with it; for I knew they were a parcel of refractory, ungoverned villains, and were fit for any manner of mischief.

While I was saying this, the man came whom he had sent back, and with him eleven more. In the dress they were in it was impossible to guess what nation they were of; but he made all clear, both to them and to me. First, he turned to me, and pointing to them, said, "These, sir, are some of the gentlemen who owe their lives to you;" and then turning to them, and pointing to me, he let them know who I was; upon which they all came up, one by one, not as if they had been sailors, and ordinary fellows, and the like, but really as if they had been ambassadors or noblemen, and I a monarch or great conqueror: their behaviour was, to the last degree, obliging and courteous, and yet mixed with a manly, majestic gravity, which very well became them; and, in short, they had so much more manners than I, that I scarce knew how to receive their civilities, much less how to return them in kind.

The history of their coming to, and conduct in, the island after my going away is so very remarkable, and has so many incidents which the former part of my relation will help to understand, and which will in most of the particulars, refer to the account I have already given, that I cannot but commit them, with great delight, to the reading of those that come after me.

In order to do this as intelligibly as I can, I must go back to the circumstances in which I left the island, and the persons on it, of whom I am to speak. And first, it is necessary to repeat that I had sent away Friday's father and the Spaniard (the two whose lives I had rescued from the savages) in a large canoe to the main, as I then thought it, to fetch over the Spaniard's companions that he left behind him, in order to save them from the like calamity that he had been in, and in order to succour them for the present; and that, if possible, we might together find some way for our deliverance afterwards. When I sent them away I had no visible appearance of, or the least room to hope for, my own deliverance, any more than I had twenty years before—much less had I any foreknowledge of what afterwards happened, I mean, of an English ship coming on shore there to fetch me off; and it could not be but a very great surprise to them, when they came back, not only to find that I was gone, but to find three strangers left on the spot, possessed of all that I had left behind me, which would otherwise have been their own.

The first thing, however, which I inquired into, that I might begin where I left off, was of their own part; and I desired the Spaniard would give me a particular account of his voyage back to his countrymen with the boat, when I sent him to fetch them over. He told me there was little variety in that part, for nothing remarkable happened to them on the way, having had very calm weather and a smooth sea. As for his countrymen, it could not be doubted, he said, but that they were overjoyed to see him (it seems he was the principal man among them, the captain of the vessel they had been shipwrecked in having been dead some time): they were, he said, the more surprised to see him, because they knew that he was fallen into the hands of the savages, who, they were satisfied, would devour him as they did all the rest of their prisoners; that when he told them the story of his deliverance, and in what manner he was furnished for carrying them away, it was like a dream to them, and their astonishment, he said, was somewhat like that of Joseph's brethren when he told them who he was, and the story of his exaltation in Pharaoh's court; but when he showed them the arms, the powder, the ball, the provisions that he brought them for their journey or voyage, they were restored to themselves, took a just share of the joy of their deliverance, and immediately prepared to come away with him.

Their first business was to get canoes; and in this they were obliged not to stick so much upon the honesty of it, but to trespass upon their friendly savages, and to borrow two large canoes, or periaguas, on pretence of going out a-fishing, or for pleasure. In these they came away the next morning. It seems they wanted no time to get themselves ready; for they had neither clothes nor provisions, nor anything in the world but what they had on them, and a few roots to eat, of which they used to make their bread. They were in all three weeks absent; and in that time, unluckily for them, I had the occasion offered for my escape, as I mentioned in the other part, and to get off from the island, leaving three of the most impudent, hardened, ungoverned, disagreeable villains behind me that any man could desire to meet with—to the poor Spaniards' great grief and disappointment.

The only just thing the rogues did was, that when the Spaniards came ashore, they gave my letter to them, and gave them provisions, and other relief, as I had ordered them to do; also they gave them the long paper of directions which I had left with them, containing the particular methods which I took for managing every part of my life there; the way I baked my bread, bred up tame goats, and planted my corn; how I cured my grapes, made my pots, and, in a word, everything I did. All this being written down, they gave to the Spaniards (two of them understood English well enough): nor did they refuse to accommodate the Spaniards with anything else, for they agreed very well for some time. They gave them an equal admission into the house or cave, and they began to live very sociably; and the head Spaniard, who had seen pretty much of my methods, together with Friday's father, managed all their affairs; but as for the Englishmen, they did nothing but ramble about the island, shoot parrots, and catch tortoises; and when they came home at night, the Spaniards provided their suppers for them.

The Spaniards would have been satisfied with this had the others but let them alone, which, however, they could not find in their hearts to do long: but, like the dog in the manger, they would not eat themselves, neither would they let the others eat. The differences, nevertheless, were at first but trivial, and such as are not worth relating, but at last it broke out into open war: and it began with all the rudeness and insolence that can be imagined—without reason, without provocation, contrary to nature, and indeed to common sense; and though, it is true, the first relation of it came from the Spaniards themselves, whom I may call the accusers, yet when I came to examine the fellows they could not deny a word of it.

But before I come to the particulars of this part, I must supply a defect in my former relation; and this was, I forgot to set down among the rest, that just as we were weighing the anchor to set sail, there happened a little quarrel on board of our ship, which I was once afraid would have turned to a second mutiny; nor was it appeased till the captain, rousing up his courage, and taking us all to his assistance, parted them by force, and making two of the most refractory fellows prisoners, he laid them in irons: and as they had been active in the former disorders, and let fall some ugly, dangerous words the second time, he threatened to carry them in irons to England, and have them hanged there for mutiny and running away with the ship. This, it seems, though the captain did not intend to do it, frightened some other men in the ship; and some of them had put it into the head of the rest that the captain only gave them good words for the present, till they should come to same English port, and that then they should be all put into gaol, and tried for their lives. The mate got intelligence of this, and acquainted us with it, upon which it was desired that I, who still passed for a great man among them, should go down with the mate and satisfy the men, and tell them that they might be assured, if they behaved well the rest of the voyage, all they had done for the time past should be pardoned. So I went, and after passing my honour's word to them they appeared easy, and the more so when I caused the two men that were in irons to be released and forgiven.

But this mutiny had brought us to an anchor for that night; the wind also falling calm next morning, we found that our two men who had been laid in irons had stolen each of them a musket and some other weapons (what powder or shot they had we knew not), and had taken the ship's pinnace, which was not yet hauled up, and run away with her to their companions in roguery on shore. As soon as we found this, I ordered the long-boat on shore, with twelve men and the mate, and away they went to seek the rogues; but they could neither find them nor any of the rest, for they all fled into the woods when they saw the boat coming on shore. The mate was once resolved, in justice to their roguery, to have destroyed their plantations, burned all their household stuff and furniture, and left them to shift without it; but having no orders, he let it all alone, left everything as he found it, and bringing the pinnace way, came on board without them. These two men made their number five; but the other three villains were so much more wicked than they, that after they had been two or three days together they turned the two newcomers out of doors to shift for themselves, and would have nothing to do with them; nor could they for a good while be persuaded to give them any food: as for the Spaniards, they were not yet come.

When the Spaniards came first on shore, the business began to go forward: the Spaniards would have persuaded the three English brutes to have taken in their countrymen again, that, as they said, they might be all one family; but they would not hear of it, so the two poor fellows lived by themselves; and finding nothing but industry and application would make them live comfortably, they pitched their tents on the north shore of the island, but a little more to the west, to be out of danger of the savages, who always landed on the east parts of the island. Here they built them two huts, one to lodge in, and the other to lay up their magazines and stores in; and the Spaniards having given them some corn for seed, and some of the peas which I had left them, they dug, planted, and enclosed, after the pattern I had set for them all, and began to live pretty well. Their first crop of corn was on the ground; and though it was but a little bit of land which they had dug up at first, having had but a little time, yet it was enough to relieve them, and find them with bread and other eatables; and one of the fellows being the cook's mate of the ship, was very ready at making soup, puddings, and such other preparations as the rice and the milk, and such little flesh as they got, furnished him to do.

They were going on in this little thriving position when the three unnatural rogues, their own countrymen too, in mere humour, and to insult them, came and bullied them, and told them the island was theirs: that the governor, meaning me, had given them the possession of it, and nobody else had any right to it; and that they should build no houses upon their ground unless they would pay rent for them. The two men, thinking they were jesting at first, asked them to come in and sit down, and see what fine houses they were that they had built, and to tell them what rent they demanded; and one of them merrily said if they were the ground-landlords, he hoped if they built tenements upon their land, and made improvements, they would, according to the custom of landlords, grant a long lease: and desired they would get a scrivener to draw the writings. One of the three, cursing and raging, told them they should see they were not in jest; and going to a little place at a distance, where the honest men had made a fire to dress their victuals, he takes a firebrand, and claps it to the outside of their hut, and set it on fire: indeed, it would have been all burned down in a few minutes if one of the two had not run to the fellow, thrust him away, and trod the fire out with his feet, and that not without some difficulty too.

The fellow was in such a rage at the honest man's thrusting him away, that he returned upon him, with a pole he had in his hand, and had not the man avoided the blow very nimbly, and run into the hut, he had ended his days at once. His comrade, seeing the danger they were both in, ran after him, and immediately they came both out with their muskets, and the man that was first struck at with the pole knocked the fellow down that began the quarrel with the stock of his musket, and that before the other two could come to help him; and then, seeing the rest come at them, they stood together, and presenting the other ends of their pieces to them, bade them stand off.

The others had firearms with them too; but one of the two honest men, bolder than his comrade, and made desperate by his danger, told them if they offered to move hand or foot they were dead men, and boldly commanded them to lay down their arms. They did not, indeed, lay down their arms, but seeing him so resolute, it brought them to a parley, and they consented to take their wounded man with them and be gone: and, indeed, it seems the fellow was wounded sufficiently with the blow. However, they were much in the wrong, since they had the advantage, that they did not disarm them effectually, as they might have done, and have gone immediately to the Spaniards, and given them an account how the rogues had treated them; for the three villains studied nothing but revenge, and every day gave them some intimation that they did so.

Chapter 3

Fight with Cannibals

But not to crowd this part with an account of the lesser part of the rogueries with which they plagued them continually, night and day, it forced the two men to such a desperation that they resolved to fight them all three, the first time they had a fair opportunity. In order to do this they resolved to go to the castle (as they called my old dwelling), where the three rogues and the Spaniards all lived together at that time, intending to have a fair battle, and the Spaniards should stand by to see fair play: so they got up in the morning before day, and came to the place, and called the Englishmen by their names telling a Spaniard that answered that they wanted to speak with them.

It happened that the day before two of the Spaniards, having been in the woods, had seen one of the two Englishmen, whom, for distinction, I called the honest men, and he had made a sad complaint to the Spaniards of the barbarous usage they had met with from their three countrymen, and how they had ruined their plantation, and destroyed their corn, that they had laboured so hard to bring forward, and killed the milch-goat and their three kids, which was all they had provided for their sustenance, and that if he and his friends, meaning the Spaniards, did not assist them again, they should be starved. When the Spaniards came home at night, and they were all at supper, one of them took the freedom to reprove the three Englishmen, though in very gentle and mannerly terms, and asked them how they could be so cruel, they being harmless, inoffensive fellows: that they were putting themselves in a way to subsist by their labour, and that it had cost them a great deal of pains to bring things to such perfection as they were then in.

One of the Englishmen returned very briskly, "What had they to do there? that they came on shore without leave; and that they should not plant or build upon the island; it was none of their ground." "Why," says the Spaniard, very calmly, "Seignior Inglese, they must not starve." The Englishman replied, like a rough tarpaulin, "They might starve; they should not plant nor build in that place." "But what must they do then, seignior?" said the Spaniard. Another of the brutes returned, "Do? they should be servants, and work for them." "But how can you expect that of them?" says the Spaniard; "they are not bought with your money; you have no right to make them servants." The Englishman answered, "The island was theirs; the governor had given it to them, and no man had anything to do there but themselves;" and with that he swore that he would go and burn all their new huts; they should build none upon their land. "Why, seignior," says the Spaniard, "by the same rule, we must be your servants, too." "Ay," returned the bold dog, "and so you shall, too, before we have done with you;" mixing two or three oaths in the proper intervals of his speech. The Spaniard only smiled at that, and made him no answer. However, this little discourse had heated them; and starting up, one says to the other. (I think it was he they called Will Atkins), "Come, Jack, let's go and have t'other brush with them; we'll demolish their castle, I'll warrant you; they shall plant no colony in our dominions."

Upon this they were all trooping away, with every man a gun, a pistol, and a sword, and muttered some insolent things among themselves of what they would do to the Spaniards, too, when opportunity offered; but the Spaniards, it seems, did not so perfectly understand them as to know all the particulars, only that in general they threatened them hard for taking the two Englishmen's part. Whither they went, or how they bestowed their time that evening, the Spaniards said they did not know; but it seems they wandered about the country part of the night, and them lying down in the place which I used to call my bower, they were weary and overslept themselves. The case was this: they had resolved to stay till midnight, and so take the two poor men when they were asleep, and as they acknowledged afterwards, intended to set fire to their huts while they were in them, and either burn them there or murder them as they came out. As malice seldom sleeps very sound, it was very strange they should not have been kept awake. However, as the two men had also a design upon them, as I have said, though a much fairer one than that of burning and murdering, it happened, and very luckily for them all, that they were up and gone abroad before the bloody-minded rogues came to their huts.

When they came there, and found the men gone, Atkins, who it seems was the forwardest man, called out to his comrade, "Ha, Jack, here's the nest, but the birds are flown." They mused a while, to think what should be the occasion of their being gone abroad so soon, and suggested presently that the Spaniards had given them notice of it; and with that they shook hands, and swore to one another that they would be revenged of the Spaniards. As soon as they had made this bloody bargain they fell to work with the poor men's habitation; they did not set fire, indeed, to anything, but they pulled down both their houses, and left not the least stick standing, or scarce any sign on the ground where they stood; they tore all their household stuff in pieces, and threw everything about in such a manner, that the poor men afterwards found some of their things a mile off. When they had done this, they pulled up all the young trees which the poor men had planted; broke down an enclosure they had made to secure their cattle and their corn; and, in a word, sacked and plundered everything as completely as a horde of Tartars would have done.

The two men were at this juncture gone to find them out, and had resolved to fight them wherever they had been, though they were but two to three; so that, had they met, there certainly would have been blood shed among them, for they were all very stout, resolute fellows, to give them their due.

But Providence took more care to keep them asunder than they themselves could do to meet; for, as if they had dogged one another, when the three were gone thither, the two were here; and afterwards, when the two went back to find them, the three were come to the old habitation again: we shall see their different conduct presently. When the three came back like furious creatures, flushed with the rage which the work they had been about had put them into, they came up to the Spaniards, and told them what they had done, by way of scoff and bravado; and one of them stepping up to one of the Spaniards, as if they had been a couple of boys at play, takes hold of his hat as it was upon his head, and giving it a twirl about, fleering in his face, says to him, "And you, Seignior Jack Spaniard, shall have the same sauce if you do not mend your manners." The Spaniard, who, though a quiet civil man, was as brave a man as could be, and withal a strong, well-made man, looked at him for a good while, and then, having no weapon in his hand, stepped gravely up to him, and, with one blow of his fist, knocked him down, as an ox is felled with a

60

pole-axe; at which one of the rogues, as insolent as the first, fired his pistol at the Spaniard immediately; he missed his body, indeed, for the bullets went through his hair, but one of them touched the tip of his ear, and he bled pretty much. The blood made the Spaniard believe he was more hurt than he really was, and that put him into some heat, for before he acted all in a perfect calm; but now resolving to go through with his work, he stooped, and taking the fellow's musket whom he had knocked down, was just going to shoot the man who had fired at him, when the rest of the Spaniards, being in the cave, came out, and calling to him not to shoot, they stepped in, secured the other two, and took their arms from them.

When they were thus disarmed, and found they had made all the Spaniards their enemies, as well as their own countrymen, they began to cool, and giving the Spaniards better words, would have their arms again; but the Spaniards, considering the feud that was between them and the other two Englishmen, and that it would be the best method they could take to keep them from killing one another, told them they would do them no harm, and if they would live peaceably, they would be very willing to assist and associate with them as they did before; but that they could not think of giving them their arms again, while they appeared so resolved to do mischief with them to their own countrymen, and had even threatened them all to make them their servants.

The rogues were now quite deaf to all reason, and being refused their arms, they raved away like madmen, threatening what they would do, though they had no firearms. But the Spaniards, despising their threatening, told them they should take care how they offered any injury to their plantation or cattle; for if they did they would shoot them as they would ravenous beasts, wherever they found them; and if they fell into their hands alive, they should certainly be hanged. However, this was far from cooling them, but away they went, raging and swearing like furies. As soon as they were gone, the two men came back, in passion and rage enough also, though of another kind; for having been at their plantation, and finding it all demolished and destroyed, as above mentioned, it will easily be supposed they had provocation enough. They could scarce have room to tell their tale, the Spaniards were so eager to tell them theirs: and it was strange enough to find that three men should thus bully nineteen, and receive no punishment at all.

The Spaniards, indeed, despised them, and especially, having thus disarmed them, made light of their threatenings; but the two Englishmen resolved to have their remedy against them, what pains soever it cost to find them out. But the Spaniards interposed here too, and told them that as they had disarmed them, they could not consent that they (the two) should pursue them with firearms, and perhaps kill them. "But," said the grave Spaniard, who was their governor, "we will endeavour to make them do you justice, if you will leave it to us: for there is no doubt but they will come to us again, when their passion is over, being not able to subsist without our assistance. We promise you to make no peace with them without having full satisfaction for you; and upon this condition we hope you will promise to use no violence with them, other than in your own defence." The two Englishmen yielded to this very awkwardly, and with great reluctance; but the Spaniards protested that they did it only to keep them from bloodshed, and to make them all easy at last. "For," said they, "we are not so many of us; here is room enough for us all, and it is a great pity that we should not be all good friends." At length they did consent, and waited for the issue of the thing, living for some days with the Spaniards; for their own habitation was destroyed.

In about five days' time the vagrants, tired with wandering, and almost starved with hunger, having chiefly lived on turtles' eggs all that while, came back to the grove; and finding my Spaniard, who, as I have said, was the governor, and two more with him, walking by the side of the creek, they came up in a very submissive, humble manner, and begged to be received again into the society. The Spaniards used them civilly, but told them they had acted so unnaturally to their countrymen, and so very grossly to themselves, that they could not come to any conclusion without consulting the two Englishmen and the rest; but, however, they would go to them and discourse about it, and they should know in half-an-hour. It may be guessed that they were very hard put to it; for, as they were to wait this half-hour for an answer, they begged they would send them out some bread in the meantime, which they did, sending at the same time a large piece of goat's flesh and a boiled parrot, which they ate very eagerly.

After half-an-hour's consultation they were called in, and a long debate ensued, their two countrymen charging them with the ruin of all their labour, and a design to murder them; all which they owned before, and therefore could not deny now. Upon the whole, the Spaniards acted the moderators between them; and as they had obliged the two Englishmen not to hurt the three while they were naked and unarmed, so they now obliged the three to go and rebuild their fellows' two huts, one to be of the same and the other of larger dimensions than they were before; to fence their ground again, plant trees in the room of those pulled up, dig up the land again for planting corn, and, in a word, to restore everything to the same state as they found it, that is, as near as they could.

Well, they submitted to all this; and as they had plenty of provisions given them all the while, they grew very orderly, and the whole society began to live pleasantly and agreeably together again; only that these three fellows could never be persuaded to work—I mean for themselves—except now and then a little, just as they pleased. However, the Spaniards told them plainly that if they would but live sociably and friendly together, and study the good of the whole plantation, they would be content to work for them, and let them walk about and be as idle as they pleased; and thus, having lived pretty well together for a month or two, the Spaniards let them have arms again, and gave them liberty to go abroad with them as before.

It was not above a week after they had these arms, and went abroad, before the ungrateful creatures began to be as insolent and troublesome as ever. However, an accident happened presently upon this, which endangered the safety of them all, and they were obliged to lay by all private resentments, and look to the preservation of their lives.

It happened one night that the governor, the Spaniard whose life I had saved, who was now the governor of the rest, found himself very uneasy in the night, and could by no means get any sleep: he was perfectly well in body, only found his thoughts tumultuous; his mind ran upon men fighting and killing one another; but he was broad awake, and could not by any means get any sleep; in short, he lay a great while, but growing more and more uneasy, he resolved to rise. As they lay, being so many of them, on goat-skins laid thick upon such couches and pads as they made for themselves, so they had little to do, when they were willing to rise, but to get upon their feet, and perhaps put on a coat, such as it was, and their pumps, and they were ready for going any way that their thoughts guided them. Being thus got up, he looked out; but being dark, he could see little or nothing, and besides, the trees which I had planted, and which were now grown tall, intercepted his sight, so that he could only look up, and see that it was a starlight night, and hearing no noise, he returned and lay down again; but to no purpose; he could not compose himself to anything like rest; but his thoughts were to the last degree uneasy, and he knew not for what. Having made some noise with rising and walking about, going out and coming in, another of them waked, and asked who it was that was up. The governor told him how it had been with him. "Say you so?" says the other Spaniard; "such things are not to be slighted, I assure you; there is certainly some mischief working near us;" and presently he asked him, "Where are the Englishmen?" "They are all in their huts," says he, "safe enough." It seems the Spaniards had kept possession of the main apartment, and had made a place for the three Englishmen, who, since their last mutiny, were always quartered by themselves, and could not come at the rest. "Well," says the Spaniard, "there is something in it, I am persuaded, from my own experience. I am satisfied that our spirits embodied have a converse with and receive intelligence from the spirits unembodied, and inhabiting the invisible world; and this friendly notice is given for our advantage, if we knew how to make use of it. Come, let us go and look abroad; and if we find nothing at all in it to justify the trouble, I'll tell you a story to the purpose, that shall convince you of the justice of my proposing it."

They went out presently to go up to the top of the hill, where I used to go; but they being strong, and a good company, nor alone, as I was, used none of my cautions to go up by the ladder, and pulling it up after them, to go up a second stage to the top, but were going round through the grove unwarily, when they were surprised with seeing a light as of fire, a very little way from them, and hearing the voices of men, not of one or two, but of a great number.

Among the precautions I used to take on the savages landing on the island, it was my constant care to prevent them making the least discovery of there being any inhabitant upon the place: and when by any occasion they came to know it, they felt it so effectually that they that got away were scarce able to give any account of it; for we disappeared as soon as possible, nor did ever any that had seen me escape to tell any one else, except it was the three savages in our last encounter who jumped into the boat; of whom, I mentioned, I was afraid they should go home and bring more help. Whether it was the consequence of the escape of those men that so great a number came now together, or whether they came ignorantly, and by accident, on their usual bloody errand, the Spaniards could not understand; but whatever it was, it was their business either to have concealed themselves or not to have seen them at all, much less to have let the savages have seen there were any inhabitants in the place; or to have fallen upon them so effectually as not a man of them should have escaped, which could only have been by getting in between them and their boats; but this presence of mind was wanting to them, which was the ruin of their tranquillity for a great while.

We need not doubt but that the governor and the man with him, surprised with this sight, ran back immediately and raised their fellows, giving them an account of the imminent danger they were all in, and they again as readily took the alarm; but it was impossible to persuade them to stay close within where they were, but they must all run out to see how things stood. While it was dark, indeed, they were safe, and they had opportunity enough for some hours to view the savages by the light of three fires they had made at a distance from one another; what they were doing they knew not, neither did they know what to do themselves. For, first, the enemy were too many; and secondly, they did not keep together, but were divided into several parties, and were on shore in several places.

The Spaniards were in no small consternation at this sight; and, as they found that the fellows went straggling all over the shore, they made no doubt but, first or last, some of them would chop in upon their habitation, or upon some other place where they would see the token of inhabitants; and they were in great perplexity also for fear of their flock of goats, which, if they should be destroyed, would have been little less than starving them. So the first thing they resolved upon was to despatch three men away before it was light, two Spaniards and one Englishman, to drive away all the goats to the great valley where the cave was, and, if need were, to drive them into the very cave itself. Could they have seen the savages all together in one body, and at a distance from their canoes, they were resolved, if there had been a hundred of them, to attack them; but that could not be done, for they were some of them two miles off from the other, and, as it appeared afterwards, were of two different nations.

After having mused a great while on the course they should take, they resolved at last, while it was still dark, to send the old savage, Friday's father, out as a spy, to learn, if possible, something concerning them, as what they came for, what they intended to do, and the like. The old man readily undertook it; and stripping himself quite naked, as most of the savages were, away he went. After he had been gone an hour or two, he brings word that he had been among them undiscovered, that he found they were two parties, and of two several nations, who had war with one another, and had a great battle in their own country; and that both sides having had several prisoners taken in the fight, they were, by mere chance, landed all on the same island, for the devouring their prisoners and making merry; but their coming so by chance to the same place had spoiled all their mirth—that they were in a great rage at one another, and were so near that he believed they would fight again as soon as daylight began to appear; but he did not perceive that they had any notion of anybody being on the island but themselves. He had hardly made an end of telling his story, when they could perceive, by the unusual noise they made, that the two little armies were engaged in a bloody fight. Friday's father used all the arguments he could to persuade our people to lie close, and not be seen; he told them their safety consisted in it, and that they had nothing to do but lie still, and the savages would kill one another to their hands, and then the rest would go away; and it was so to a tittle. But it was impossible to prevail, especially upon the Englishmen; their curiosity was so importunate that they must run out and see the battle. However, they used some caution too: they did not go openly, just by their own dwelling, but went farther into the woods, and placed themselves to advantage, where they might securely see them manage the fight, and, as they thought, not be seen by them; but the savages did see them, as we shall find hereafter.

The battle was very fierce, and, if I might believe the Englishmen, one of them said he could perceive that some of them were men of great bravery, of invincible spirit, and of great policy in guiding the fight. The battle, they said, held two hours before they could guess which party would be beaten; but then that party which was nearest our people's habitation began to appear weakest, and after some time more some of them began to fly; and this put our men again into a great consternation, lest any one of those that fled should run into the grove before their dwelling for shelter, and thereby involuntarily discover the place; and that, by consequence, the pursuers would also do the like in search of them. Upon this, they resolved that they would stand armed within the wall, and whoever came into the grove, they resolved to sally out over the wall and kill them, so that, if possible, not one should return to give an account of it; they ordered also that it should be done with their swords, or by knocking them down with the stocks of their muskets, but not by shooting them, for fear of raising an alarm by the noise.

As they expected it fell out; three of the routed army fled for life, and crossing the creek, ran directly into the place, not in the least knowing whither they went, but running as into a thick wood for shelter. The scout they kept to look abroad gave notice of this within, with this comforting addition, that the conquerors had not pursued them, or seen which way they were gone; upon this the Spanish governor, a man of humanity, would not suffer them to kill the three fugitives, but sending three men out by the top of the hill, ordered them to go round, come in behind them, and surprise and take them prisoners, which was done. The residue of the conquered people fled to their canoes, and got off to sea; the victors retired, made no pursuit, or very little, but drawing themselves into a body together, gave two great screaming shouts, most likely by way of triumph, and so the fight ended; the same day, about three o'clock in the afternoon, they also marched to their canoes. And thus the Spaniards had the island again free to themselves, their fright was over, and they saw no savages for several years after.

After they were all gone, the Spaniards came out of their den, and viewing the field of battle, they found about two-and-thirty men dead on the spot; some were killed with long arrows, which were found sticking in their bodies; but most of them were killed with great wooden swords, sixteen or seventeen of which they found in the field of battle, and as many bows, with a great many arrows. These swords were strange, unwieldy things, and they must be very strong men that used them; most of those that were killed with them had their heads smashed to pieces, as we may say, or, as we call it in English, their brains knocked out, and several their arms and legs broken; so that it is evident they fight with inexpressible rage and fury. We found not one man that was not stone dead; for either they stay by their enemy till they have killed him, or they carry all the wounded men that are not quite dead away with them.

This deliverance tamed our ill-disposed Englishmen for a great while; the sight had filled them with horror, and the consequences appeared terrible to the last degree, especially upon supposing that some time or other they should fall into the hands of those creatures, who would not only kill them as enemies, but for food, as we kill our cattle; and they professed to me that the thoughts of being eaten up like beef and mutton, though it was supposed it was not to be till they were dead, had something in it so horrible that it nauseated their very stomachs, made them sick when they thought of it, and filled their minds with such unusual terror, that they were not themselves for some weeks after. This, as I said, tamed even the three English brutes I have been speaking of; and for a great while after they were tractable, and went about the common business of the whole society well enough—planted, sowed, reaped, and began to be all naturalised to the country. But some time after this they fell into such simple measures again as brought them into a great deal of trouble.

They had taken three prisoners, as I observed; and these three being stout young fellows, they made them servants, and taught them to work for them, and as slaves they did well enough; but they did not take their measures as I did by my man Friday, viz. to begin with them upon the principle of having saved their lives, and then instruct them in the rational principles of life; much less did they think of teaching them religion, or attempt civilising and reducing them by kind usage and affectionate arguments. As they gave them their food every day, so they gave them their work too, and kept them fully employed in drudgery enough; but they failed in this by it, that they never had them to assist them and fight for them as I had my man Friday, who was as true to me as the very flesh upon my bones.

But to come to the family part. Being all now good friends—for common danger, as I said above, had effectually reconciled them— they began to consider their general circumstances; and the first thing that came under consideration was whether, seeing the savages particularly haunted that side of the island, and that there were more remote and retired parts of it equally adapted to their way of living, and manifestly to their advantage, they should not rather move their habitation, and plant in some more proper place for their safety, and especially for the security of their cattle and corn.

Upon this, after long debate, it was concluded that they would not remove their habitation; because that, some time or other, they thought they might hear from their governor again, meaning me; and if I should send any one to seek them, I should be sure to direct them to that side, where, if they should find the place demolished, they would conclude the savages had killed us all, and we were gone, and so our supply would go too. But as to their corn and cattle, they agreed to remove them into the valley where my cave was, where the land was as proper for both, and where indeed there was land enough. However, upon second thoughts they altered one part of their resolution too, and resolved only to remove part of their cattle thither, and part of their corn there; so that if one part was destroyed the other might be saved. And one part of prudence they luckily used: they never trusted those three savages which they had taken prisoners with knowing anything of the plantation they had made in that valley, or of any cattle they had there, much less of the cave at that place, which they kept, in case of necessity, as a safe retreat; and thither they carried also the two barrels of powder which I had sent them at my coming away. They resolved, however, not to change their habitation; yet, as I had carefully covered it first with a wall or fortification, and then with a grove of trees, and as they were now fully convinced their safety consisted entirely in their being concealed, they set to work to cover and conceal the place yet more effectually than before. For this purpose, as I planted trees, or rather thrust in stakes, which in time all grew up to be trees, for some good distance before the entrance into my apartments, they went on in the same manner, and filled up the rest of that whole space of ground from the trees I had set quite down to the side of the creek, where I landed my floats, and even into the very ooze where the tide flowed, not so much as leaving any place to land, or any sign that there had been any landing thereabouts: these stakes also being of a wood very forward to grow, they took care to have them generally much larger and taller than those which I had planted. As they grew apace, they planted them so very thick and close together, that when they had been three or four years grown there was no piercing with the eye any considerable way into the plantation. As for that part which I had planted, the trees were grown as thick as a man's thigh, and among them they had placed so many other short ones, and so thick, that it stood like a palisado a quarter of a mile thick, and it was next to impossible to penetrate it, for a little dog could hardly get between the trees, they stood so close.

But this was not all; for they did the same by all the ground to the right hand and to the left, and round even to the side of the hill, leaving no way, not so much as for themselves, to come out but by the ladder placed up to the side of the hill, and then lifted up, and placed again from the first stage up to the top: so that when the ladder was taken down, nothing but what had wings or witchcraft to assist it could come at them. This was excellently well contrived: nor was it less than what they afterwards found occasion for, which served to convince me, that as human prudence has the authority of Providence to justify it, so it has doubtless the direction of Providence to set it to work; and if we listened carefully to the voice of it, I am persuaded we might prevent many of the disasters which our lives are now, by our own negligence, subjected to.

They lived two years after this in perfect retirement, and had no more visits from the savages. They had, indeed, an alarm given them one morning, which put them into a great consternation; for some of the Spaniards being out early one morning on the west side or end of the island (which was that end where I never went, for fear of being discovered), they were surprised with seeing about twenty canoes of Indians just coming on shore. They made the best of their way home in hurry enough; and giving the alarm to their comrades, they kept close all that day and the next, going out only at night to make their observation: but they had the good luck to be undiscovered, for wherever the savages went, they did not land that time on the island, but pursued some other design.

Chapter 4

Renewed Invasion of Savages

And now they had another broil with the three Englishmen; one of whom, a most turbulent fellow, being in a rage at one of the three captive slaves, because the fellow had not done something right which he bade him do, and seemed a little untractable in his showing him, drew a hatchet out of a frog-belt which he wore by his side, and fell upon the poor savage, not to correct him, but to kill him. One of the Spaniards who was by, seeing him give the fellow a barbarous cut with the hatchet, which he aimed at his head, but stuck into his shoulder, so that he thought he had cut the poor creature's arm off, ran to him, and entreating him not to murder the poor man, placed himself between him and the savage, to prevent the mischief. The fellow, being enraged the more at this, struck at the Spaniard with his hatchet, and swore he would serve him as he intended to serve the savage; which the Spaniard perceiving, avoided the blow, and with a shovel, which he had in his hand (for they were all working in the field about their corn land), knocked the brute down. Another of the Englishmen, running up at the same time to help his comrade, knocked the Spaniard down; and then two Spaniards more came in to help their man, and a third Englishman fell in upon them. They had none of them any firearms or any other weapons but hatchets and other tools, except this third Englishman; he had one of

75

my rusty cutlasses, with which he made at the two last Spaniards, and wounded them both. This fray set the whole family in an uproar, and more help coming in they took the three Englishmen prisoners. The next question was, what should be done with them? They had been so often mutinous, and were so very furious, so desperate, and so idle withal, they knew not what course to take with them, for they were mischievous to the highest degree, and cared not what hurt they did to any man; so that, in short, it was not safe to live with them.

The Spaniard who was governor told them, in so many words, that if they had been of his own country he would have hanged them; for all laws and all governors were to preserve society, and those who were dangerous to the society ought to be expelled out of it; but as they were Englishmen, and that it was to the generous kindness of an Englishman that they all owed their preservation and deliverance, he would use them with all possible lenity, and would leave them to the judgment of the other two Englishmen, who were their countrymen. One of the two honest Englishmen stood up, and said they desired it might not be left to them. "For," says he, "I am sure we ought to sentence them to the gallows;" and with that he gives an account how Will Atkins, one of the three, had proposed to have all the five Englishmen join together and murder all the Spaniards when they were in their sleep.

When the Spanish governor heard this, he calls to Will Atkins, "How, Seignior Atkins, would you murder us all? What have you to say to that?" The hardened villain was so far from denying it, that he said it was true, and swore they would do it still before they had done with them. "Well, but Seignior Atkins," says the Spaniard, "what have we done to you that you will kill us? What would you get by killing us? And what must we do to prevent you killing us? Must we kill you, or you kill us? Why will you put us to the necessity of this, Seignior Atkins?" says the Spaniard very calmly, and smiling. Seignior Atkins was in such a rage at the Spaniard's making a jest of it, that, had he not been held by three men, and withal had no weapon near him, it was thought he would have attempted to kill the Spaniard in the middle of all the company. This hare-brained carriage obliged them to consider seriously what was to be done. The two Englishmen and the Spaniard who saved the poor savage were of the opinion that they should hang one of the three for an example to the rest, and that particularly it should be he that had twice attempted to commit murder with his hatchet; indeed, there was some reason to believe he had done it, for the poor savage was in such a miserable condition with the wound he had received that it was thought he could not live. But the governor Spaniard still said No; it was an Englishman that had saved all their lives, and he would never consent to put an Englishman to death, though he had murdered half of them; nay, he said if he had been killed himself by an Englishman, and had time left to speak, it should be that they should pardon him.

This was so positively insisted on by the governor Spaniard, that there was no gainsaying it; and as merciful counsels are most apt to prevail where they are so earnestly pressed, so they all came into it. But then it was to be considered what should be done to keep them from doing the mischief they designed; for all agreed, governor and all, that means were to be used for preserving the society from danger. After a long debate, it was agreed that they should be disarmed, and not permitted to have either gun, powder, shot, sword, or any weapon; that they should be turned out of the society, and left to live where they would and how they would, by themselves; but that none of the rest, either Spaniards or English, should hold any kind of converse with them, or have anything to do with them; that they should be forbid to come within a certain distance of the place where the rest dwelt; and if they offered to commit any disorder, so as to spoil, burn, kill, or destroy any of the corn, plantings, buildings, fences, or cattle belonging to the society, they should die without mercy, and they would shoot them wherever they could find them.

The humane governor, musing upon the sentence, considered a little upon it; and turning to the two honest Englishmen, said, "Hold; you must reflect that it will be long ere they can raise corn and cattle of their own, and they must not starve; we must therefore allow them provisions." So he caused to be added, that they should have a proportion of corn given them to last them eight months, and for seed to sow, by which time they might be supposed to raise some of their own; that they should have six milch-goats, four he-goats, and six kids given them, as well for present subsistence as for a store; and that they should have tools given them for their work in the fields, but they should have none of these tools or provisions unless they would swear solemnly that they would not hurt or injure any of the Spaniards with them, or of their fellow-Englishmen.

Thus they dismissed them the society, and turned them out to shift for themselves. They went away sullen and refractory, as neither content to go away nor to stay: but, as there was no remedy, they went, pretending to go and choose a place where they would settle themselves; and some provisions were given them, but no weapons. About four or five days after, they came again for some victuals, and gave the governor an account where they had pitched their tents, and marked themselves out a habitation and plantation; and it was a very convenient place indeed, on the remotest part of the island, NE., much about the place where I providentially landed in my first voyage, when I was driven out to sea in my foolish attempt to sail round the island.

Here they built themselves two handsome huts, and contrived them in a manner like my first habitation, being close under the side of a hill, having some trees already growing on three sides of it, so that by planting others it would be very easily covered from the sight, unless narrowly searched for. They desired some dried goat- skins for beds and covering, which were given them; and upon giving their words that they would not disturb the rest, or injure any of their plantations, they gave them hatchets, and what other tools they could spare; some peas, barley, and rice, for sowing; and, in a word, anything they wanted, except arms and ammunition.

They lived in this separate condition about six months, and had got in their first harvest, though the quantity was but small, the parcel of land they had planted being but little. Indeed, having all their plantation to form, they had a great deal of work upon their hands; and when they came to make boards and pots, and such things, they were quite out of their element, and could make nothing of it; therefore when the rainy season came on, for want of a cave in the earth, they could not keep their grain dry, and it was in great danger of spoiling. This humbled them much: so they came and begged the Spaniards to help them, which they very readily did; and in four days worked a great hole in the side of the hill for them, big enough to secure their corn and other things from the rain: but it was a poor place at best compared to mine, and especially as mine was then, for the Spaniards had greatly enlarged it, and made several new apartments in it.

About three quarters of a year after this separation, a new frolic took these rogues, which, together with the former villainy they had committed, brought mischief enough upon them, and had very near been the ruin of the whole colony. The three new associates began, it seems, to be weary of the laborious life they led, and that without hope of bettering their circumstances: and a whim took them that they would make a voyage to the continent, from whence the savages came, and would try if they could seize upon some prisoners among the natives there, and bring them home, so as to make them do the laborious part of the work for them.

The project was not so preposterous, if they had gone no further. But they did nothing, and proposed nothing, but had either mischief in the design, or mischief in the event. And if I may give my opinion, they seemed to be under a blast from Heaven: for if we will not allow a visible curse to pursue visible crimes, how shall we reconcile the events of things with the divine justice? It was certainly an apparent vengeance on their crime of mutiny and piracy that brought them to the state they were in; and they showed not the least remorse for the crime, but added new villanies to it, such as the piece of monstrous cruelty of wounding a poor slave because he did not, or perhaps could not, understand to do what he was directed, and to wound him in such a manner as made him a cripple all his life, and in a place where no surgeon or medicine could be had for his cure; and, what was still worse, the intentional murder, for such to be sure it was, as was afterwards the formed design they all laid to murder the Spaniards in cold blood, and in their sleep.

The three fellows came down to the Spaniards one morning, and in very humble terms desired to be admitted to speak with them. The Spaniards very readily heard what they had to say, which was this: that they were tired of living in the manner they did, and that they were not handy enough to make the necessaries they wanted, and that having no help, they found they should be starved; but if the Spaniards would give them leave to take one of the canoes which they came over in, and give them arms and ammunition proportioned to their defence, they would go over to the main, and seek their fortunes, and so deliver them from the trouble of supplying them with any other provisions.

The Spaniards were glad enough to get rid of them, but very honestly represented to them the certain destruction they were running into; told them they had suffered such hardships upon that very spot, that they could, without any spirit of prophecy, tell them they would be starved or murdered, and bade them consider of it. The men replied audaciously, they should be starved if they stayed here, for they could not work, and would not work, and they could but be starved abroad; and if they were murdered, there was an end of them; they had no wives or children to cry after them; and, in short, insisted importunately upon their demand, declaring they would go, whether they gave them any arms or not.

The Spaniards told them, with great kindness, that if they were resolved to go they should not go like naked men, and be in no condition to defend themselves; and that though they could ill spare firearms, not having enough for themselves, yet they would let them have two muskets, a pistol, and a cutlass, and each man a hatchet, which they thought was sufficient for them. In a word, they accepted the offer; and having baked bread enough to serve them a month given them, and as much goats' flesh as they could eat while it was sweet, with a great basket of dried grapes, a pot of fresh water, and a young kid alive, they boldly set out in the canoe for a voyage over the sea, where it was at least forty miles broad. The boat, indeed, was a large one, and would very well have carried fifteen or twenty men, and therefore was rather too big for them to manage; but as they had a fair breeze and flood-tide with them, they did well enough. They had made a mast of a long pole, and a sail of four large goat-skins dried, which they had sewed or laced together; and away they went merrily together. The Spaniards called after them "Bon voyajo;" and no man ever thought of seeing them any more.

The Spaniards were often saying to one another, and to the two honest Englishmen who remained behind, how quietly and comfortably they lived, now these three turbulent fellows were gone. As for their coming again, that was the remotest thing from their thoughts that could be imagined; when, behold, after two-and-twenty days' absence, one of the Englishmen being abroad upon his planting work, sees three strange men coming towards him at a distance, with guns upon their shoulders.

Away runs the Englishman, frightened and amazed, as if he was bewitched, to the governor Spaniard, and tells him they were all undone, for there were strangers upon the island, but he could not tell who they were. The Spaniard, pausing a while, says to him, "How do you mean—you cannot tell who? They are the savages, to be sure." "No, no," says the Englishman, "they are men in clothes, with arms." "Nay, then," says the Spaniard, "why are you so concerned! If they are not savages they must be friends; for there is no Christian nation upon earth but will do us good rather than harm." While they were debating thus, came up the three Englishmen, and standing without the wood, which was new planted, hallooed to them. They presently knew their voices, and so all the wonder ceased. But now the admiration was turned upon another question—What could be the matter, and what made them come back again?

It was not long before they brought the men in, and inquiring where they had been, and what they had been doing, they gave them a full account of their voyage in a few words: that they reached the land in less than two days, but finding the people alarmed at their coming, and preparing with bows and arrows to fight them, they durst not go on, shore, but sailed on to the northward six or seven hours, till they came to a great opening, by which they perceived that the land they saw from our island was not the main, but an island: that upon entering that opening of the sea they saw another island on the right hand north, and several more west; and being resolved to land somewhere, they put over to one of the islands which lay west, and went boldly on shore; that they found the people very courteous and friendly to them; and they gave them several roots and some dried fish, and appeared very sociable; and that the women, as well as the men, were very forward to supply them with anything they could get for them to eat, and brought it to them a great way, on their heads. They continued here for four days, and inquired as well as they could of them by signs, what nations were this way, and that way, and were told of several fierce and terrible people that lived almost every way, who, as they made known by signs to them, used to eat men; but, as for themselves, they said they never ate men or women, except only such as they took in the wars; and then they owned they made a great feast, and ate their prisoners.

The Englishmen inquired when they had had a feast of that kind; and they told them about two moons ago, pointing to the moon and to two fingers; and that their great king had two hundred prisoners now, which he had taken in his war, and they were feeding them to make them fat for the next feast. The Englishmen seemed mighty desirous of seeing those prisoners; but the others mistaking them, thought they were desirous to have some of them to carry away for their own eating. So they beckoned to them, pointing to the setting of the sun, and then to the rising; which was to signify that the next morning at sunrising they would bring some for them; and accordingly the next morning they brought down five women and eleven men, and gave them to the Englishmen to carry with them on their voyage, just as we would bring so many cows and oxen down to a seaport town to victual a ship.

As brutish and barbarous as these fellows were at home, their stomachs turned at this sight, and they did not know what to do. To refuse the prisoners would have been the highest affront to the savage gentry that could be offered them, and what to do with them they knew not. However, after some debate, they resolved to accept of them: and, in return, they gave the savages that brought them one of their hatchets, an old key, a knife, and six or seven of their bullets; which, though they did not understand their use, they seemed particularly pleased with; and then tying the poor creatures' hands behind them, they dragged the prisoners into the boat for our men.

The Englishmen were obliged to come away as soon as they had them, or else they that gave them this noble present would certainly have expected that they should have gone to work with them, have killed two or three of them the next morning, and perhaps have invited the donors to dinner. But having taken their leave, with all the respect and thanks that could well pass between people, where on either side they understood not one word they could say, they put off with their boat, and came back towards the first island; where, when they arrived, they set eight of their prisoners at liberty, there being too many of them for their occasion. In their voyage they endeavoured to have some communication with their prisoners; but it was impossible to make them understand anything. Nothing they could say to them, or give them, or do for them, but was looked upon as going to murder them. They first of all unbound them; but the poor creatures screamed at that, especially the women, as if they had just felt the knife at their throats; for they immediately concluded they were unbound on purpose to be killed. If they gave them thing to eat, it was the same thing; they then concluded it was for fear they should sink in flesh, and so not be fat enough to kill. If they looked at one of them more particularly, the party presently concluded it was to see whether he or she was fattest, and fittest to kill first; nay, after they had brought them quite over, and began to use them kindly, and treat them well, still they expected every day to make a dinner or supper for their new masters.

When the three wanderers had give this unaccountable history or journal of their voyage, the Spaniard asked them where their new family was; and being told that they had brought them on shore, and put them into one of their huts, and were come up to beg some victuals for them, they (the Spaniards) and the other two Englishmen, that is to say, the whole colony, resolved to go all down to the place and see them; and did so, and Friday's father with them. When they came into the hut, there they sat, all bound; for when they had brought them on shore they bound their hands that they might not take the boat and make their escape; there, I say, they sat, all of them stark naked. First, there were three comely fellows, well shaped, with straight limbs, about thirty to thirty- five years of age; and five women, whereof two might be from thirty to forty, two more about four or five and twenty; and the fifth, a tall, comely maiden, about seventeen. The women were well- favoured, agreeable persons, both in shape and features, only tawny; and two of them, had they been perfect white, would have passed for very handsome women, even in London, having pleasant countenances, and of a very modest behaviour; especially when they came afterwards to be clothed and dressed, though that dress was very indifferent, it must be confessed.

The sight, you may be sure, was something uncouth to our Spaniards, who were, to give them a just character, men of the most calm, sedate tempers, and perfect good humour, that ever I met with: and, in particular, of the utmost modesty: I say, the sight was very uncouth, to see three naked men and five naked women, all together bound, and in the most miserable circumstances that human nature could be supposed to be, viz. to be expecting every moment to be dragged out and have their brains knocked out, and then to be eaten up like a calf that is killed for a dainty.

The first thing they did was to cause the old Indian, Friday's father, to go in, and see first if he knew any of them, and then if he understood any of their speech. As soon as the old man came in, he looked seriously at them, but knew none of them; neither could any of them understand a word he said, or a sign he could make, except one of the women. However, this was enough to answer the end, which was to satisfy them that the men into whose hands they were fallen were Christians; that they abhorred eating men or women; and that they might be sure they would not be killed. As soon as they were assured of this, they discovered such a joy, and by such awkward gestures, several ways, as is hard to describe; for it seems they were of several nations. The woman who was their interpreter was bid, in the next place, to ask them if they were willing to be servants, and to work for the men who had brought them away, to save their lives; at which they all fell a-dancing; and presently one fell to taking up this, and another that, anything that lay next, to carry on their shoulders, to intimate they were willing to work.

The governor, who found that the having women among them would presently be attended with some inconvenience, and might occasion some strife, and perhaps blood, asked the three men what they intended to do with these women, and how they intended to use them, whether as servants or as wives? One of the Englishmen answered, very boldly and readily, that they would use them as both; to which the governor said: "I am not going to restrain you from it—you are your own masters as to that; but this I think is but just, for avoiding disorders and quarrels among you, and I desire it of you for that reason only, viz. that you will all engage, that if any of you take any of these women as a wife, he shall take but one; and that having taken one, none else shall touch her; for though we cannot marry any one of you, yet it is but reasonable that, while you stay here, the woman any of you takes shall be maintained by the man that takes her, and should be his wife—I mean," says he, "while he continues here, and that none else shall have anything to do with her." All this appeared so just, that every one agreed to it without any difficulty.

Then the Englishmen asked the Spaniards if they designed to take any of them? But every one of them answered "No." Some of them said they had wives in Spain, and the others did not like women that were not Christians; and all together declared that they would not touch one of them, which was an instance of such virtue as I have not met with in all my travels. On the other hand, the five Englishmen took them every one a wife, that is to say, a temporary wife; and so they set up a new form of living; for the Spaniards and Friday's father lived in my old habitation, which they had enlarged exceedingly within. The three servants which were taken in the last battle of the savages lived with them; and these carried on the main part of the colony, supplied all the rest with food, and assisted them in anything as they could, or as they found necessity required.

But the wonder of the story was, how five such refractory, ill- matched fellows should agree about these women, and that some two of them should not choose the same woman, especially seeing two or three of them were, without comparison, more agreeable than the others; but they took a good way enough to prevent quarrelling among themselves, for they set the five women by themselves in one of their huts, and they went all into the other hut, and drew lots among them who should choose first.

Him that drew to choose first went away by himself to the hut where the poor naked creatures were, and fetched out her he chose; and it was worth observing, that he that chose first took her that was reckoned the homeliest and oldest of the five, which made mirth enough amongst the rest; and even the Spaniards laughed at it; but the fellow considered better than any of them, that it was application and business they were to expect assistance in, as much as in anything else; and she proved the best wife of all the parcel.

When the poor women saw themselves set in a row thus, and fetched out one by one, the terrors of their condition returned upon them again, and they firmly believed they were now going to be devoured. Accordingly, when the English sailor came in and fetched out one of them, the rest set up a most lamentable cry, and hung about her, and took their leave of her with such agonies and affection as would have grieved the hardest heart in the world: nor was it possible for the Englishmen to satisfy them that they were not to be immediately murdered, till they fetched the old man, Friday's father, who immediately let them know that the five men, who were to fetch them out one by one, had chosen them for their wives. When they had done, and the fright the women were in was a little over, the men went to work, and the Spaniards came and helped them: and in a few hours they had built them every one a new hut or tent for their lodging apart; for those they had already were crowded with their tools, household stuff, and provisions. The three wicked ones had pitched farthest off, and the two honest ones nearer, but both on the north shore of the island, so that they continued separated as before; and thus my island was peopled in three places, and, as I might say, three towns were begun to be built.

And here it is very well worth observing that, as it often happens in the world (what the wise ends in God's providence are, in such a disposition of things, I cannot say), the two honest fellows had the two worst wives; and the three reprobates, that were scarce worth hanging, that were fit for nothing, and neither seemed born to do themselves good nor any one else, had three clever, careful, and ingenious wives; not that the first two were bad wives as to their temper or humour, for all the five were most willing, quiet, passive, and subjected creatures, rather like slaves than wives; but my meaning is, they were not alike capable, ingenious, or industrious, or alike cleanly and neat. Another observation I must make, to the honour of a diligent application on one hand, and to the disgrace of a slothful, negligent, idle temper on the other, that when I came to the place, and viewed the several improvements, plantings, and management of the several little colonies, the two men had so far out-gone the three, that there was no comparison. They had, indeed, both of them as much ground laid out for corn as they wanted, and the reason was, because, according to my rule, nature dictated that it was to no purpose to sow more corn than they wanted; but the difference of the cultivation, of the planting, of the fences, and indeed, of everything else, was easy to be seen at first view.

The two men had innumerable young trees planted about their huts, so that, when you came to the place, nothing was to be seen but a wood; and though they had twice had their plantation demolished, once by their own countrymen, and once by the enemy, as shall be shown in its place, yet they had restored all again, and everything was thriving and flourishing about them; they had grapes planted in order, and managed like a vineyard, though they had themselves never seen anything of that kind; and by their good ordering their vines, their grapes were as good again as any of the others. They had also found themselves out a retreat in the thickest part of the woods, where, though there was not a natural cave, as I had found, yet they made one with incessant labour of their hands, and where, when the mischief which followed happened, they secured their wives and children so as they could never be found; they having, by sticking innumerable stakes and poles of the wood which, as I said, grew so readily, made the grove impassable, except in some places, when they climbed up to get over the outside part, and then went on by ways of their own leaving.

As to the three reprobates, as I justly call them, though they were much civilised by their settlement compared to what they were before, and were not so quarrelsome, having not the same opportunity; yet one of the certain companions of a profligate mind never left them, and that was their idleness. It is true, they planted corn and made fences; but Solomon's words were never better verified than in them, "I went by the vineyard of the slothful, and it was all overgrown with thorns": for when the Spaniards came to view their crop they could not see it in some places for weeds, the hedge had several gaps in it, where the wild goats had got in and eaten up the corn; perhaps here and there a dead bush was crammed in, to stop them out for the present, but it was only shutting the stable-door after the steed was stolen. Whereas, when they looked on the colony of the other two, there was the very face of industry and success upon all they did; there was not a weed to be seen in all their corn, or a gap in any of their hedges; and they, on the other hand, verified Solomon's words in another place, "that the diligent hand maketh rich"; for everything grew and thrived, and they had plenty within and without; they had more tame cattle than the others, more utensils and necessaries within doors, and yet more pleasure and diversion too.

It is true, the wives of the three were very handy and cleanly within doors; and having learned the English ways of dressing, and cooking from one of the other Englishmen, who, as I said, was a cook's mate on board the ship, they dressed their husbands' victuals very nicely and well; whereas the others could not be brought to understand it; but then the husband, who, as I say, had been cook's mate, did it himself. But as for the husbands of the three wives, they loitered about, fetched turtles' eggs, and caught fish and birds: in a word, anything but labour; and they fared accordingly. The diligent lived well and comfortably, and the slothful hard and beggarly; and so, I believe, generally speaking, it is all over the world.

But I now come to a scene different from all that had happened before, either to them or to me; and the origin of the story was this: Early one morning there came on shore five or six canoes of Indians or savages, call them which you please, and there is no room to doubt they came upon the old errand of feeding upon their slaves; but that part was now so familiar to the Spaniards, and to our men too, that they did not concern themselves about it, as I did: but having been made sensible, by their experience, that their only business was to lie concealed, and that if they were not seen by any of the savages they would go off again quietly, when their business was done, having as yet not the least notion of there being any inhabitants in the island; I say, having been made sensible of this, they had nothing to do but to give notice to all the three plantations to keep within doors, and not show themselves, only placing a scout in a proper place, to give notice when the boats went to sea again.

This was, without doubt, very right; but a disaster spoiled all these measures, and made it known among the savages that there were inhabitants there; which was, in the end, the desolation of almost the whole colony. After the canoes with the savages were gone off, the Spaniards peeped abroad again; and some of them had the curiosity to go to the place where they had been, to see what they had been doing. Here, to their great surprise, they found three savages left behind, and lying fast asleep upon the ground. It was supposed they had either been so gorged with their inhuman feast, that, like beasts, they were fallen asleep, and would not stir when the others went, or they had wandered into the woods, and did not come back in time to be taken in.

The Spaniards were greatly surprised at this sight and perfectly at a loss what to do. The Spaniard governor, as it happened, was with them, and his advice was asked, but he professed he knew not what to do. As for slaves, they had enough already; and as to killing them, there were none of them inclined to do that: the Spaniard governor told me they could not think of shedding innocent blood; for as to them, the poor creatures had done them no wrong, invaded none of their property, and they thought they had no just quarrel against them, to take away their lives. And here I must, in justice to these Spaniards, observe that, let the accounts of

Spanish cruelty in Mexico and Peru be what they will, I never met with seventeen men of any nation whatsoever, in any foreign country, who were so universally modest, temperate, virtuous, so very good-humoured, and so courteous, as these Spaniards: and as to cruelty, they had nothing of it in their very nature; no inhumanity, no barbarity, no outrageous passions; and yet all of them men of great courage and spirit. Their temper and calmness had appeared in their bearing the insufferable usage of the three Englishmen; and their justice and humanity appeared now in the case of the savages above. After some consultation they resolved upon this; that they would lie still a while longer, till, if possible, these three men might be gone. But then the governor recollected that the three savages had no boat; and if they were left to rove about the island, they would certainly discover that there were inhabitants in it; and so they should be undone that way. Upon this, they went back again, and there lay the fellows fast asleep still, and so they resolved to awaken them, and take them prisoners; and they did so. The poor fellows were strangely frightened when they were seized upon and bound; and afraid, like the women, that they should be murdered and eaten: for it seems those people think all the world does as they do, in eating men's flesh; but they were soon made easy as to that, and away they carried them.

It was very happy for them that they did not carry them home to the castle, I mean to my palace under the hill; but they carried them first to the bower, where was the chief of their country work, such as the keeping the goats, the planting the corn, &c.; and afterward they carried them to the habitation of the two Englishmen. Here they were set to work, though it was not much they had for them to do; and whether it was by negligence in guarding them, or that they thought the fellows could not mend themselves, I know not, but one of them ran away, and, taking to the woods, they could never hear of him any more. They had good reason to believe he got home again soon after in some other boats or canoes of savages who came on shore three or four weeks afterwards, and who, carrying on their revels as usual, went off in two days' time. This thought terrified them exceedingly; for they concluded, and that not without good cause indeed, that if this fellow came home safe among his comrades, he would certainly give them an account that there were people in the island, and also how few and weak they were; for this savage, as observed before, had never been told, and it was very happy he had not, how many there were or where they lived; nor had he ever seen or heard the fire of any of their guns, much less had they shown him any of their other retired places; such as the cave in the valley, or the new retreat which the two Englishmen had made, and the like.

The first testimony they had that this fellow had given intelligence of them was, that about two mouths after this six canoes of savages, with about seven, eight, or ten men in a canoe, came rowing along the north side of the island, where they never used to come before, and landed, about an hour after sunrise, at a convenient place, about a mile from the habitation of the two Englishmen, where this escaped man had been kept. As the chief Spaniard said, had they been all there the damage would not have been so much, for not a man of them would have escaped; but the case differed now very much, for two men to fifty was too much odds. The two men had the happiness to discover them about a league off, so that it was above an hour before they landed; and as they landed a mile from their huts, it was some time before they could come at them. Now, having great reason to believe that they were betrayed, the first thing they did was to bind the two slaves which were left, and cause two of the three men whom they brought with the women (who, it seems, proved very faithful to them) to lead them, with their two wives, and whatever they could carry away with them, to their retired places in the woods, which I have spoken of above, and there to bind the two fellows hand and foot, till they heard farther. In the next place, seeing the savages were all come on shore, and that they had bent their course directly that way, they opened the fences where the milch cows were kept, and drove them all out; leaving their goats to straggle in the woods, whither they pleased, that the savages might think they were all bred wild; but the rogue who came with them was too cunning for that, and gave them an account of it all, for they went directly to the place.

When the two poor frightened men had secured their wives and goods, they sent the other slave they had of the three who came with the women, and who was at their place by accident, away to the Spaniards with all speed, to give them the alarm, and desire speedy help, and, in the meantime, they took their arms and what ammunition they had, and retreated towards the place in the wood where their wives were sent; keeping at a distance, yet so that they might see, if possible, which way the savages took. They had not gone far but that from a rising ground they could see the little army of their enemies come on directly to their habitation, and, in a moment more, could see all their huts and household stuff flaming up together, to their great grief and mortification; for this was a great loss to them, irretrievable, indeed, for some time. They kept their station for a while, till they found the savages, like wild beasts, spread themselves all over the place, rummaging every way, and every place they could think of, in search of prey; and in particular for the people, of whom now it plainly appeared they had intelligence.

The two Englishmen seeing this, thinking themselves not secure where they stood, because it was likely some of the wild people might come that way, and they might come too many together, thought it proper to make another retreat about half a mile farther; believing, as it afterwards happened, that the further they strolled, the fewer would be together. Their next halt was at the entrance into a very thick-grown part of the woods, and where an old trunk of a tree stood, which was hollow and very large; and in this tree they both took their standing, resolving to see there what might offer. They had not stood there long before two of the savages appeared running directly that way, as if they had already had notice where they stood, and were coming up to attack them; and a little way farther they espied three more coming after them, and five more beyond them, all coming the same way; besides which, they saw seven or eight more at a distance, running another way; for in a word, they ran every way, like sportsmen beating for their game.

The poor men were now in great perplexity whether they should stand and keep their posture or fly; but after a very short debate with themselves, they considered that if the savages ranged the country thus before help came, they might perhaps find their retreat in the woods, and then all would be lost; so they resolved to stand them there, and if they were too many to deal with, then they would get up to the top of the tree, from whence they doubted not to defend themselves, fire excepted, as long as their ammunition lasted, though all the savages that were landed, which was near fifty, were to attack them.

Having resolved upon this, they next considered whether they should fire at the first two, or wait for the three, and so take the middle party, by which the two and the five that followed would be separated; at length they resolved to let the first two pass by, unless they should spy them the tree, and come to attack them. The first two savages confirmed them also in this resolution, by turning a little from them towards another part of the wood; but the three, and the five after them, came forward directly to the tree, as if they had known the Englishmen were there. Seeing them come so straight towards them, they resolved to take them in a line as they came: and as they resolved to fire but one at a time, perhaps the first shot might hit them all three; for which purpose the man who was to fire put three or four small bullets into his piece; and having a fair loophole, as it were, from a broken hole in the tree, he took a sure aim, without being seen, waiting till they were within about thirty yards of the tree, so that he could not miss.

While they were thus waiting, and the savages came on, they plainly saw that one of the three was the runaway savage that had escaped from them; and they both knew him distinctly, and resolved that, if possible, he should not escape, though they should both fire; so the other stood ready with his piece, that if he did not drop at the first shot, he should be sure to have a second. But the first was too good a marksman to miss his aim; for as the savages kept near one another, a little behind in a line, he fired, and hit two of them directly; the foremost was killed outright, being shot in the head; the second, which was the runaway Indian, was shot through the body, and fell, but was not quite dead; and the third had a little scratch in the shoulder, perhaps by the same ball that went through the body of the second; and being dreadfully frightened, though not so much hurt, sat down upon the ground, screaming and yelling in a hideous manner.

The five that were behind, more frightened with the noise than sensible of the danger, stood still at first; for the woods made the sound a thousand times bigger than it really was, the echoes rattling from one side to another, and the fowls rising from all parts, screaming, and every sort making a different noise, according to their kind; just as it was when I fired the first gun that perhaps was ever shot off in the island.

However, all being silent again, and they not knowing what the matter was, came on unconcerned, till they came to the place where their companions lay in a condition miserable enough. Here the poor ignorant creatures, not sensible that they were within reach of the same mischief, stood all together over the wounded man, talking, and, as may be supposed, inquiring of him how he came to be hurt; and who, it is very rational to believe, told them that a flash of fire first, and immediately after that thunder from their gods, had killed those two and wounded him. This, I say, is rational; for nothing is more certain than that, as they saw no man near them, so they had never heard a gun in all their lives, nor so much as heard of a gun; neither knew they anything of killing and wounding at a distance with fire and bullets: if they had, one might reasonably believe they would not have stood so unconcerned to view the fate of their fellows, without some apprehensions of their own.

Our two men, as they confessed to me, were grieved to be obliged to kill so many poor creatures, who had no notion of their danger; yet, having them all thus in their power, and the first having loaded his piece again, resolved to let fly both together among them; and singling out, by agreement, which to aim at, they shot together, and killed, or very much wounded, four of them; the fifth, frightened even to death, though not hurt, fell with the rest; so that our men, seeing them all fall together, thought they had killed them all.

The belief that the savages were all killed made our two men come boldly out from the tree before they had charged their guns, which was a wrong step; and they were under some surprise when they came to the place, and found no less than four of them alive, and of them two very little hurt, and one not at all. This obliged them to fall upon them with the stocks of their muskets; and first they made sure of the runaway savage, that had been the cause of all the mischief, and of another that was hurt in the knee, and put them out of their pain; then the man that was not hurt at all came and kneeled down to them, with his two hands held up, and made piteous moans to them, by gestures and signs, for his life, but could not say one word to them that they could understand. However, they made signs to him to sit down at the foot of a tree hard by; and one of the Englishmen, with a piece of rope-yarn, which he had by great chance in his pocket, tied his two hands behind him, and there they left him; and with what speed they could made after the other two, which were gone before, fearing they, or any more of them, should find way to their covered place in the woods, where their wives, and the few goods they had left, lay. They came once in sight of the two men, but it was at a great distance; however, they had the satisfaction to see them cross over a valley towards the sea, quite the contrary way from that which led to their retreat, which they were afraid of; and being satisfied with that, they went back to the tree where they left their prisoner, who, as they supposed, was delivered by his comrades, for he was gone, and the two pieces of rope-yarn with which they had bound him lay just at the foot of the tree.

They were now in as great concern as before, not knowing what course to take, or how near the enemy might be, or in what number; so they resolved to go away to the place where their wives were, to see if all was well there, and to make them easy. These were in fright enough, to be sure; for though the savages were their own countrymen, yet they were most terribly afraid of them, and perhaps the more for the knowledge they had of them. When they came there, they found the savages had been in the wood, and very near that place, but had not found it; for it was indeed inaccessible, from the trees standing so thick, unless the persons seeking it had been directed by those that knew it, which these did not: they found, therefore, everything very safe, only the women in a terrible fright. While they were here they had the comfort to have seven of the Spaniards come to their assistance; the other ten, with their servants, and Friday's father, were gone in a body to defend their bower, and the corn and cattle that were kept there, in case the savages should have roved over to that side of the country, but they did not spread so far. With the seven Spaniards came one of the three savages, who, as I said, were their prisoners formerly; and with them also came the savage whom the Englishmen had left bound hand and foot at the tree; for it seems they came that way, saw the slaughter of the seven men, and unbound the eighth, and brought him along with them; where, however, they were obliged to bind again, as they had the two others who were left when the third ran away.

The prisoners now began to be a burden to them; and they were so afraid of their escaping, that they were once resolving to kill them all, believing they were under an absolute necessity to do so for their own preservation. However, the chief of the Spaniards would not consent to it, but ordered, for the present, that they should be sent out of the way to my old cave in the valley, and be kept there, with two Spaniards to guard them, and have food for their subsistence, which was done; and they were bound there hand and foot for that night.

When the Spaniards came, the two Englishmen were so encouraged, that they could not satisfy themselves to stay any longer there; but taking five of the Spaniards, and themselves, with four muskets and a pistol among them, and two stout quarter-staves, away they went in quest of the savages. And first they came to the tree where the men lay that had been killed; but it was easy to see that some more of the savages had been there, for they had attempted to carry their dead men away, and had dragged two of them a good way, but had given it over. From thence they advanced to the first rising ground, where they had stood and seen their camp destroyed, and where they had the mortification still to see some of the smoke; but neither could they here see any of the savages. They then resolved, though with all possible caution, to go forward towards their ruined plantation; but, a little before they came thither, coming in sight of the sea-shore, they saw plainly the savages all embarked again in their canoes, in order to be gone. They seemed sorry at first that there was no way to come at them, to give them a parting blow; but, upon the whole, they were very well satisfied to be rid of them.

The poor Englishmen being now twice ruined, and all their improvements destroyed, the rest all agreed to come and help them to rebuild, and assist them with needful supplies. Their three countrymen, who were not yet noted for having the least inclination to do any good, yet as soon as they heard of it (for they, living remote eastward, knew nothing of the matter till all was over), came and offered their help and assistance, and did, very friendly, work for several days to restore their habitation and make necessaries for them. And thus in a little time they were set upon their legs again.

About two days after this they had the farther satisfaction of seeing three of the savages' canoes come driving on shore, and, at some distance from them, two drowned men, by which they had reason to believe that they had met with a storm at sea, which had overset some of them; for it had blown very hard the night after they went off. However, as some might miscarry, so, on the other hand, enough of them escaped to inform the rest, as well of what they had done as of what had happened to them; and to whet them on to another enterprise of the same nature, which they, it seems, resolved to attempt, with sufficient force to carry all before them; for except what the first man had told them of inhabitants, they could say little of it of their own knowledge, for they never saw one man; and the fellow being killed that had affirmed it, they had no other witness to confirm it to, them.

ROBINSON CRUSOE AT HOME IN THE CASTLE.

Chapter 5

A Great Victory

It was five or six months after this before they heard any more of the savages, in which time our men were in hopes they had either forgot their former bad luck, or given over hopes of better; when, on a sudden, they were invaded with a most formidable fleet of no less than eight-and-twenty canoes, full of savages, armed with bows and arrows, great clubs, wooden swords, and such like engines of war; and they brought such numbers with them, that, in short, it put all our people into the utmost consternation.

As they came on shore in the evening, and at the easternmost side of the island, our men had that night to consult and consider what to do. In the first place, knowing that their being entirely concealed was their only safety before and would be much more so now, while the number of their enemies would be so great, they resolved, first of all, to take down the huts which were built for the two Englishmen, and drive away their goats to the old cave; because they supposed the savages would go directly thither, as soon as it was day, to play the old game over again, though they did not now land within two leagues of it. In the next place, they drove away all the flocks of goats they had at the old bower, as I called it, which belonged to the Spaniards; and, in short, left as little appearance of inhabitants anywhere as was possible; and the next morning early they posted themselves, with all their force, at the plantation of the two men, to wait for their coming. As they guessed, so it happened: these new invaders, leaving their canoes at the east end of the island, came ranging along the shore, directly towards the place, to the number of two hundred and fifty, as near as our men could judge. Our army was but small indeed; but, that which was worse, they had not arms for all their number. The whole account, it seems, stood thus: first, as to men, seventeen Spaniards, five Englishmen, old Friday, the three slaves taken with the women, who proved very faithful, and three other slaves, who lived with the Spaniards. To arm these, they had eleven muskets, five pistols, three fowling-pieces, five muskets or fowling-pieces which were taken by me from the mutinous seamen whom I reduced, two swords, and three old halberds.

To their slaves they did not give either musket or fusee; but they had each a halberd, or a long staff, like a quarter-staff, with a great spike of iron fastened into each end of it, and by his side a hatchet; also every one of our men had a hatchet. Two of the women could not be prevailed upon but they would come into the fight, and they had bows and arrows, which the Spaniards had taken from the savages when the first action happened, which I have spoken of, where the Indians fought with one another; and the women had hatchets too.

The chief Spaniard, whom I described so often, commanded the whole; and Will Atkins, who, though a dreadful fellow for wickedness, was a most daring, bold fellow, commanded under him. The savages came forward like lions; and our men, which was the worst of their fate, had no advantage in their situation; only that Will Atkins, who now proved a most useful fellow, with six men, was planted just behind a small thicket of bushes as an advanced guard, with orders to let the first of them pass by and then fire into the middle of them, and as soon as he had fired, to make his retreat as nimbly as he could round a part of the wood, and so come in behind the Spaniards, where they stood, having a thicket of trees before them.

When the savages came on, they ran straggling about every way in heaps, out of all manner of order, and Will Atkins let about fifty of them pass by him; then seeing the rest come in a very thick throng, he orders three of his men to fire, having loaded their muskets with six or seven bullets apiece, about as big as large pistol-bullets. How many they killed or wounded they knew not, but the consternation and surprise was inexpressible among the savages; they were frightened to the last degree to hear such a dreadful noise, and see their men killed, and others hurt, but see nobody that did it; when, in the middle of their fright, Will Atkins and his other three let fly again among the thickest of them; and in less than a minute the first three, being loaded again, gave them a third volley.

Had Will Atkins and his men retired immediately, as soon as they had fired, as they were ordered to do, or had the rest of the body been at hand to have poured in their shot continually, the savages had been effectually routed; for the terror that was among them came principally from this, that they were killed by the gods with thunder and lightning, and could see nobody that hurt them. But Will Atkins, staying to load again, discovered the cheat: some of the savages who were at a distance spying them, came upon them behind; and though Atkins and his men fired at them also, two or three times, and killed above twenty, retiring as fast as they could, yet they wounded Atkins himself, and killed one of his fellow-Englishmen with their arrows, as they did afterwards one Spaniard, and one of the Indian slaves who came with the women. This slave was a most gallant fellow, and fought most desperately, killing five of them with his own hand, having no weapon but one of the armed staves and a hatchet.

Our men being thus hard laid at, Atkins wounded, and two other men killed, retreated to a rising ground in the wood; and the Spaniards, after firing three volleys upon them, retreated also; for their number was so great, and they were so desperate, that though above fifty of them were killed, and more than as many wounded, yet they came on in the teeth of our men, fearless of danger, and shot their arrows like a cloud; and it was observed that their wounded men, who were not quite disabled, were made outrageous by their wounds, and fought like madmen.

When our men retreated, they left the Spaniard and the Englishman that were killed behind them: and the savages, when they came up to them, killed them over again in a wretched manner, breaking their arms, legs, and heads, with their clubs and wooden swords, like true savages; but finding our men were gone, they did not seem inclined to pursue them, but drew themselves up in a ring, which is, it seems, their custom, and shouted twice, in token of their victory; after which, they had the mortification to see several of their wounded men fall, dying with the mere loss of blood.

The Spaniard governor having drawn his little body up together upon a rising ground, Atkins, though he was wounded, would have had them march and charge again all together at once: but the Spaniard replied, "Seignior Atkins, you see how their wounded men fight; let them alone till morning; all the wounded men will be stiff and sore with their wounds, and faint with the loss of blood; and so we shall have the fewer to engage." This advice was good: but Will Atkins replied merrily, "That is true, seignior, and so shall I too; and that is the reason I would go on while I am warm." "Well, Seignior Atkins," says the Spaniard, "you have behaved gallantly, and done your part; we will fight for you if you cannot come on; but I think it best to stay till morning:" so they waited.

But as it was a clear moonlight night, and they found the savages in great disorder about their dead and wounded men, and a great noise and hurry among them where they lay, they afterwards resolved to fall upon them in the night, especially if they could come to give them but one volley before they were discovered, which they had a fair opportunity to do; for one of the Englishmen in whose quarter it was where the fight began, led them round between the woods and the seaside westward, and then turning short south, they came so near where the thickest of them lay, that before they were seen or heard eight of them fired in among them, and did dreadful execution upon them; in half a minute more eight others fired after them, pouring in their small shot in such a quantity that abundance were killed and wounded; and all this while they were not able to see who hurt them, or which way to fly.

The Spaniards charged again with the utmost expedition, and then divided themselves into three bodies, and resolved to fall in among them all together. They had in each body eight persons, that is to say, twenty-two men and the two women, who, by the way, fought desperately. They divided the firearms equally in each party, as well as the halberds and staves. They would have had the women kept back, but they said they were resolved to die with their husbands. Having thus formed their little army, they marched out from among the trees, and came up to the teeth of the enemy, shouting and hallooing as loud as they could; the savages stood all together, but were in the utmost confusion, hearing the noise of our men shouting from three quarters together. They would have fought if they had seen us; for as soon as we came near enough to be seen, some arrows were shot, and poor old Friday was wounded, though not dangerously. But our men gave them no time, but running up to them, fired among them three ways, and then fell in with the butt-ends of their muskets, their swords, armed staves, and hatchets, and laid about them so well that, in a word, they set up a dismal screaming and howling, flying to save their lives which way soever they could.

Our men were tired with the execution, and killed or mortally wounded in the two fights about one hundred and eighty of them; the rest, being frightened out of their wits, scoured through the woods and over the hills, with all the speed that fear and nimble feet could help them to; and as we did not trouble ourselves much to pursue them, they got all together to the seaside, where they landed, and where their canoes lay. But their disaster was not at an end yet; for it blew a terrible storm of wind that evening from the sea, so that it was impossible for them to go off; nay, the storm continuing all night, when the tide came up their canoes were most of them driven by the surge of the sea so high upon the shore that it required infinite toil to get them off; and some of them were even dashed to pieces against the beach. Our men, though glad of their victory, yet got little rest that night; but having refreshed themselves as well as they could, they resolved to march to that part of the island where the savages were fled, and see what posture they were in. This necessarily led them over the place where the fight had been, and where they found several of the poor creatures not quite dead, and yet past recovering life; a sight disagreeable enough to generous minds, for a truly great man though obliged by the law of battle to destroy his enemy, takes no delight in his misery. However, there was no need to give any orders in this case; for their own savages, who were their servants, despatched these poor creatures with their hatchets.

At length they came in view of the place where the more miserable remains of the savages' army lay, where there appeared about a hundred still; their posture was generally sitting upon the ground, with their knees up towards their mouth, and the head put between the two hands, leaning down upon the knees. When our men came within two musket-shots of them, the Spaniard governor ordered two muskets to be fired without ball, to alarm them; this he did, that by their countenance he might know what to expect, whether they were still in heart to fight, or were so heartily beaten as to be discouraged, and so he might manage accordingly. This stratagem took: for as soon as the savages heard the first gun, and saw the flash of the second, they started up upon their feet in the greatest consternation imaginable; and as our men advanced swiftly towards them, they all ran screaming and yelling away, with a kind of howling noise, which our men did not understand, and had never heard before; and thus they ran up the hills into the country.

At first our men had much rather the weather had been calm, and they had all gone away to sea: but they did not then consider that this might probably have been the occasion of their coming again in such multitudes as not to be resisted, or, at least, to come so many and so often as would quite desolate the island, and starve them. Will Atkins, therefore, who notwithstanding his wound kept always with them, proved the best counsellor in this case: his advice was, to take the advantage that offered, and step in between them and their boats, and so deprive them of the capacity of ever returning any more to plague the island. They consulted long about this; and some were against it for fear of making the wretches fly to the woods and live there desperate, and so they should have them to hunt like wild beasts, be afraid to stir out about their business, and have their plantations continually rifled, all their tame goats destroyed, and, in short, be reduced to a life of continual distress.

Will Atkins told them they had better have to do with a hundred men than with a hundred nations; that, as they must destroy their boats, so they must destroy the men, or be all of them destroyed themselves. In a word, he showed them the necessity of it so plainly that they all came into it; so they went to work immediately with the boats, and getting some dry wood together from a dead tree, they tried to set some of them on fire, but they were so wet that they would not burn; however, the fire so burned the upper part that it soon made them unfit for use at sea.

When the Indians saw what they were about, some of them came running out of the woods, and coming as near as they could to our men, kneeled down and cried, "Oa, Oa, Waramokoa," and some other words of their language, which none of the others understood anything of; but as they made pitiful gestures and strange noises, it was easy to understand they begged to have their boats spared, and that they would be gone, and never come there again. But our men were now satisfied that they had no way to preserve themselves, or to save their colony, but effectually to prevent any of these people from ever going home again; depending upon this, that if even so much as one of them got back into their country to tell the story, the colony was undone; so that, letting them know that they should not have any mercy, they fell to work with their canoes, and destroyed every one that the storm had not destroyed before; at the sight of which, the savages raised a hideous cry in the woods, which our people heard plain enough, after which they ran about the island like distracted men, so that, in a word, our men did not really know what at first to do with them. Nor did the Spaniards, with all their prudence, consider that while they made those people thus desperate, they ought to have kept a good guard at the same time upon their plantations; for though it is true they had driven away their cattle, and the Indians did not find out their main retreat, I mean my old castle at the hill, nor the cave in the valley, yet they found out my plantation at the bower, and pulled it all to pieces, and all the fences and planting about it; trod all the corn under foot, tore up the vines and grapes, being just then almost ripe, and did our men inestimable damage, though to themselves not one farthing's worth of service.

Though our men were able to fight them upon all occasions, yet they were in no condition to pursue them, or hunt them up and down; for as they were too nimble of foot for our people when they found them single, so our men durst not go abroad single, for fear of being surrounded with their numbers. The best was they had no weapons; for though they had bows, they had no arrows left, nor any materials to make any; nor had they any edge-tool among them. The extremity and distress they were reduced to was great, and indeed deplorable; but, at the same time, our men were also brought to very bad circumstances by them, for though their retreats were preserved, yet their provision was destroyed, and their harvest spoiled, and what to do, or which way to turn themselves, they knew not. The only refuge they had now was the stock of cattle they had in the valley by the cave, and some little corn which grew there, and the plantation of the three Englishmen. Will Atkins and his comrades were now reduced to two; one of them being killed by an arrow, which struck him on the side of his head, just under the temple, so that he never spoke more; and it was very remarkable that this was the same barbarous fellow that cut the poor savage slave with his hatchet, and who afterwards intended to have murdered the Spaniards.

I looked upon their case to have been worse at this time than mine was at any time, after I first discovered the grains of barley and rice, and got into the manner of planting and raising my corn, and my tame cattle; for now they had, as I may say, a hundred wolves upon the island, which would devour everything they could come at, yet could be hardly come at themselves.

When they saw what their circumstances were, the first thing they concluded was, that they would, if possible, drive the savages up to the farther part of the island, south-west, that if any more came on shore they might not find one another; then, that they would daily hunt and harass them, and kill as many of them as they could come at, till they had reduced their number; and if they could at last tame them, and bring them to anything, they would give them corn, and teach them how to plant, and live upon their daily labour. In order to do this, they so followed them, and so terrified them with their guns, that in a few days, if any of them fired a gun at an Indian, if he did not hit him, yet he would fall down for fear. So dreadfully frightened were they that they kept out of sight farther and farther; till at last our men followed them, and almost every day killing or wounding some of them, they kept up in the woods or hollow places so much, that it reduced them to the utmost misery for want of food; and many were afterwards found dead in the woods, without any hurt, absolutely starved to death.

When our men found this, it made their hearts relent, and pity moved them, especially the generous-minded Spaniard governor; and he proposed, if possible, to take one of them alive and bring him to understand what they meant, so far as to be able to act as interpreter, and go among them and see if they might be brought to some conditions that might be depended upon, to save their lives and do us no harm.

It was some while before any of them could be taken; but being weak and half-starved, one of them was at last surprised and made a prisoner. He was sullen at first, and would neither eat nor drink; but finding himself kindly used, and victuals given to him, and no violence offered him, he at last grew tractable, and came to himself. They often brought old Friday to talk to him, who always told him how kind the others would be to them all; that they would not only save their lives, but give them part of the island to live in, provided they would give satisfaction that they would keep in their own bounds, and not come beyond it to injure or prejudice others; and that they should have corn given them to plant and make it grow for their bread, and some bread given them for their present subsistence; and old Friday bade the fellow go and talk with the rest of his countrymen, and see what they said to it; assuring them that, if they did not agree immediately, they should be all destroyed.

The poor wretches, thoroughly humbled, and reduced in number to about thirty-seven, closed with the proposal at the first offer, and begged to have some food given them; upon which twelve Spaniards and two Englishmen, well armed, with three Indian slaves and old Friday, marched to the place where they were. The three Indian slaves carried them a large quantity of bread, some rice boiled up to cakes and dried in the sun, and three live goats; and they were ordered to go to the side of a hill, where they sat down, ate their provisions very thankfully, and were the most faithful fellows to their words that could be thought of; for, except when they came to beg victuals and directions, they never came out of their bounds; and there they lived when I came to the island and I went to see them. They had taught them both to plant corn, make bread, breed tame goats, and milk them: they wanted nothing but wives in order for them soon to become a nation. They were confined to a neck of land, surrounded with high rocks behind them, and lying plain towards the sea before them, on the south-east corner of the island. They had land enough, and it was very good and fruitful; about a mile and a half broad, and three or four miles in length. Our men taught them to make wooden spades, such as I made for myself, and gave among them twelve hatchets and three or four knives; and there they lived, the most subjected, innocent creatures that ever were heard of.

After this the colony enjoyed a perfect tranquillity with respect to the savages, till I came to revisit them, which was about two years after; not but that, now and then, some canoes of savages came on shore for their triumphal, unnatural feasts; but as they were of several nations, and perhaps had never heard of those that came before, or the reason of it, they did not make any search or inquiry after their countrymen; and if they had, it would have been very hard to have found them out.

Thus, I think, I have given a full account of all that happened to them till my return, at least that was worth notice. The Indians were wonderfully civilised by them, and they frequently went among them; but they forbid, on pain of death, any one of the Indians coming to them, because they would not have their settlement betrayed again. One thing was very remarkable, viz. that they taught the savages to make wicker-work, or baskets, but they soon outdid their masters: for they made abundance of ingenious things in wicker-work, particularly baskets, sieves, bird-cages, cupboards, &c.; as also chairs, stools, beds, couches, being very ingenious at such work when they were once put in the way of it.

My coming was a particular relief to these people, because we furnished them with knives, scissors, spades, shovels, pick-axes, and all things of that kind which they could want. With the help of those tools they were so very handy that they came at last to build up their huts or houses very handsomely, raddling or working it up like basket-work all the way round. This piece of ingenuity, although it looked very odd, was an exceeding good fence, as well against heat as against all sorts of vermin; and our men were so taken with it that they got the Indians to come and do the like for them; so that when I came to see the two Englishmen's colonies, they looked at a distance as if they all lived like bees in a hive.

As for Will Atkins, who was now become a very industrious, useful, and sober fellow, he had made himself such a tent of basket-work as I believe was never seen; it was one hundred and twenty paces round on the outside, as I measured by my steps; the walls were as close worked as a basket, in panels or squares of thirty-two in number, and very strong, standing about seven feet high; in the middle was another not above twenty-two paces round, but built stronger, being octagon in its form, and in the eight corners stood eight very strong posts; round the top of which he laid strong pieces, knit together with wooden pins, from which he raised a pyramid for a handsome roof of eight rafters, joined together very well, though he had no nails, and only a few iron spikes, which he made himself, too, out of the old iron that I had left there. Indeed, this fellow showed abundance of ingenuity in several things which he had no knowledge of: he made him a forge, with a pair of wooden bellows to blow the fire; he made himself charcoal for his work; and he formed out of the iron crows a middling good anvil to hammer upon: in this manner he made many things, but especially hooks, staples, and spikes, bolts and hinges. But to return to the house: after he had pitched the roof of his innermost tent, he worked it up between the rafters with basket-work, so firm, and thatched that over again so ingeniously with rice-straw, and over that a large leaf of a tree, which covered the top, that his house was as dry as if it had been tiled or slated. He owned, indeed, that the savages had made the basket-work for him. The outer circuit was covered as a lean-to all round this inner apartment, and long rafters lay from the thirty-two angles to the top posts of the inner house, being about twenty feet distant, so that there was a space like a walk within the outer wicker-wall, and without the inner, near twenty feet wide.

The inner place he partitioned off with the same wickerwork, but much fairer, and divided into six apartments, so that he had six rooms on a floor, and out of every one of these there was a door: first into the entry, or coming into the main tent, another door into the main tent, and another door into the space or walk that was round it; so that walk was also divided into six equal parts, which served not only for a retreat, but to store up any necessaries which the family had occasion for. These six spaces not taking up the whole circumference, what other apartments the outer circle had were thus ordered: As soon as you were in at the door of the outer circle you had a short passage straight before you to the door of the inner house; but on either side was a wicker partition and a door in it, by which you went first into a large room or storehouse, twenty feet wide and about thirty feet long, and through that into another not quite so long; so that in the outer circle were ten handsome rooms, six of which were only to be come at through the apartments of the inner tent, and served as closets or retiring rooms to the respective chambers of the inner circle; and four large warehouses, or barns, or what you please to call them, which went through one another, two on either hand of the passage, that led through the outer door to the inner tent. Such a piece of basket-work, I believe, was never seen in the world, nor a house or tent so neatly contrived, much less so built. In this great bee-hive lived the three families, that is to say, Will Atkins and his companion; the third was killed, but his wife remained with three children, and the other two were not at all backward to give the widow her full share of everything, I mean as to their corn, milk, grapes, &c., and when they killed a kid, or found a turtle on the shore; so that they all lived well enough; though it was true they were not so industrious as the other two, as has been observed already.

One thing, however, cannot be omitted, viz. that as for religion, I do not know that there was anything of that kind among them; they often, indeed, put one another in mind that there was a God, by the very common method of seamen, swearing by His name: nor were their poor ignorant savage wives much better for having been married to Christians, as we must call them; for as they knew very little of God themselves, so they were utterly incapable of entering into any discourse with their wives about a God, or to talk anything to them concerning religion.

The utmost of all the improvement which I can say the wives had made from them was, that they had taught them to speak English pretty well; and most of their children, who were near twenty in all, were taught to speak English too, from their first learning to speak, though they at first spoke it in a very broken manner, like their mothers. None of these children were above six years old when I came thither, for it was not much above seven years since they had fetched these five savage ladies over; they had all children, more or less: the mothers were all a good sort of well- governed, quiet, laborious women, modest and decent, helpful to one another, mighty observant, and subject to their masters (I cannot call them husbands), and lacked nothing but to be well instructed in the Christian religion, and to be legally married; both of which were happily brought about afterwards by my means, or at least in consequence of my coming among them.

Chapter 6

The French Clergyman's Counsel

Having thus given an account of the colony in general, and pretty much of my runagate Englishmen, I must say something of the Spaniards, who were the main body of the family, and in whose story there are some incidents also remarkable enough.

I had a great many discourses with them about their circumstances when they were among the savages. They told me readily that they had no instances to give of their application or ingenuity in that country; that they were a poor, miserable, dejected handful of people; that even if means had been put into their hands, yet they had so abandoned themselves to despair, and were so sunk under the weight of their misfortune, that they thought of nothing but starving. One of them, a grave and sensible man, told me he was convinced they were in the wrong; that it was not the part of wise men to give themselves up to their misery, but always to take hold of the helps which reason offered, as well for present support as for future deliverance: he told me that grief was the most senseless, insignificant passion in the world, for that it regarded only things past, which were generally impossible to be recalled or to be remedied, but had no views of things to come, and had no share in anything that looked like deliverance, but rather added to the affliction than proposed a remedy; and upon this he repeated a Spanish proverb, which, though I cannot repeat in the same words that he spoke it in, yet I remember I made it into an English proverb of my own, thus:-

"In trouble to be troubled, Is to have your trouble doubled."

He then ran on in remarks upon all the little improvements I had made in my solitude: my unwearied application, as he called it; and how I had made a condition, which in its circumstances was at first much worse than theirs, a thousand times more happy than theirs was, even now when they were all together. He told me it was remarkable that Englishmen had a greater presence of mind in their distress than any people that ever he met with; that their unhappy nation and the Portuguese were the worst men in the world to struggle with misfortunes; for that their first step in dangers, after the common efforts were over, was to despair, lie down under it, and die, without rousing their thoughts up to proper remedies for escape.

I told him their case and mine differed exceedingly; that they were cast upon the shore without necessaries, without supply of food, or present sustenance till they could provide for it; that, it was true, I had this further disadvantage and discomfort, that I was alone; but then the supplies I had providentially thrown into my hands, by the unexpected driving of the ship on the shore, was such a help as would have encouraged any creature in the world to have applied himself as I had done. "Seignior," says the Spaniard, "had we poor Spaniards been in your case, we should never have got half those things out of the ship, as you did: nay," says he, "we should never have found means to have got a raft to carry them, or to have got the raft on shore without boat or sail: and how much less should we have done if any of us had been alone!" Well, I desired him to abate his compliments, and go on with the history of their coming on shore, where they landed. He told me they unhappily landed at a place where there were people without provisions; whereas, had they had the common sense to put off to sea again, and gone to another island a little further, they had found provisions, though without people: there being an island that way, as they had been told, where there were provisions, though no people— that is to say, that the Spaniards of Trinidad had frequently been there, and had filled the island with goats and hogs at several times, where they had bred in such multitudes, and where turtle and sea-fowls were in such plenty, that they could have been in no want of flesh, though they had found no bread; whereas, here they were only sustained with a few roots and herbs, which they understood not, and which had no substance in them, and which the inhabitants gave them sparingly enough; and they could treat them no better, unless they would turn cannibals and eat men's flesh.

They gave me an account how many ways they strove to civilise the savages they were with, and to teach them rational customs in the ordinary way of living, but in vain; and how they retorted upon them as unjust that they who came there for assistance and support should attempt to set up for instructors to those that gave them food; intimating, it seems, that none should set up for the instructors of others but those who could live without them. They gave me dismal accounts of the extremities they were driven to; how sometimes they were many days without any food at all, the island they were upon being inhabited by a sort of savages that lived more indolent, and for that reason were less supplied with the necessaries of life, than they had reason to believe others were in the same part of the world; and yet they found that these savages were less ravenous and voracious than those who had better supplies of food. Also, they added, they could not but see with what demonstrations of wisdom and goodness the governing providence of God directs the events of things in this world, which, they said, appeared in their circumstances: for if, pressed by the hardships they were under, and the barrenness of the country where they were, they had searched after a better to live in, they had then been out of the way of the relief that happened to them by my means.

They then gave me an account how the savages whom they lived amongst expected them to go out with them into their wars; and, it was true, that as they had firearms with them, had they not had the disaster to lose their ammunition, they could have been serviceable not only to their friends, but have made themselves terrible both to friends and enemies; but being without powder and shot, and yet in a condition that they could not in reason decline to go out with their landlords to their wars; so when they came into the field of battle they were in a worse condition than the savages themselves, for they had neither bows nor arrows, nor could they use those the savages gave them. So they could do nothing but stand still and be wounded with arrows, till they came up to the teeth of the enemy; and then, indeed, the three halberds they had were of use to them; and they would often drive a whole little army before them with those halberds, and sharpened sticks put into the muzzles of their muskets. But for all this they were sometimes surrounded with multitudes, and in great danger from their arrows, till at last they found the way to make themselves large targets of wood, which they covered with skins of wild beasts, whose names they knew not, and these covered them from the arrows of the savages: that, notwithstanding these, they were sometimes in great danger; and five of them were once knocked down together with the clubs of the savages, which was the time when one of them was taken prisoner— that is to say, the Spaniard whom I relieved. At first they thought he had been killed; but when they afterwards heard he was taken prisoner, they were under the greatest grief imaginable, and would willingly have all ventured their lives to have rescued him.

They told me that when they were so knocked down, the rest of their company rescued them, and stood over them fighting till they were come to themselves, all but him whom they thought had been dead; and then they made their way with their halberds and pieces, standing close together in a line, through a body of above a thousand savages, beating down all that came in their way, got the victory over their enemies, but to their great sorrow, because it was with the loss of their friend, whom the other party finding alive, carried off with some others, as I gave an account before. They described, most affectionately, how they were surprised with joy at the return of their friend and companion in misery, who they thought had been devoured by wild beasts of the worst kind—wild men; and yet, how more and more they were surprised with the account he gave them of his errand, and that there was a Christian in any place near, much more one that was able, and had humanity enough, to contribute to their deliverance.

They described how they were astonished at the sight of the relief I sent them, and at the appearance of loaves of bread—things they had not seen since their coming to that miserable place; how often they crossed it and blessed it as bread sent from heaven; and what a reviving cordial it was to their spirits to taste it, as also the other things I had sent for their supply; and, after all, they would have told me something of the joy they were in at the sight of a boat and pilots, to carry them away to the person and place from whence all these new comforts came. But it was impossible to express it by words, for their excessive joy naturally driving them to unbecoming extravagances, they had no way to describe them but by telling me they bordered upon lunacy, having no way to give vent to their passions suitable to the sense that was upon them; that in some it worked one way and in some another; and that some of them, through a surprise of joy, would burst into tears, others be stark mad, and others immediately faint. This discourse extremely affected me, and called to my mind Friday's ecstasy when he met his father, and the poor people's ecstasy when I took them up at sea after their ship was on fire; the joy of the mate of the ship when he found himself delivered in the place where he expected to perish; and my own joy, when, after twenty-eight years' captivity, I found a good ship ready to carry me to my own country. All these things made me more sensible of the relation of these poor men, and more affected with it.

Having thus given a view of the state of things as I found them, I must relate the heads of what I did for these people, and the condition in which I left them. It was their opinion, and mine too, that they would be troubled no more with the savages, or if they were, they would be able to cut them off, if they were twice as many as before; so they had no concern about that. Then I entered into a serious discourse with the Spaniard, whom I call governor, about their stay in the island; for as I was not come to carry any of them off, so it would not be just to carry off some and leave others, who, perhaps, would be unwilling to stay if their strength was diminished. On the other hand, I told them I came to establish them there, not to remove them; and then I let them know that I had brought with me relief of sundry kinds for them; that I had been at a great charge to supply them with all things necessary, as well for their convenience as their defence; and that I had such and such particular persons with me, as well to increase and recruit their number, as by the particular necessary employments which they were bred to, being artificers, to assist them in those things in which at present they were in want.

They were all together when I talked thus to them; and before I delivered to them the stores I had brought, I asked them, one by one, if they had entirely forgot and buried the first animosities that had been among them, and would shake hands with one another, and engage in a strict friendship and union of interest, that so there might be no more misunderstandings and jealousies.

Will Atkins, with abundance of frankness and good humour, said they had met with affliction enough to make them all sober, and enemies enough to make them all friends; that, for his part, he would live and die with them, and was so far from designing anything against the Spaniards, that he owned they had done nothing to him but what his own mad humour made necessary, and what he would have done, and perhaps worse, in their case; and that he would ask them pardon, if I desired it, for the foolish and brutish things he had done to them, and was very willing and desirous of living in terms of entire friendship and union with them, and would do anything that lay in his power to convince them of it; and as for going to England, he cared not if he did not go thither these twenty years.

The Spaniards said they had, indeed, at first disarmed and excluded Will Atkins and his two countrymen for their ill conduct, as they had let me know, and they appealed to me for the necessity they were under to do so; but that Will Atkins had behaved himself so bravely in the great fight they had with the savages, and on several occasions since, and had showed himself so faithful to, and concerned for, the general interest of them all, that they had forgotten all that was past, and thought he merited as much to be trusted with arms and supplied with necessaries as any of them; that they had testified their satisfaction in him by committing the command to him next to the governor himself; and as they had entire confidence in him and all his countrymen, so they acknowledged they had merited that confidence by all the methods that honest men could merit to be valued and trusted; and they most heartily embraced the occasion of giving me this assurance, that they would never have any interest separate from one another.

Upon these frank and open declarations of friendship, we appointed the next day to dine all together; and, indeed, we made a splendid feast. I caused the ship's cook and his mate to come on shore and dress our dinner, and the old cook's mate we had on shore assisted. We brought on shore six pieces of good beef and four pieces of pork, out of the ship's provisions, with our punch-bowl and materials to fill it; and in particular I gave them ten bottles of French claret, and ten bottles of English beer; things that neither the Spaniards nor the English had tasted for many years, and which it may be supposed they were very glad of. The Spaniards added to our feast five whole kids, which the cooks roasted; and three of them were sent, covered up close, on board the ship to the seamen, that they might feast on fresh meat from on shore, as we did with their salt meat from on board.

After this feast, at which we were very innocently merry, I brought my cargo of goods; wherein, that there might be no dispute about dividing, I showed them that there was a sufficiency for them all, desiring that they might all take an equal quantity, when made up, of the goods that were for wearing. As, first, I distributed linen sufficient to make every one of them four shirts, and, at the Spaniard's request, afterwards made them up six; these were exceeding comfortable to them, having been what they had long since forgot the use of, or what it was to wear them. I allotted the thin English stuffs, which I mentioned before, to make every one a light coat, like a frock, which I judged fittest for the heat of the season, cool and loose; and ordered that whenever they decayed, they should make more, as they thought fit; the like for pumps, shoes, stockings, hats, &c. I cannot express what pleasure sat upon the countenances of all these poor men when they saw the care I had taken of them, and how well I had furnished them. They told me I was a father to them; and that having such a correspondent as I was in so remote a part of the world, it would make them forget that they were left in a desolate place; and they all voluntarily engaged to me not to leave the place without my consent.

Then I presented to them the people I had brought with me, particularly the tailor, the smith, and the two carpenters, all of them most necessary people; but, above all, my general artificer, than whom they could not name anything that was more useful to them; and the tailor, to show his concern for them, went to work immediately, and, with my leave, made them every one a shirt, the first thing he did; and, what was still more, he taught the women not only how to sew and stitch, and use the needle, but made them assist to make the shirts for their husbands, and for all the rest. As to the carpenters, I scarce need mention how useful they were; for they took to pieces all my clumsy, unhandy things, and made clever convenient tables, stools, bedsteads, cupboards, lockers, shelves, and everything they wanted of that kind. But to let them see how nature made artificers at first, I carried the carpenters to see Will Atkins' basket-house, as I called it; and they both owned they never saw an instance of such natural ingenuity before, nor anything so regular and so handily built, at least of its kind; and one of them, when he saw it, after musing a good while, turning about to me, "I am sure," says he, "that man has no need of us; you need do nothing but give him tools."

Then I brought them out all my store of tools, and gave every man a digging-spade, a shovel, and a rake, for we had no barrows or ploughs; and to every separate place a pickaxe, a crow, a broad axe, and a saw; always appointing, that as often as any were broken or worn out, they should be supplied without grudging out of the general stores that I left behind. Nails, staples, hinges, hammers, chisels, knives, scissors, and all sorts of ironwork, they had without reserve, as they required; for no man would take more than he wanted, and he must be a fool that would waste or spoil them on any account whatever; and for the use of the smith I left two tons of unwrought iron for a supply.

My magazine of powder and arms which I brought them was such, even to profusion, that they could not but rejoice at them; for now they could march as I used to do, with a musket upon each shoulder, if there was occasion; and were able to fight a thousand savages, if they had but some little advantages of situation, which also they could not miss, if they had occasion.

I carried on shore with me the young man whose mother was starved to death, and the maid also; she was a sober, well-educated, religious young woman, and behaved so inoffensively that every one gave her a good word; she had, indeed, an unhappy life with us, there being no woman in the ship but herself, but she bore it with patience. After a while, seeing things so well ordered, and in so fine a way of thriving upon my island, and considering that they had neither business nor acquaintance in the East Indies, or reason for taking so long a voyage, both of them came to me and desired I would give them leave to remain on the island, and be entered among my family, as they called it. I agreed to this readily; and they had a little plot of ground allotted to them, where they had three tents or houses set up, surrounded with a basket-work, palisadoed like Atkins's, adjoining to his plantation. Their tents were contrived so that they had each of them a room apart to lodge in, and a middle tent like a great storehouse to lay their goods in, and to eat and to drink in. And now the other two Englishmen removed their habitation to the same place; and so the island was divided into three colonies, and no more—viz. the Spaniards, with old Friday and the first servants, at my habitation under the hill, which was, in a word, the capital city, and where they had so enlarged and extended their works, as well under as on the outside of the hill, that they lived, though perfectly concealed, yet full at large. Never was there such a little city in a wood, and so hid, in any part of the world; for I verify believe that a thousand men might have ranged the island a month, and, if they had not known there was such a thing, and looked on purpose for it, they would not have found it. Indeed the trees stood so thick and so close, and grew so fast woven one into another, that nothing but cutting them down first could discover the place, except the only two narrow entrances where they went in and out could be found, which was not very easy; one of them was close down at the water's edge, on the side of the creek, and it was afterwards above two hundred yards to the place; and the other was up a ladder at twice, as I have already described it; and they had also a large wood, thickly planted, on the top of the hill, containing above an acre, which grew apace, and concealed the place from all discovery there, with only one narrow place between two trees, not easily to be discovered, to enter on that side.

The other colony was that of Will Atkins, where there were four families of Englishmen, I mean those I had left there, with their wives and children; three savages

129

that were slaves, the widow and children of the Englishman that was killed, the young man and the maid, and, by the way, we made a wife of her before we went away. There were besides the two carpenters and the tailor, whom I brought with me for them: also the smith, who was a very necessary man to them, especially as a gunsmith, to take care of their arms; and my other man, whom I called Jack-of-all-trades, who was in himself as good almost as twenty men; for he was not only a very ingenious fellow, but a very merry fellow, and before I went away we married him to the honest maid that came with the youth in the ship I mentioned before.

And now I speak of marrying, it brings me naturally to say something of the French ecclesiastic that I had brought with me out of the ship's crew whom I took up at sea. It is true this man was a Roman, and perhaps it may give offence to some hereafter if I leave anything extraordinary upon record of a man whom, before I begin, I must (to set him out in just colours) represent in terms very much to his disadvantage, in the account of Protestants; as, first, that he was a Papist; secondly, a Popish priest; and thirdly, a French Popish priest. But justice demands of me to give him a due character; and I must say, he was a grave, sober, pious, and most religious person; exact in his life, extensive in his charity, and exemplary in almost everything he did. What then can any one say against being very sensible of the value of such a man, notwithstanding his profession? though it may be my opinion perhaps, as well as the opinion of others who shall read this, that he was mistaken.

The first hour that I began to converse with him after he had agreed to go with me to the East Indies, I found reason to delight exceedingly in his conversation; and he first began with me about religion in the most obliging manner imaginable. "Sir," says he, "you have not only under God" (and at that he crossed his breast) "saved my life, but you have admitted me to go this voyage in your ship, and by your obliging civility have taken me into your family, giving me an opportunity of free conversation. Now, sir, you see by my habit what my profession is, and I guess by your nation what yours is; I may think it is my duty, and doubtless it is so, to use my utmost endeavours, on all occasions, to bring all the souls I can to the knowledge of the truth, and to embrace the Catholic doctrine; but as I am here under your permission, and in your family, I am bound, in justice to your kindness as well as in decency and good manners, to be under your government; and therefore I shall not, without your leave, enter into any debate on the points of religion in which we may not agree, further than you shall give me leave."

I told him his carriage was so modest that I could not but acknowledge it; that it was true we were such people as they call heretics, but that he was not the first Catholic I had conversed with without falling into inconveniences, or carrying the questions to any height in debate; that he should not find himself the worse used for being of a different opinion from us, and if we did not converse without any dislike on either side, it should be his fault, not ours.

He replied that he thought all our conversation might be easily separated from disputes; that it was not his business to cap principles with every man he conversed with; and that he rather desired me to converse with him as a gentleman than as a religionist; and that, if I would give him leave at any time to discourse upon religious subjects, he would readily comply with it, and that he did not doubt but I would allow him also to defend his own opinions as well as he could; but that without my leave he would not break in upon me with any such thing. He told me further, that he would not cease to do all that became him, in his office as a priest, as well as a private Christian, to procure the good of the ship, and the safety of all that was in her; and though, perhaps, we would not join with him, and he could not pray with us, he hoped he might pray for us, which he would do upon all occasions. In this manner we conversed; and as he was of the most obliging, gentlemanlike behaviour, so he was, if I may be allowed to say so, a man of good sense, and, as I believe, of great learning.

He gave me a most diverting account of his life, and of the many extraordinary events of it; of many adventures which had befallen him in the few years that he had been abroad in the world; and particularly, it was very remarkable, that in the voyage he was now engaged in he had had the misfortune to be five times shipped and unshipped, and never to go to the place whither any of the ships he was in were at first designed. That his first intent was to have gone to Martinico, and that he went on board a ship bound thither at St. Malo; but being forced into Lisbon by bad weather, the ship received some damage by running aground in the mouth of the river Tagus, and was obliged to unload her cargo there; but finding a Portuguese ship there bound for the Madeiras, and ready to sail, and supposing he should meet with a ship there bound to Martinico, he went on board, in order to sail to the Madeiras; but the master of the Portuguese ship being but an indifferent mariner, had been out of his reckoning, and they drove to Fayal; where, however, he happened to find a very good market for his cargo, which was corn, and therefore resolved not to go to the Madeiras, but to load salt at the Isle of May, and to go away to Newfoundland. He had no remedy in this exigence but to go with the ship, and had a pretty good voyage as far as the Banks (so they call the place where they catch the fish), where, meeting with a French ship bound from France to Quebec, and from thence to Martinico, to carry provisions, he thought he should have an opportunity to complete his first design, but when he came to Quebec, the master of the ship died, and the vessel proceeded no further; so the next voyage he shipped himself for France, in the ship that was burned when we took them up at sea, and then shipped with us for the East Indies, as I have already said. Thus he had been disappointed in five voyages; all, as I may call it, in one voyage, besides what I shall have occasion to mention further of him.

But I shall not make digression into other men's stories which have no relation to my own; so I return to what concerns our affair in the island. He came to me one morning (for he lodged among us all the while we were upon the island), and it happened to be just when I was going to visit the Englishmen's colony, at the furthest part of the island; I say, he came to me, and told me, with a very grave countenance, that he had for two or three days desired an opportunity of some discourse with me, which he hoped would not be displeasing to me, because he thought it might in some measure correspond with my general design, which was the prosperity of my new colony, and perhaps might put it, at least more than he yet thought it was, in the way of God's blessing.

I looked a little surprised at the last of his discourse, and turning a little short, "How, sir," said I, "can it be said that we are not in the way of God's blessing, after such visible assistances and deliverances as we have seen here, and of which I have given you a large account?" "If you had pleased, sir," said he, with a world of modesty, and yet great readiness, "to have heard me, you would have found no room to have been displeased, much less to think so hard of me, that I should suggest that you have not had wonderful assistances and deliverances; and I hope, on your behalf, that you are in the way of God's blessing, and your design is exceeding good, and will prosper. But, sir, though it were more so than is even possible to you, yet there may be some among you that are not equally right in their actions: and you know that in the story of the children of Israel, one Achan in the camp removed God's blessing from them, and turned His hand so against them, that six-and-thirty of them, though not concerned in the crime, were the objects of divine vengeance, and bore the weight of that punishment."

I was sensibly touched with this discourse, and told him his inference was so just, and the whole design seemed so sincere, and was really so religious in its own nature, that I was very sorry I had interrupted him, and begged him to go on; and, in the meantime, because it seemed that what we had both to say might take up some time, I told him I was going to the Englishmen's plantations, and asked him to go with me, and we might discourse of it by the way. He told me he would the more willingly wait on me thither, because there partly the thing was acted which he desired to speak to me about; so we walked on, and I pressed him to be free and plain with me in what he had to say.

"Why, then, sir," said he, "be pleased to give me leave to lay down a few propositions, as the foundation of what I have to say, that we may not differ in the general principles, though we may be of some differing opinions in the practice of particulars. First, sir, though we differ in some of the doctrinal articles of religion (and it is very unhappy it is so, especially in the case before us, as I shall show afterwards), yet there are some general principles in which we both agree—that there is a God; and that this God having given us some stated general rules for our service and obedience, we ought not willingly and knowingly to offend Him, either by neglecting to do what He has commanded, or by doing what He has expressly forbidden. And let our different religions be what they will, this general principle is readily owned by us all, that the blessing of God does not ordinarily follow presumptuous sinning against His command; and every good Christian will be affectionately concerned to prevent any that are under his care living in a total neglect of God and His commands. It is not your men being Protestants, whatever my opinion may be of such, that discharges me from being concerned for their souls, and from endeavouring, if it lies before me, that they should live in as little distance from enmity with their Maker as possible, especially if you give me leave to meddle so far in your circuit."

I could not yet imagine what he aimed at, and told him I granted all he had said, and thanked him that he would so far concern himself for us: and begged he would explain the particulars of what he had observed, that like Joshua, to take his own parable, I might put away the accursed thing from us.

"Why, then, sir," says he, "I will take the liberty you give me; and there are three things, which, if I am right, must stand in the way of God's blessing upon your endeavours here, and which I should rejoice, for your sake and their own, to see removed. And, sir, I promise myself that you will fully agree with me in them all, as soon as I name them; especially because I shall convince you, that every one of them may, with great ease, and very much to your satisfaction, be remedied. First, sir," says he, "you have here four Englishmen, who have fetched women from among the savages, and have taken them as their wives, and have had many children by them all, and yet are not married to them after any stated legal manner, as the laws of God and man require. To this, sir, I know, you will object that there was no clergyman or priest of any kind to perform the ceremony; nor any pen and ink, or paper, to write down a contract of marriage, and have it signed between them. And I know also, sir, what the Spaniard governor has told you, I mean of the agreement that he obliged them to make when they took those women, viz. that they should choose them out by consent, and keep separately to them; which, by the way, is nothing of a marriage, no agreement with the women as wives, but only an agreement among themselves, to keep them from quarrelling. But, sir, the essence of the sacrament of matrimony" (so he called it, being a Roman) "consists not only in the mutual consent of the parties to take one another as man and wife, but in the formal and legal obligation that there is in the contract to compel the man and woman, at all times, to own and acknowledge each other; obliging the man to abstain from all other women, to engage in no other contract while these subsist; and, on all occasions, as ability allows, to provide honestly for them and their children; and to oblige the women to the same or like conditions, on their side. Now, sir," says he, "these men may, when they please, or when occasion presents, abandon these women, disown their children, leave them to perish, and take other women, and marry them while these are living;" and here he added, with some warmth, "How, sir, is God honoured in this unlawful liberty? And how shall a blessing succeed your endeavours in this place, however good in themselves, and however sincere in your design, while these men, who at present are your subjects, under your absolute government and dominion, are allowed by you to live in open adultery?"

I confess I was struck with the thing itself, but much more with the convincing arguments he supported it with; but I thought to have got off my young priest by telling him that all that part was done when I was not there: and that they had lived so many years with them now, that if it was adultery, it was past remedy; nothing could be done in it now.

"Sir," says he, "asking your pardon for such freedom, you are right in this, that, it being done in your absence, you could not be charged with that part of the crime; but, I beseech you, flatter not yourself that you are not, therefore, under an obligation to do your utmost now to put an end to it. You should legally and effectually marry them; and as, sir, my way of marrying may not be easy to reconcile them to, though it will be effectual, even by your own laws, so your way may be as well before God, and as valid among men. I mean by a written contract signed by both man and woman, and by all the witnesses present, which all the laws of Europe would decree to be valid."

I was amazed to see so much true piety, and so much sincerity of zeal, besides the unusual impartiality in his discourse as to his own party or church, and such true warmth for preserving people that he had no knowledge of or relation to from transgressing the laws of God. But recollecting what he had said of marrying them by a written contract, which I knew he would stand to, I returned it back upon him, and told him I granted all that he had said to be just, and on his part very kind; that I would discourse with the men upon the point now, when I came to them; and I knew no reason why they should scruple to let him marry them all, which I knew well enough would be granted to be as authentic and valid in England as if they were married by one of our own clergymen.

I then pressed him to tell me what was the second complaint which he had to make, acknowledging that I was very much his debtor for the first, and thanking him heartily for it. He told me he would use the same freedom and plainness in the second, and hoped I would take it as well; and this was, that notwithstanding these English subjects of mine, as he called them, had lived with these women almost seven years, had taught them to speak English, and even to read it, and that they were, as he perceived, women of tolerable understanding, and capable of instruction, yet they had not, to this hour, taught them anything of the Christian religion—no, not so much as to know there was a God, or a worship, or in what manner God was to be served, or that their own idolatry, and worshipping they knew not whom, was false and absurd. This he said was an unaccountable neglect, and what God would certainly call them to account for, and perhaps at last take the work out of their hands. He spoke this very affectionately and warmly.

"I am persuaded," says he, "had those men lived in the savage country whence their wives came, the savages would have taken more pains to have brought them to be idolaters, and to worship the devil, than any of these men, so far as I can see, have taken with them to teach the knowledge of the true God. Now, sir," said he, "though I do not acknowledge your religion, or you mine, yet we would be glad to see the devil's servants and the subjects of his kingdom taught to know religion; and that they might, at least, hear of God and a Redeemer, and the resurrection, and of a future state—things which we all believe; that they might, at least, be so much nearer coming into the bosom of the true Church than they are now in the public profession of idolatry and devil-worship."

I could hold no longer: I took him in my arms and embraced him eagerly. "How far," said I to him, "have I been from understanding the most essential part of a Christian, viz. to love the interest of the Christian Church, and the good of other men's souls! I scarce have known what belongs to the being a Christian."—"Oh, sir! do not say so," replied he; "this thing is not your fault."— "No," said I; "but why did I never lay it to heart as well as you?"—"It is not too late yet," said he; "be not too forward to condemn yourself."—"But what can be done now?" said I: "you see I am going away."— "Will you give me leave to talk with these poor men about it?"—"Yes, with all my heart," said I: "and oblige them to give heed to what you say too."—"As to that," said he, "we must leave them to the mercy of Christ; but it is your business to assist them, encourage them, and instruct them; and if you give me leave, and God His blessing, I do not doubt but the poor ignorant souls shall be brought home to the great circle of Christianity, if not into the particular faith we all embrace, and that even while you stay here." Upon this I said, "I shall not only give you leave, but give you a thousand thanks for it."

I now pressed him for the third article in which we were to blame. "Why, really," says he, "it is of the same nature. It is about your poor savages, who are, as I may say, your conquered subjects. It is a maxim, sir, that is or ought to be received among all Christians, of what church or pretended church soever, that the Christian knowledge ought to be propagated by all possible means and on all possible occasions. It is on this principle that our Church sends missionaries into Persia, India, and China; and that our clergy, even of the superior sort, willingly engage in the most hazardous voyages, and the most dangerous residence amongst murderers and barbarians, to teach them the knowledge of the true God, and to bring them over to embrace the Christian faith. Now, sir, you have such an opportunity here to have six or seven and thirty poor savages brought over from a state of idolatry to the knowledge of God, their Maker and Redeemer, that I wonder how you can pass such an occasion of doing good, which is really worth the expense of a man's whole life."

139

I was now struck dumb indeed, and had not one word to say. I had here the spirit of true Christian zeal for God and religion before me. As for me, I had not so much as entertained a thought of this in my heart before, and I believe I should not have thought of it; for I looked upon these savages as slaves, and people whom, had we not had any work for them to do, we would have used as such, or would have been glad to have transported them to any part of the world; for our business was to get rid of them, and we would all have been satisfied if they had been sent to any country, so they had never seen their own. I was confounded at his discourse, and knew not what answer to make him.

He looked earnestly at me, seeing my confusion. "Sir," says he, "I shall be very sorry if what I have said gives you any offence."— "No, no," said I, "I am offended with nobody but myself; but I am perfectly confounded, not only to think that I should never take any notice of this before, but with reflecting what notice I am able to take of it now. You know, sir," said I, "what circumstances I am in; I am bound to the East Indies in a ship freighted by merchants, and to whom it would be an insufferable piece of injustice to detain their ship here, the men lying all this while at victuals and wages on the owners' account. It is true, I agreed to be allowed twelve days here, and if I stay more, I must pay three pounds sterling per diem demurrage; nor can I stay upon demurrage above eight days more, and I have been here thirteen already; so that I am perfectly unable to engage in this work unless I would suffer myself to be left behind here again; in which case, if this single ship should miscarry in any part of her voyage, I should be just in the same condition that I was left in here at first, and from which I have been so wonderfully delivered." He owned the case was very hard upon me as to my voyage; but laid it home upon my conscience whether the blessing of saving thirty-seven souls was not worth venturing all I had in the world for. I was not so sensible of that as he was. I replied to him thus: "Why, sir, it is a valuable thing, indeed, to be an instrument in God's hand to convert thirty-seven heathens to the knowledge of Christ: but as you are an ecclesiastic, and are given over to the work, so it seems so naturally to fall in the way of your profession; how is it, then, that you do not rather offer yourself to undertake it than to press me to do it?"

Upon this he faced about just before me, as he walked along, and putting me to a full stop, made me a very low bow. "I most heartily thank God and you, sir," said he, "for giving me so evident a call to so blessed a work; and if you think yourself discharged from it, and desire me to undertake it, I will most readily do it, and think it a happy reward for all the hazards and difficulties of such a broken, disappointed voyage as I have met with, that I am dropped at last into so glorious a work."

I discovered a kind of rapture in his face while he spoke this to me; his eyes sparkled like fire; his face glowed, and his colour came and went; in a word, he was fired with the joy of being embarked in such a work. I paused a considerable while before I could tell what to say to him; for I was really surprised to find a man of such sincerity, and who seemed possessed of a zeal beyond the ordinary rate of men. But after I had considered it a while, I asked him seriously if he was in earnest, and that he would venture, on the single consideration of an attempt to convert those poor people, to be locked up in an unplanted island for perhaps his life, and at last might not know whether he should be able to do them good or not? He turned short upon me, and asked me what I called a venture? "Pray, sir," said he, "what do you think I consented to go in your ship to the East Indies for?"—"ay," said I, "that I

141

know not, unless it was to preach to the Indians."—
"Doubtless it was," said he; "and do you think, if I can
convert these thirty-seven men to the faith of Jesus
Christ, it is not worth my time, though I should never be
fetched off the island again?—nay, is it not infinitely of
more worth to save so many souls than my life is, or the
life of twenty more of the same profession? Yes, sir,"
says he, "I would give God thanks all my days if I could
be made the happy instrument of saving the souls of
those poor men, though I were never to get my foot off
this island or see my native country any more. But since
you will honour me with putting me into this work, for
which I will pray for you all the days of my life, I have
one humble petition to you besides."— "What is that?"
said I.—"Why," says he, "it is, that you will leave your
man Friday with me, to be my interpreter to them, and
to assist me; for without some help I cannot speak to
them, or they to me."

I was sensibly touched at his requesting Friday,
because I could not think of parting with him, and that
for many reasons: he had been the companion of my
travels; he was not only faithful to me, but sincerely
affectionate to the last degree; and I had resolved to do
something considerable for him if he out-lived me, as it
was probable he would. Then I knew that, as I had bred
Friday up to be a Protestant, it would quite confound
him to bring him to embrace another religion; and he
would never, while his eyes were open, believe that his
old master was a heretic, and would be damned; and this
might in the end ruin the poor fellow's principles, and so
turn him back again to his first idolatry. However, a
sudden thought relieved me in this strait, and it was this:
I told him I could not say that I was willing to part with
Friday on any account whatever, though a work that to
him was of more value than his life ought to be of much
more value than the keeping or parting with a servant.

On the other hand, I was persuaded that Friday would by no means agree to part with me; and I could not force him to it without his consent, without manifest injustice; because I had promised I would never send him away, and he had promised and engaged that he would never leave me, unless I sent him away.

He seemed very much concerned at it, for he had no rational access to these poor people, seeing he did not understand one word of their language, nor they one of his. To remove this difficulty, I told him Friday's father had learned Spanish, which I found he also understood, and he should serve him as an interpreter. So he was much better satisfied, and nothing could persuade him but he would stay and endeavour to convert them; but Providence gave another very happy turn to all this.

I come back now to the first part of his objections. When we came to the Englishmen, I sent for them all together, and after some account given them of what I had done for them, viz. what necessary things I had provided for them, and how they were distributed, which they were very sensible of, and very thankful for, I began to talk to them of the scandalous life they led, and gave them a full account of the notice the clergyman had taken of it; and arguing how unchristian and irreligious a life it was, I first asked them if they were married men or bachelors? They soon explained their condition to me, and showed that two of them were widowers, and the other three were single men, or bachelors. I asked them with what conscience they could take these women, and call them their wives, and have so many children by them, and not be lawfully married to them? They all gave me the answer I expected, viz. that there was nobody to marry them; that they agreed before the governor to keep them as their wives, and to maintain them and own them as their wives; and they thought, as things stood with them, they

143

were as legally married as if they had been married by a parson and with all the formalities in the world.

I told them that no doubt they were married in the sight of God, and were bound in conscience to keep them as their wives; but that the laws of men being otherwise, they might desert the poor women and children hereafter; and that their wives, being poor desolate women, friendless and moneyless, would have no way to help themselves. I therefore told them that unless I was assured of their honest intent, I could do nothing for them, but would take care that what I did should be for the women and children without them; and that, unless they would give me some assurances that they would marry the women, I could not think it was convenient they should continue together as man and wife; for that it was both scandalous to men and offensive to God, who they could not think would bless them if they went on thus.

All this went on as I expected; and they told me, especially Will Atkins, who now seemed to speak for the rest, that they loved their wives as well as if they had been born in their own native country, and would not leave them on any account whatever; and they did verily believe that their wives were as virtuous and as modest, and did, to the utmost of their skill, as much for them and for their children, as any woman could possibly do: and they would not part with them on any account. Will Atkins, for his own particular, added that if any man would take him away, and offer to carry him home to England, and make him captain of the best man-of-war in the navy, he would not go with him if he might not carry his wife and children with him; and if there was a clergyman in the ship, he would be married to her now with all his heart.

This was just as I would have it. The priest was not with me at that moment, but he was not far off; so to try him further, I told him I had a clergyman with me, and, if he was sincere, I would have him married next morning, and bade him consider of it, and talk with the rest. He said, as for himself, he need not consider of it at all, for he was very ready to do it, and was glad I had a minister with me, and he believed they would be all willing also. I then told him that my friend, the minister, was a Frenchman, and could not speak English, but I would act the clerk between them. He never so much as asked me whether he was a Papist or Protestant, which was, indeed, what I was afraid of. We then parted, and I went back to my clergyman, and Will Atkins went in to talk with his companions. I desired the French gentleman not to say anything to them till the business was thoroughly ripe; and I told him what answer the men had given me.

Before I went from their quarter they all came to me and told me they had been considering what I had said; that they were glad to hear I had a clergyman in my company, and they were very willing to give me the satisfaction I desired, and to be formally married as soon as I pleased; for they were far from desiring to part with their wives, and that they meant nothing but what was very honest when they chose them. So I appointed them to meet me the next morning; and, in the meantime, they should let their wives know the meaning of the marriage law; and that it was not only to prevent any scandal, but also to oblige them that they should not forsake them, whatever might happen.

The women were easily made sensible of the meaning of the thing, and were very well satisfied with it, as, indeed, they had reason to be: so they failed not to attend all together at my apartment next morning, where I brought out my clergyman; and though he had not on a minister's gown, after the manner of England, or the habit of a priest, after the manner of France, yet having a black vest something like a cassock, with a sash round it, he did not look very unlike a minister; and as for his language, I was his interpreter. But the seriousness of his behaviour to them, and the scruples he made of marrying the women, because they were not baptized and professed Christians, gave them an exceeding reverence for his person; and there was no need, after that, to inquire whether he was a clergyman or not. Indeed, I was afraid his scruples would have been carried so far as that he would not have married them at all; nay, notwithstanding all I was able to say to him, he resisted me, though modestly, yet very steadily, and at last refused absolutely to marry them, unless he had first talked with the men and the women too; and though at first I was a little backward to it, yet at last I agreed to it with a good will, perceiving the sincerity of his design.

When he came to them he let them know that I had acquainted him with their circumstances, and with the present design; that he was very willing to perform that part of his function, and marry them, as I had desired; but that before he could do it, he must take the liberty to talk with them. He told them that in the sight of all indifferent men, and in the sense of the laws of society, they had lived all this while in a state of sin; and that it was true that nothing but the consenting to marry, or effectually separating them from one another, could now put an end to it; but there was a difficulty in it, too, with respect to the laws of Christian matrimony, which he was not fully satisfied about, that of marrying one that is a professed Christian to a savage, an idolater, and a heathen—one that is not baptized; and yet that he did not see that there was time left to endeavour to persuade the women to be baptized, or to profess the name of Christ, whom they had, he doubted, heard nothing of, and without which they could not be baptized. He told them he doubted they were but indifferent Christians themselves; that they had but little knowledge of God or of His ways, and, therefore, he could not expect that they had said much to their wives on that head yet; but that unless they would promise him to use their endeavours with their wives to persuade them to become Christians, and would, as well as they could, instruct them in the knowledge and belief of God that made them, and to worship Jesus Christ that redeemed them, he could not marry them; for he would have no hand in joining Christians with savages, nor was it consistent with the principles of the Christian religion, and was, indeed, expressly forbidden in God's law.

They heard all this very attentively, and I delivered it very faithfully to them from his mouth, as near his own words as I could; only sometimes adding something of my own, to convince them how just it was, and that I was of his mind; and I always very carefully distinguished between what I said from myself and what were the clergyman's words. They told me it was very true what the gentleman said, that they were very indifferent Christians themselves, and that they had never talked to their wives about religion. "Lord, sir," says Will Atkins, "how should we teach them religion? Why, we know nothing ourselves; and besides, sir," said he, "should we talk to them of God and Jesus Christ, and heaven and hell, it would make them laugh at us, and ask us what we believe ourselves. And if we should tell them that we believe all the things we speak of to them, such as of good people going to heaven, and wicked people to the devil, they would ask us where we intend to go ourselves, that believe all this, and are such wicked fellows as we indeed are? Why, sir; 'tis enough to give them a surfeit of religion at first hearing; folks must have some religion themselves before they begin to teach other people."—"Will Atkins," said I to him, "though I am afraid that what you say has too much

147

truth in it, yet can you not tell your wife she is in the wrong; that there is a God and a religion better than her own; that her gods are idols; that they can neither hear nor speak; that there is a great Being that made all things, and that can destroy all that He has made; that He rewards the good and punishes the bad; and that we are to be judged by Him at last for all we do here? You are not so ignorant but even nature itself will teach you that all this is true; and I am satisfied you know it all to be true, and believe it yourself."—"That is true, sir," said Atkins; "but with what face can I say anything to my wife of all this, when she will tell me immediately it cannot be true?"—"Not true!" said I; "what do you mean by that?"—"Why, sir," said he, "she will tell me it cannot be true that this God I shall tell her of can be just, or can punish or reward, since I am not punished and sent to the devil, that have been such a wicked creature as she knows I have been, even to her, and to everybody else; and that I should be suffered to live, that have been always acting so contrary to what I must tell her is good, and to what I ought to have done."—"Why, truly, Atkins," said I, "I am afraid thou speakest too much truth;" and with that I informed the clergyman of what Atkins had said, for he was impatient to know. "Oh," said the priest, "tell him there is one thing will make him the best minister in the world to his wife, and that is repentance; for none teach repentance like true penitents. He wants nothing but to repent, and then he will be so much the better qualified to instruct his wife; he will then be able to tell her that there is not only a God, and that He is the just rewarder of good and evil, but that He is a merciful Being, and with infinite goodness and long-suffering forbears to punish those that offend; waiting to be gracious, and willing not the death of a sinner, but rather that he should return and live; and even reserves damnation to the general day of retribution; that it is a clear evidence of God and of a future state that righteous men receive not their reward, or wicked men their punishment, till they come into another world; and this will lead him to teach his wife the doctrine of the resurrection and of the last judgment. Let him but repent himself, he will be an excellent preacher of repentance to his wife."

I repeated all this to Atkins, who looked very serious all the while, and, as we could easily perceive, was more than ordinarily affected with it; when being eager, and hardly suffering me to make an end, "I know all this, master," says he, "and a great deal more; but I have not the impudence to talk thus to my wife, when God and my conscience know, and my wife will be an undeniable evidence against me, that I have lived as if I had never heard of a God or future state, or anything about it; and to talk of my repenting, alas!" (and with that he fetched a deep sigh, and I could see that the tears stood in his eyes) "'tis past all that with me."—"Past it, Atkins?" said I: "what dost thou mean by that?"—"I know well enough what I mean," says he; "I mean 'tis too late, and that is too true."

I told the clergyman, word for word, what he said, and this affectionate man could not refrain from tears; but, recovering himself, said to me, "Ask him but one question. Is he easy that it is too late; or is he troubled, and wishes it were not so?" I put the question fairly to Atkins; and he answered with a great deal of passion, "How could any man be easy in a condition that must certainly end in eternal destruction? that he was far from being easy; but that, on the contrary, he believed it would one time or other ruin him."—"What do you mean by that?" said I.—"Why," he said, "he believed he should one time or other cut his throat, to put an end to the terror of it."

The clergyman shook his head, with great concern in his face, when I told him all this; but turning quick to me upon it, says, "If that be his case, we may assure him it is not too late; Christ will give him repentance. But pray," says he, "explain this to him: that as no man is saved but by Christ, and the merit of His passion procuring divine mercy for him, how can it be too late for any man to receive mercy? Does he think he is able to sin beyond the power or reach of divine mercy? Pray tell him there may be a time when provoked mercy will no longer strive, and when God may refuse to hear, but that it is never too late for men to ask mercy; and we, that are Christ's servants, are commanded to preach mercy at all times, in the name of Jesus Christ, to all those that sincerely repent: so that it is never too late to repent."

I told Atkins all this, and he heard me with great earnestness; but it seemed as if he turned off the discourse to the rest, for he said to me he would go and have some talk with his wife; so he went out a while, and we talked to the rest. I perceived they were all stupidly ignorant as to matters of religion, as much as I was when I went rambling away from my father; yet there were none of them backward to hear what had been said; and all of them seriously promised that they would talk with their wives about it, and do their endeavours to persuade them to turn Christians.

The clergyman smiled upon me when I reported what answer they gave, but said nothing a good while; but at last, shaking his head, "We that are Christ's servants," says he, "can go no further than to exhort and instruct: and when men comply, submit to the reproof, and promise what we ask, 'tis all we can do; we are bound to accept their good words; but believe me, sir," said he, "whatever you may have known of the life of that man you call Will Atkin's, I believe he is the only sincere convert among them: I will not despair of the rest; but that man is apparently struck with the sense of his past life, and I doubt not, when he comes to talk of religion to his wife, he will talk himself effectually into it: for attempting to teach others is sometimes the best way of teaching ourselves. If that poor Atkins begins but once to talk seriously of Jesus Christ to his wife, he will assuredly talk himself into a thorough convert, make himself a penitent, and who knows what may follow."

Upon this discourse, however, and their promising, as above, to endeavour to persuade their wives to embrace Christianity, he married the two other couple; but Will Atkins and his wife were not yet come in. After this, my clergyman, waiting a while, was curious to know where Atkins was gone, and turning to me, said, "I entreat you, sir, let us walk out of your labyrinth here and look; I daresay we shall find this poor man somewhere or other talking seriously to his wife, and teaching her already something of religion." I began to be of the same mind; so we went out together, and I carried him a way which none knew but myself, and where the trees were so very thick that it was not easy to see through the thicket of leaves, and far harder to see in than to see out: when, coming to the edge of the wood, I saw Atkins and his tawny wife sitting under the shade of a bush, very eager in discourse: I stopped short till my clergyman came up to me, and then having showed him where they were, we stood and looked very steadily at them a good while. We observed him very earnest with her, pointing up to the sun, and to every quarter of the heavens, and then down to the earth, then out to the sea, then to himself, then to her, to the woods, to the trees. "Now," says the clergyman, "you see my words are made good, the man preaches to her; mark him now, he is telling her that our God has made him, her, and the heavens, the earth, the sea, the woods, the trees, &c."—"I believe he is," said I.

Immediately we perceived Will Atkins start upon his feet, fall down on his knees, and lift up both his hands. We supposed he said something, but we could not hear him; it was too far for that. He did not continue kneeling half a minute, but comes and sits down again by his wife, and talks to her again; we perceived then the woman very attentive, but whether she said anything to him we could not tell. While the poor fellow was upon his knees I could see the tears run plentifully down my clergyman's cheeks, and I could hardly forbear myself; but it was a great affliction to us both that we were not near enough to hear anything that passed between them. Well, however, we could come no nearer for fear of disturbing them: so we resolved to see an end of this piece of still conversation, and it spoke loud enough to us without the help of voice. He sat down again, as I have said, close by her, and talked again earnestly to her, and two or three times we could see him embrace her most passionately; another time we saw him take out his handkerchief and wipe her eyes, and then kiss her again with a kind of transport very unusual; and after several of these things, we saw him on a sudden jump up again, and lend her his hand to help her up, when immediately leading her by the hand a step or two, they both kneeled down together, and continued so about two minutes.

My friend could bear it no longer, but cries out aloud, "St. Paul! St. Paul! behold he prayeth." I was afraid Atkins would hear him, therefore I entreated him to withhold himself a while, that we might see an end of the scene, which to me, I must confess, was the most affecting that ever I saw in my life. Well, he strove with himself for a while, but was in such raptures to think that the poor heathen woman was become a Christian, that he was not able to contain himself; he wept several times, then throwing up his hands and crossing his breast, said over several things ejaculatory, and by the way of giving God thanks for so miraculous a testimony of the success of our endeavours. Some he spoke softly, and I could not well hear others; some things he said in Latin, some in French; then two or three times the tears would interrupt him, that he could not speak at all; but I begged that he would contain himself, and let us more narrowly and fully observe what was before us, which he did for a time, the scene not being near ended yet; for after the poor man and his wife were risen again from their knees, we observed he stood talking still eagerly to her, and we observed her motion, that she was greatly affected with what he said, by her frequently lifting up her hands, laying her hand to her breast, and such other postures as express the greatest seriousness and attention; this continued about half a quarter of an hour, and then they walked away, so we could see no more of them in that situation.

I took this interval to say to the clergyman, first, that I was glad to see the particulars we had both been witnesses to; that, though I was hard enough of belief in such cases, yet that I began to think it was all very sincere here, both in the man and his wife, however ignorant they might both be, and I hoped such a beginning would yet have a more happy end. "But, my friend," added I, "will you give me leave to start one difficulty here? I cannot tell how to object the least thing against that affectionate concern which you show for the turning of the poor people from their paganism to the Christian religion; but how does this comfort you, while these people are, in your account, out of the pale of the Catholic Church, without which you believe there is no salvation? so that you esteem these but heretics, as effectually lost as the pagans themselves."

To this he answered, with abundance of candour, thus: "Sir, I am a Catholic of the Roman Church, and a priest of the order of St. Benedict, and I embrace all the principles of the Roman faith; but yet, if you will believe me, and that I do not speak in compliment to you, or in respect to my circumstances and your civilities; I say nevertheless, I do not look upon you, who call yourselves reformed, without some charity. I dare not say (though I know it is our opinion in general) that you cannot be saved; I will by no means limit the mercy of Christ so far as think that He cannot receive you into the bosom of His Church, in a manner to us unperceivable; and I hope you have the same charity for us: I pray daily for you being all restored to Christ's Church, by whatsoever method He, who is all-wise, is pleased to direct. In the meantime, surely you will allow it consists with me as a Roman to distinguish far between a Protestant and a pagan; between one that calls on Jesus Christ, though in a way which I do not think is according to the true faith, and a savage or a barbarian, that knows no God, no Christ, no Redeemer; and if you are not within the pale of the Catholic Church, we hope you are nearer being restored to it than those who know nothing of God or of His Church: and I rejoice, therefore, when I see this poor man, who you say has been a profligate, and almost a murderer kneel down and pray to Jesus Christ, as we suppose he did, though not fully enlightened; believing that God, from whom every such work proceeds, will sensibly touch his heart, and bring him to the further knowledge of that truth in His own time; and if God shall influence this poor man to convert and instruct the ignorant savage, his wife, I can never believe that he shall be cast away himself. And have I not reason, then, to rejoice, the nearer any are brought to the knowledge of Christ, though they may not be brought quite home into the bosom of the Catholic Church just at the time when I desire it, leaving it to the goodness of Christ to perfect His work in His own time, and in his own way? Certainly, I would rejoice if all the savages in America were brought, like this poor woman, to pray to God, though they were all to be Protestants at first, rather than they should continue pagans or heathens; firmly believing, that He that had bestowed the first light on them would farther illuminate them with a beam of His heavenly grace, and bring them into the pale of His Church when He should see good."

Chapter 7

Conversation betwixt Will Atkins and His Wife

I was astonished at the sincerity and temper of this pious Papist, as much as I was oppressed by the power of his reasoning; and it presently occurred to my thoughts, that if such a temper was universal, we might be all Catholic Christians, whatever Church or particular profession we joined in; that a spirit of charity would soon work us all up into right principles; and as he thought that the like charity would make us all Catholics, so I told him I believed, had all the members of his Church the like moderation, they would soon all be Protestants. And there we left that part; for we never disputed at all. However, I talked to him another way, and taking him by the hand, "My friend," says I, "I wish all the clergy of the Romish Church were blessed with such moderation, and had an equal share of your charity. I am entirely of your opinion; but I must tell you that if you should preach such doctrine in Spain or Italy, they would put you into the Inquisition."—"It may be so," said he; "I know not what they would do in Spain or Italy; but I will not say they would be the better Christians for that severity; for I am sure there is no heresy in abounding with charity."

Well, as Will Atkins and his wife were gone, our business there was over, so we went back our own way; and when we came back, we found them waiting to be

156

called in. Observing this, I asked my clergyman if we should discover to him that we had seen him under the bush or not; and it was his opinion we should not, but that we should talk to him first, and hear what he would say to us; so we called him in alone, nobody being in the place but ourselves, and I began by asking him some particulars about his parentage and education. He told me frankly enough that his father was a clergyman who would have taught him well, but that he, Will Atkins, despised all instruction and correction; and by his brutish conduct cut the thread of all his father's comforts and shortened his days, for that he broke his heart by the most ungrateful, unnatural return for the most affectionate treatment a father ever gave.

In what he said there seemed so much sincerity of repentance, that it painfully affected me. I could not but reflect that I, too, had shortened the life of a good, tender father by my bad conduct and obstinate self-will. I was, indeed, so surprised with what he had told me, that I thought, instead of my going about to teach and instruct him, the man was made a teacher and instructor to me in a most unexpected manner.

I laid all this before the young clergyman, who was greatly affected with it, and said to me, "Did I not say, sir, that when this man was converted he would preach to us all? I tell you, sir, if this one man be made a true penitent, there will be no need of me; he will make Christians of all in the island."—But having a little composed myself, I renewed my discourse with Will Atkins. "But, Will," said I, "how comes the sense of this matter to touch you just now?"

W.A.—Sir, you have set me about a work that has struck a dart though my very soul; I have been talking about God and religion to my wife, in order, as you directed me, to make a Christian of her, and she has preached such a sermon to me as I shall never forget while I live.

R.C.—No, no, it is not your wife has preached to you; but when you were moving religious arguments to her, conscience has flung them back upon you.

W.A.—Ay, sir, with such force as is not to be resisted.

R.C.—Pray, Will, let us know what passed between you and your wife; for I know something of it already.

W.A.—Sir, it is impossible to give you a full account of it; I am too full to hold it, and yet have no tongue to express it; but let her have said what she will, though I cannot give you an account of it, this I can tell you, that I have resolved to amend and reform my life.

R.C.—But tell us some of it: how did you begin, Will? For this has been an extraordinary case, that is certain. She has preached a sermon, indeed, if she has wrought this upon you.

W.A.—Why, I first told her the nature of our laws about marriage, and what the reasons were that men and women were obliged to enter into such compacts as it was neither in the power of one nor other to break; that otherwise, order and justice could not be maintained, and men would run from their wives, and abandon their children, mix confusedly with one another, and neither families be kept entire, nor inheritances be settled by legal descent.

R.C.—You talk like a civilian, Will. Could you make her understand what you meant by inheritance and families? They know no such things among the savages, but marry anyhow, without regard to relation, consanguinity, or family; brother and sister, nay, as I have been told, even the father and the daughter, and the son and the mother.

W.A.—I believe, sir, you are misinformed, and my wife assures me of the contrary, and that they abhor it;

perhaps, for any further relations, they may not be so exact as we are; but she tells me never in the near relationship you speak of.

R.C.—Well, what did she say to what you told her?

W.A.—She said she liked it very well, as it was much better than in her country.

R.C.—But did you tell her what marriage was?

W.A.—Ay, ay, there began our dialogue. I asked her if she would be married to me our way. She asked me what way that was; I told her marriage was appointed by God; and here we had a strange talk together, indeed, as ever man and wife had, I believe.

N.B.—This dialogue between Will Atkins and his wife, which I took down in writing just after he told it me, was as follows:-

Wife.—Appointed by your God!—Why, have you a God in your country?

W.A.—Yes, my dear, God is in every country.

Wife.—No your God in my country; my country have the great old Benamuckee God.

W.A.—Child, I am very unfit to show you who God is; God is in heaven and made the heaven and the earth, the sea, and all that in them is.

Wife.—No makee de earth; no you God makee all earth; no makee my country.

[Will Atkins laughed a little at her expression of God not making her country.]

Wife.—No laugh; why laugh me? This no ting to laugh.

[He was justly reproved by his wife, for she was more serious than he at first.]

W.A.—That's true, indeed; I will not laugh any more, my dear.

Wife.—Why you say you God makee all?

W.A.—Yes, child, our God made the whole world, and you, and me, and all things; for He is the only true

159

God, and there is no God but Him. He lives for ever in heaven.

Wife.—Why you no tell me long ago?

W.A.—That's true, indeed; but I have been a wicked wretch, and have not only forgotten to acquaint thee with anything before, but have lived without God in the world myself.

Wife.—What, have you a great God in your country, you no know Him? No say O to Him? No do good ting for Him? That no possible.

W.A.—It is true; though, for all that, we live as if there was no God in heaven, or that He had no power on earth.

Wife.—But why God let you do so? Why He no makee you good live?

W.A.—It is all our own fault.

Wife.—But you say me He is great, much great, have much great power; can makee kill when He will: why He no makee kill when you no serve Him? no say O to Him? no be good mans?

W.A.—That is true, He might strike me dead; and I ought to expect it, for I have been a wicked wretch, that is true; but God is merciful, and does not deal with us as we deserve.

Wife.—But then do you not tell God thankee for that too?

W. A.—No, indeed, I have not thanked God for His mercy, any more than I have feared God from His power.

Wife.—Then you God no God; me no think, believe He be such one, great much power, strong: no makee kill you, though you make Him much angry.

W.A.—What, will my wicked life hinder you from believing in God? What a dreadful creature am I! and what a sad truth is it, that the horrid lives of Christians hinder the conversion of heathens!

Wife.—How me tink you have great much God up there [she points up to heaven], and yet no do well, no do good ting? Can He tell? Sure He no tell what you do?

W.A.—Yes, yes, He knows and sees all things; He hears us speak, sees what we do, knows what we think though we do not speak.

Wife.—What! He no hear you curse, swear, speak de great damn?

W.A.—Yes, yes, He hears it all.

Wife.—Where be then the much great power strong?

W.A.—He is merciful, that is all we can say for it; and this proves Him to be the true God; He is God, and not man, and therefore we are not consumed.

[Here Will Atkins told us he was struck with horror to think how he could tell his wife so clearly that God sees, and hears, and knows the secret thoughts of the heart, and all that we do, and yet that he had dared to do all the vile things he had done.]

Wife.—Merciful! What you call dat?

W.A.—He is our Father and Maker, and He pities and spares us.

Wife.—So then He never makee kill, never angry when you do wicked; then He no good Himself, or no great able.

W.A.—Yes, yes, my dear, He is infinitely good and infinitely great, and able to punish too; and sometimes, to show His justice and vengeance, He lets fly His anger to destroy sinners and make examples; many are cut off in their sins.

Wife.—But no makee kill you yet; then He tell you, maybe, that He no makee you kill: so you makee the bargain with Him, you do bad thing, He no be angry at you when He be angry at other mans.

W.A.—No, indeed, my sins are all presumptions upon His goodness; and He would be infinitely just if He destroyed me, as He has done other men.

161

Wife.—Well, and yet no kill, no makee you dead: what you say to Him for that? You no tell Him thankee for all that too?

W.A.—I am an unthankful, ungrateful dog, that is true.

Wife.—Why He no makee you much good better? you say He makee you.

W.A.—He made me as He made all the world: it is I have deformed myself and abused His goodness, and made myself an abominable wretch.

Wife.—I wish you makee God know me. I no makee Him angry—I no do bad wicked thing.

[Here Will Atkins said his heart sunk within him to hear a poor untaught creature desire to be taught to know God, and he such a wicked wretch, that he could not say one word to her about God, but what the reproach of his own carriage would make most irrational to her to believe; nay, that already she had told him that she could not believe in God, because he, that was so wicked, was not destroyed.]

W.A.—My dear, you mean, you wish I could teach you to know God, not God to know you; for He knows you already, and every thought in your heart.

Wife.—Why, then, He know what I say to you now: He know me wish to know Him. How shall me know who makee me?

W.A.—Poor creature, He must teach thee: I cannot teach thee. I will pray to Him to teach thee to know Him, and forgive me, that am unworthy to teach thee.

[The poor fellow was in such an agony at her desiring him to make her know God, and her wishing to know Him, that he said he fell down on his knees before her, and prayed to God to enlighten her mind with the saving knowledge of Jesus Christ, and to pardon his sins, and accept of his being the unworthy instrument of instructing her in the principles of religion: after which he sat down by her again, and their dialogue went on. This was the time when we saw him kneel down and hold up his hands.]

Wife.—What you put down the knee for? What you hold up the hand for? What you say? Who you speak to? What is all that?

W.A.—My dear, I bow my knees in token of my submission to Him that made me: I said O to Him, as you call it, and as your old men do to their idol Benamuckee; that is, I prayed to Him.

Wife.—What say you O to Him for?

W.A.—I prayed to Him to open your eyes and your understanding, that you may know Him, and be accepted by Him.

Wife.—Can He do that too?

W.A.—Yes, He can: He can do all things.

Wife.—But now He hear what you say?

W.A.—Yes, He has bid us pray to Him, and promised to hear us.

Wife.—Bid you pray? When He bid you? How He bid you? What you hear Him speak?

W.A.—No, we do not hear Him speak; but He has revealed Himself many ways to us.

[Here he was at a great loss to make her understand that God has revealed Himself to us by His word, and what His word was; but at last he told it to her thus.]

W.A.—God has spoken to some good men in former days, even from heaven, by plain words; and God has inspired good men by His Spirit; and they have written all His laws down in a book.

Wife.—Me no understand that; where is book?

W.A.—Alas! my poor creature, I have not this book; but I hope I shall one time or other get it for you, and help you to read it.

[Here he embraced her with great affection, but with inexpressible grief that he had not a Bible.]

Wife.—But how you makee me know that God teachee them to write that book?

W.A.—By the same rule that we know Him to be God.

Wife.—What rule? What way you know Him?

W.A.—Because He teaches and commands nothing but what is good, righteous, and holy, and tends to make us perfectly good, as well as perfectly happy; and because He forbids and commands us to avoid all that is wicked, that is evil in itself, or evil in its consequence.

Wife.—That me would understand, that me fain see; if He teachee all good thing, He makee all good thing, He give all thing, He hear me when I say O to Him, as you do just now; He makee me good if I wish to be good; He spare me, no makee kill me, when I no be good: all this you say He do, yet He be great God; me take, think, believe Him to be great God; me say O to Him with you, my dear.

Here the poor man could forbear no longer, but raised her up, made her kneel by him, and he prayed to God aloud to instruct her in the knowledge of Himself, by His Spirit; and that by some good providence, if possible, she might, some time or other, come to have a Bible, that she might read the word of God, and be taught by it to know Him. This was the time that we saw him lift her up by the hand, and saw him kneel down by her, as above.

They had several other discourses, it seems, after this; and particularly she made him promise that, since he confessed his own life had been a wicked, abominable course of provocations against God, that he would reform it, and not make God angry any more, lest He should make him dead, as she called it, and then she would be left alone, and never be taught to know this God better; and lest he should be miserable, as he had told her wicked men would be after death.

This was a strange account, and very affecting to us both, but particularly to the young clergyman; he was, indeed, wonderfully surprised with it, but under the greatest affliction imaginable that he could not talk to her, that he could not speak English to make her understand him; and as she spoke but very broken English, he could not understand her; however, he turned himself to me, and told me that he believed that there must be more to do with this woman than to marry her. I did not understand him at first; but at length he explained himself, viz. that she ought to be baptized. I agreed with him in that part readily, and wished it to be done presently. "No, no; hold, sir," says he; "though I would have her be baptized, by all means, for I must observe that Will Atkins, her husband, has indeed brought her, in a wonderful manner, to be willing to embrace a religious life, and has given her just ideas of the being of a God; of His power, justice, and mercy: yet I desire to know of him if he has said anything to her of Jesus Christ, and of the salvation of sinners; of the nature of faith in Him, and redemption by Him; of the Holy Spirit, the resurrection, the last judgment, and the future state."

I called Will Atkins again, and asked him; but the poor fellow fell immediately into tears, and told us he had said something to her of all those things, but that he was himself so wicked a creature, and his own conscience so reproached him with his horrid, ungodly life, that he trembled at the apprehensions that her knowledge of him should lessen the attention she should give to those things, and make her rather contemn religion than receive it; but he was assured, he said, that her mind was so disposed to receive due impressions of all those things, and that if I would but discourse with her, she would make it appear to my satisfaction that my labour would not be lost upon her.

Accordingly I called her in, and placing myself as interpreter between my religious priest and the woman, I entreated him to begin with her; but sure such a sermon was never preached by a Popish priest in these latter ages of the world; and as I told him, I thought he had all the zeal, all the knowledge, all the sincerity of a Christian, without the error of a Roman Catholic; and that I took him to be such a clergyman as the Roman bishops were before the Church of Rome assumed spiritual sovereignty over the consciences of men. In a word, he brought the poor woman to embrace the knowledge of Christ, and of redemption by Him, not with wonder and astonishment only, as she did the first notions of a God, but with joy and faith; with an affection, and a surprising degree of understanding, scarce to be imagined, much less to be expressed; and, at her own request, she was baptized.

When he was preparing to baptize her, I entreated him that he would perform that office with some caution, that the man might not perceive he was of the Roman Church, if possible, because of other ill consequences which might attend a difference among us in that very religion which we were instructing the other in. He told me that as he had no consecrated chapel, nor proper things for the office, I should see he would do it in a manner that I should not know by it that he was a Roman Catholic myself, if I had not known it before; and so he did; for saying only some words over to himself in Latin, which I could not understand, he poured a whole dishful of water upon the woman's head, pronouncing in French, very loud, "Mary" (which was the name her husband desired me to give her, for I was her godfather), "I baptize thee in the name of the Father, and of the Son, and of the Holy Ghost;" so that none could know anything by it what religion he was of. He gave the benediction afterwards in Latin, but either Will

Atkins did not know but it was French, or else did not take notice of it at that time.

As soon as this was over we married them; and after the marriage was over, he turned to Will Atkins, and in a very affectionate manner exhorted him, not only to persevere in that good disposition he was in, but to support the convictions that were upon him by a resolution to reform his life: told him it was in vain to say he repented if he did not forsake his crimes; represented to him how God had honoured him with being the instrument of bringing his wife to the knowledge of the Christian religion, and that he should be careful he did not dishonour the grace of God; and that if he did, he would see the heathen a better Christian than himself; the savage converted, and the instrument cast away. He said a great many good things to them both; and then, recommending them to God's goodness, gave them the benediction again, I repeating everything to them in English; and thus ended the ceremony. I think it was the most pleasant and agreeable day to me that ever I passed in my whole life. But my clergyman had not done yet: his thoughts hung continually upon the conversion of the thirty-seven savages, and fain be would have stayed upon the island to have undertaken it; but I convinced him, first, that his undertaking was impracticable in itself; and, secondly, that perhaps I would put it into a way of being done in his absence to his satisfaction.

Having thus brought the affairs of the island to a narrow compass, I was preparing to go on board the ship, when the young man I had taken out of the famished ship's company came to me, and told me he understood I had a clergyman with me, and that I had caused the Englishmen to be married to the savages; that he had a match too, which he desired might be finished before I went, between two Christians, which he hoped would not be disagreeable to me.

I knew this must be the young woman who was his mother's servant, for there was no other Christian woman on the island: so I began to persuade him not to do anything of that kind rashly, or because be found himself in this solitary circumstance. I represented to him that he had some considerable substance in the world, and good friends, as I understood by himself, and the maid also; that the maid was not only poor, and a servant, but was unequal to him, she being six or seven and twenty years old, and he not above seventeen or eighteen; that he might very probably, with my assistance, make a remove from this wilderness, and come into his own country again; and that then it would be a thousand to one but he would repent his choice, and the dislike of that circumstance might be disadvantageous to both. I was going to say more, but he interrupted me, smiling, and told me, with a great deal of modesty, that I mistook in my guesses—that he had nothing of that kind in his thoughts; and he was very glad to hear that I had an intent of putting them in a way to see their own country again; and nothing should have made him think of staying there, but that the voyage I was going was so exceeding long and hazardous, and would carry him quite out of the reach of all his friends; that he had nothing to desire of me but that I would settle him in some little property in the island where he was, give him a servant or two, and some few necessaries, and he would live here like a planter, waiting the good time when, if ever I returned to England, I would redeem him. He hoped I would not be unmindful of him when I came to England: that he would give me some letters to his friends in London, to let them know how good I had been to him, and in what part of the world and what circumstances I had left him in: and he promised me that whenever I redeemed him, the plantation, and all the improvements he had made upon it, let the value be what it would, should be wholly mine.

His discourse was very prettily delivered, considering his youth, and was the more agreeable to me, because he told me positively the match was not for himself. I gave him all possible assurances that if I lived to come safe to England, I would deliver his letters, and do his business effectually; and that he might depend I should never forget the circumstances I had left him in. But still I was impatient to know who was the person to be married; upon which he told me it was my Jack-of-all-trades and his maid Susan. I was most agreeably surprised when he named the match; for, indeed, I thought it very suitable. The character of that man I have given already; and as for the maid, she was a very honest, modest, sober, and religious young woman: had a very good share of sense, was agreeable enough in her person, spoke very handsomely and to the purpose, always with decency and good manners, and was neither too backward to speak when requisite, nor impertinently forward when it was not her business; very handy and housewifely, and an excellent manager; fit, indeed, to have been governess to the whole island; and she knew very well how to behave in every respect.

The match being proposed in this manner, we married them the same day; and as I was father at the altar, and gave her away, so I gave her a portion; for I appointed her and her husband a handsome large space of ground for their plantation; and indeed this match, and the proposal the young gentleman made to give him a small property in the island, put me upon parcelling it out amongst them, that they might not quarrel afterwards about their situation.

This sharing out the land to them I left to Will Atkins, who was now grown a sober, grave, managing fellow, perfectly reformed, exceedingly pious and religious; and, as far as I may be allowed to speak positively in such a case, I verily believe he was a true penitent. He divided things so justly, and so much to every one's satisfaction, that they only desired one general writing under my hand for the whole, which I caused to be drawn up, and signed and sealed, setting out the bounds and situation of every man's plantation, and testifying that I gave them thereby severally a right to the whole possession and inheritance of the respective plantations or farms, with their improvements, to them and their heirs, reserving all the rest of the island as my own property, and a certain rent for every particular plantation after eleven years, if I, or any one from me, or in my name, came to demand it, producing an attested copy of the same writing. As to the government and laws among them, I told them I was not capable of giving them better rules than they were able to give themselves; only I made them promise me to live in love and good neighbourhood with one another; and so I prepared to leave them.

One thing I must not omit, and that is, that being now settled in a kind of commonwealth among themselves, and having much business in hand, it was odd to have seven-and-thirty Indians live in a nook of the island, independent, and, indeed, unemployed; for except the providing themselves food, which they had difficulty enough to do sometimes, they had no manner of business or property to manage. I proposed, therefore, to the governor Spaniard that he should go to them, with Friday's father, and propose to them to remove, and either plant for themselves, or be taken into their several families as servants to be maintained for their labour, but without being absolute slaves; for I would not permit them to make them slaves by force, by any means; because they had their liberty given them by capitulation, as it were articles of surrender, which they ought not to break.

They most willingly embraced the proposal, and came all very cheerfully along with him: so we allotted them land and plantations, which three or four accepted of, but all the rest chose to be employed as servants in the several families we had settled. Thus my colony was in a manner settled as follows: The Spaniards possessed my original habitation, which was the capital city, and extended their plantations all along the side of the brook, which made the creek that I have so often described, as far as my bower; and as they increased their culture, it went always eastward. The English lived in the north-east part, where Will Atkins and his comrades began, and came on southward and south-west, towards the back part of the Spaniards; and every plantation had a great addition of land to take in, if they found occasion, so that they need not jostle one another for want of room. All the east end of the island was left uninhabited, that if any of the savages should come on shore there only for their customary barbarities, they might come and go; if they disturbed nobody, nobody would disturb them: and no doubt but they were often ashore, and went away again; for I never heard that the planters were ever attacked or disturbed any more.

Chapter 8

Sails from the Island for the Brazils

It now came into my thoughts that I had hinted to my friend the clergyman that the work of converting the savages might perhaps be set on foot in his absence to his satisfaction, and I told him that now I thought that it was put in a fair way; for the savages, being thus divided among the Christians, if they would but every one of them do their part with those which came under their hands, I hoped it might have a very good effect.

He agreed presently in that, if they did their part. "But how," says he, "shall we obtain that of them?" I told him we would call them all together, and leave it in charge with them, or go to them, one by one, which he thought best; so we divided it—he to speak to the Spaniards, who were all Papists, and I to speak to the English, who were all Protestants; and we recommended it earnestly to them, and made them promise that they would never make any distinction of Papist or Protestant in their exhorting the savages to turn Christians, but teach them the general knowledge of the true God, and of their Saviour Jesus Christ; and they likewise promised us that they would never have any differences or disputes one with another about religion.

When I came to Will Atkins's house, I found that the young woman I have mentioned above, and Will Atkins's wife, were become intimates; and this prudent, religious young woman had perfected the work Will Atkins had begun; and though it was not above four days after what I have related, yet the new-baptized savage woman was made such a Christian as I have seldom heard of in all my observation or conversation in the world. It came next into my mind, in the morning before I went to them, that amongst all the needful things I had to leave with them I had not left them a Bible, in which I showed myself less considering for them than my good friend the widow was for me when she sent me the cargo of a hundred pounds from Lisbon, where she packed up three Bibles and a Prayer-book. However, the good woman's charity had a greater extent than ever she imagined, for they were reserved for the comfort and instruction of those that made much better use of them than I had done.

I took one of the Bibles in my pocket, and when I came to Will Atkins's tent, or house, and found the young woman and Atkins's baptized wife had been discoursing of religion together—for Will Atkins told it me with a great deal of joy—I asked if they were together now, and he said, "Yes"; so I went into the house, and he with me, and we found them together very earnest in discourse. "Oh, sir," says Will Atkins, "when God has sinners to reconcile to Himself, and aliens to bring home, He never wants a messenger; my wife has got a new instructor: I knew I was unworthy, as I was incapable of that work; that young woman has been sent hither from heaven—she is enough to convert a whole island of savages." The young woman blushed, and rose up to go away, but I desired her to sit-still; I told her she had a good work upon her hands, and I hoped God would bless her in it.

We talked a little, and I did not perceive that they had any book among them, though I did not ask; but I put my hand into my pocket, and pulled out my Bible.

"Here," said I to Atkins, "I have brought you an assistant that perhaps you had not before." The man was so confounded that he was not able to speak for some time; but, recovering himself, he takes it with both his hands, and turning to his wife, "Here, my dear," says he, "did not I tell you our God, though He lives above, could hear what we have said? Here's the book I prayed for when you and I kneeled down under the bush; now God has heard us and sent it." When he had said so, the man fell into such passionate transports, that between the joy of having it, and giving God thanks for it, the tears ran down his face like a child that was crying.

The woman was surprised, and was like to have run into a mistake that none of us were aware of; for she firmly believed God had sent the book upon her husband's petition. It is true that providentially it was so, and might be taken so in a consequent sense; but I believe it would have been no difficult matter at that time to have persuaded the poor woman to have believed that an express messenger came from heaven on purpose to bring that individual book. But it was too serious a matter to suffer any delusion to take place, so I turned to the young woman, and told her we did not desire to impose upon the new convert in her first and more ignorant understanding of things, and begged her to explain to her that God may be very properly said to answer our petitions, when, in the course of His providence, such things are in a particular manner brought to pass as we petitioned for; but we did not expect returns from heaven in a miraculous and particular manner, and it is a mercy that it is not so.

This the young woman did afterwards effectually, so that there was no priestcraft used here; and I should have thought it one of the most unjustifiable frauds in the world to have had it so. But the effect upon Will Atkins is really not to be expressed; and there, we may be sure, was no delusion. Sure no man was ever more thankful in the world for anything of its kind than he was for the Bible, nor, I believe, never any man was glad of a Bible from a better principle; and though he had been a most profligate creature, headstrong, furious, and desperately wicked, yet this man is a standing rule to us all for the well instructing children, viz. that parents should never give over to teach and instruct, nor ever despair of the success of their endeavours, let the children be ever so refractory, or to appearance insensible to instruction; for if ever God in His providence touches the conscience of such, the force of their education turns upon them, and the early instruction of parents is not lost, though it may have been many years laid asleep, but some time or other they may find the benefit of it. Thus it was with this poor man: however ignorant he was of religion and Christian knowledge, he found he had some to do with now more ignorant than himself, and that the least part of the instruction of his good father that now came to his mind was of use to him.

Among the rest, it occurred to him, he said, how his father used to insist so much on the inexpressible value of the Bible, and the privilege and blessing of it to nations, families, and persons; but he never entertained the least notion of the worth of it till now, when, being to talk to heathens, savages, and barbarians, he wanted the help of the written oracle for his assistance. The young woman was glad of it also for the present occasion, though she had one, and so had the youth, on board our ship among their goods, which were not yet brought on shore. And now, having said so many things of this young woman, I cannot omit telling one story more of her and myself, which has something in it very instructive and remarkable.

I have related to what extremity the poor young woman was reduced; how her mistress was starved to death, and died on board that unhappy ship we met at sea, and how the whole ship's company was reduced to the last extremity. The gentlewoman, and her son, and this maid, were first hardly used as to provisions, and at last totally neglected and starved—that is to say, brought to the last extremity of hunger. One day, being discoursing with her on the extremities they suffered, I asked her if she could describe, by what she had felt, what it was to starve, and how it appeared? She said she believed she could, and told her tale very distinctly thus:-

"First, we had for some days fared exceedingly hard, and suffered very great hunger; but at last we were wholly without food of any kind except sugar, and a little wine and water. The first day after I had received no food at all, I found myself towards evening, empty and sick at the stomach, and nearer night much inclined to yawning and sleep. I lay down on the couch in the great cabin to sleep, and slept about three hours, and awaked a little refreshed, having taken a glass of wine when I lay down; after being about three hours awake, it being about five o'clock in the morning, I found myself empty, and my stomach sickish, and lay down again, but could not sleep at all, being very faint and ill; and thus I continued all the second day with a strange variety— first hungry, then sick again, with retchings to vomit. The second night, being obliged to go to bed again without any food more than a draught of fresh water, and being asleep, I dreamed I was at Barbadoes, and that the market was mightily stocked with provisions; that I bought some for my mistress, and went and dined very heartily. I thought my stomach was full after this, as it would have been after a good dinner; but when I awaked I was exceedingly sunk in my spirits to find myself in

177

the extremity of family. The last glass of wine we had I drank, and put sugar in it, because of its having some spirit to supply nourishment; but there being no substance in the stomach for the digesting office to work upon, I found the only effect of the wine was to raise disagreeable fumes from the stomach into the head; and I lay, as they told me, stupid and senseless, as one drunk, for some time. The third day, in the morning, after a night of strange, confused, and inconsistent dreams, and rather dozing than sleeping, I awaked ravenous and furious with hunger; and I question, had not my understanding returned and conquered it, whether if I had been a mother, and had had a little child with me, its life would have been safe or not. This lasted about three hours, during which time I was twice raging mad as any creature in Bedlam, as my young master told me, and as he can now inform you.

"In one of these fits of lunacy or distraction I fell down and struck my face against the corner of a pallet-bed, in which my mistress lay, and with the blow the blood gushed out of my nose; and the cabin-boy bringing me a little basin, I sat down and bled into it a great deal; and as the blood came from me I came to myself, and the violence of the flame or fever I was in abated, and so did the ravenous part of the hunger. Then I grew sick, and retched to vomit, but could not, for I had nothing in my stomach to bring up. After I had bled some time I swooned, and they all believed I was dead; but I came to myself soon after, and then had a most dreadful pain in my stomach not to be described—not like the colic, but a gnawing, eager pain for food; and towards night it went off with a kind of earnest wishing or longing for food. I took another draught of water with sugar in it; but my stomach loathed the sugar and brought it all up again; then I took a draught of water without sugar, and that stayed with me; and I laid me down upon the bed, praying most heartily that it would please God to take me away; and composing my mind in hopes of it, I slumbered a while, and then waking, thought myself dying, being light with vapours from an empty stomach. I recommended my soul then to God, and then earnestly wished that somebody would throw me into the into the sea.

"All this while my mistress lay by me, just, as I thought, expiring, but she bore it with much more patience than I, and gave the last bit of bread she had left to her child, my young master, who would not have taken it, but she obliged him to eat it; and I believe it saved his life. Towards the morning I slept again, and when I awoke I fell into a violent passion of crying, and after that had a second fit of violent hunger. I got up ravenous, and in a most dreadful condition; and once or twice I was going to bite my own arm. At last I saw the basin in which was the blood I had bled at my nose the day before: I ran to it, and swallowed it with such haste, and such a greedy appetite, as if I wondered nobody had taken it before, and afraid it should be taken from me now. After it was down, though the thoughts of it filled me with horror, yet it checked the fit of hunger, and I took another draught of water, and was composed and refreshed for some hours after. This was the fourth day; and this I kept up till towards night, when, within the compass of three hours, I had all the several circumstances over again, one after another, viz. sick, sleepy, eagerly hungry, pain in the stomach, then ravenous again, then sick, then lunatic, then crying, then ravenous again, and so every quarter of an hour, and my strength wasted exceedingly; at night I lay me down, having no comfort but in the hope that I should die before morning.

"All this night I had no sleep; but the hunger was now turned into a disease; and I had a terrible colic and griping, by wind instead of food having found its way into the bowels; and in this condition I lay till morning, when I was surprised by the cries and lamentations of my young master, who called out to me that his mother was dead. I lifted myself up a little, for I had not strength to rise, but found she was not dead, though she was able to give very little signs of life. I had then such convulsions in my stomach, for want of some sustenance, as I cannot describe; with such frequent throes and pangs of appetite as nothing but the tortures of death can imitate; and in this condition I was when I heard the seamen above cry out, 'A sail! a sail!' and halloo and jump about as if they were distracted. I was not able to get off from the bed, and my mistress much less; and my young master was so sick that I thought he had been expiring; so we could not open the cabin door, or get any account what it was that occasioned such confusion; nor had we had any conversation with the ship's company for twelve days, they having told us that they had not a mouthful of anything to eat in the ship; and this they told us afterwards— they thought we had been dead. It was this dreadful condition we were in when you were sent to save our lives; and how you found us, sir, you know as well as I, and better too."

This was her own relation, and is such a distinct account of starving to death, as, I confess, I never met with, and was exceeding instructive to me. I am the rather apt to believe it to be a true account, because the youth gave me an account of a good part of it; though I must own, not so distinct and so feeling as the maid; and the rather, because it seems his mother fed him at the price of her own life: but the poor maid, whose constitution was stronger than that of her mistress, who was in years, and a weakly woman too, might struggle harder with it; nevertheless she might be supposed to feel the extremity something sooner than her mistress, who might be allowed to keep the last bit something longer than she parted with any to relieve her maid. No question, as the case is here related, if our ship or some other had not so providentially met them, but a few days more would have ended all their lives. I now return to my disposition of things among the people. And, first, it is to be observed here, that for many reasons I did not think fit to let them know anything of the sloop I had framed, and which I thought of setting up among them; for I found, at least at my first coming, such seeds of division among them, that I saw plainly, had I set up the sloop, and left it among them, they would, upon every light disgust, have separated, and gone away from one another; or perhaps have turned pirates, and so made the island a den of thieves, instead of a plantation of sober and religious people, as I intended it; nor did I leave the two pieces of brass cannon that I had on board, or the extra two quarter-deck guns that my nephew had provided, for the same reason. I thought it was enough to qualify them for a defensive war against any that should invade them, but not to set them up for an offensive war, or to go abroad to attack others; which, in the end, would only bring ruin and destruction upon them. I reserved the sloop, therefore, and the guns, for their service another way, as I shall observe in its place.

Having now done with the island, I left them all in good circumstances and in a flourishing condition, and went on board my ship again on the 6th of May, having been about twenty-five days among them: and as they were all resolved to stay upon the island till I came to remove them, I promised to send them further relief from the Brazils, if I could possibly find an opportunity. I particularly promised to send them some cattle, such as sheep, hogs, and cows: as to the two cows and calves which I brought from England, we had been obliged, by the length of our voyage, to kill them at sea, for want of hay to feed them.

The next day, giving them a salute of five guns at parting, we set sail, and arrived at the bay of All Saints in the Brazils in about twenty-two days, meeting nothing remarkable in our passage but this: that about three days after we had sailed, being becalmed, and the current setting strong to the ENE., running, as it were, into a bay or gulf on the land side, we were driven something out of our course, and once or twice our men cried out, "Land to the eastward!" but whether it was the continent or islands we could not tell by any means. But the third day, towards evening, the sea smooth, and the weather calm, we saw the sea as it were covered towards the land with something very black; not being able to discover what it was till after some time, our chief mate, going up the main shrouds a little way, and looking at them with a perspective, cried out it was an army. I could not imagine what he meant by an army, and thwarted him a little hastily. "Nay, sir," says he, "don't be angry, for 'tis an army, and a fleet too: for I believe there are a thousand canoes, and you may see them paddle along, for they are coming towards us apace."

I was a little surprised then, indeed, and so was my nephew the captain; for he had heard such terrible stories of them in the island, and having never been in those seas before, that he could not tell what to think of it, but said, two or three times, we should all be devoured. I must confess, considering we were becalmed, and the current set strong towards the shore, I liked it the worse; however, I bade them not be afraid, but bring the ship to an anchor as soon as we came so near as to know that we must engage them. The weather continued calm, and they came on apace towards us, so I gave orders to come to an anchor, and furl all our sails;

as for the savages, I told them they had nothing to fear but fire, and therefore they should get their boats out, and fasten them, one close by the head and the other by the stern, and man them both well, and wait the issue in that posture: this I did, that the men in the boats might he ready with sheets and buckets to put out any fire these savages might endeavour to fix to the outside of the ship.

In this posture we lay by for them, and in a little while they came up with us; but never was such a horrid sight seen by Christians; though my mate was much mistaken in his calculation of their number, yet when they came up we reckoned about a hundred and twenty-six canoes; some of them had sixteen or seventeen men in them, and some more, and the least six or seven. When they came nearer to us, they seemed to be struck with wonder and astonishment, as at a sight which doubtless they had never seen before; nor could they at first, as we afterwards understood, know what to make of us; they came boldly up, however, very near to us, and seemed to go about to row round us; but we called to our men in the boats not to let them come too near them. This very order brought us to an engagement with them, without our designing it; for five or six of the large canoes came so near our long-boat, that our men beckoned with their hands to keep them back, which they understood very well, and went back: but at their retreat about fifty arrows came on board us from those boats, and one of our men in the long-boat was very much wounded. However, I called to them not to fire by any means; but we handed down some deal boards into the boat, and the carpenter presently set up a kind of fence, like waste boards, to cover them from the arrows of the savages, if they should shoot again.

About half-an-hour afterwards they all came up in a body astern of us, and so near that we could easily discern what they were, though we could not tell their design; and I easily found they were some of my old friends, the same sort of savages that I had been used to engage with. In a short time more they rowed a little farther out to sea, till they came directly broadside with us, and then rowed down straight upon us, till they came so near that they could hear us speak; upon this, I ordered all my men to keep close, lest they should shoot any more arrows, and made all our guns ready; but being so near as to be within hearing, I made Friday go out upon the deck, and call out aloud to them in his language, to know what they meant. Whether they understood him or not, that I knew not; but as soon as he had called to them, six of them, who were in the foremost or nighest boat to us, turned their canoes from us, and stooping down, showed us their naked backs; whether this was a defiance or challenge we knew not, or whether it was done in mere contempt, or as a signal to the rest; but immediately Friday cried out they were going to shoot, and, unhappily for him, poor fellow, they let fly about three hundred of their arrows, and to my inexpressible grief, killed poor Friday, no other man being in their sight. The poor fellow was shot with no less than three arrows, and about three more fell very near him; such unlucky marksmen they were!

I was so annoyed at the loss of my old trusty servant and companion, that I immediately ordered five guns to be loaded with small shot, and four with great, and gave them such a broadside as they had never heard in their lives before. They were not above half a cable's length off when we fired; and our gunners took their aim so well, that three or four of their canoes were overset, as we had reason to believe, by one shot only. The ill manners of turning up their bare backs to us gave us no great offence; neither did I know for certain whether that which would pass for the greatest contempt among us might be understood so by them or not; therefore, in return, I had only resolved to have fired four or five guns at them with powder only, which I knew would frighten them sufficiently: but when they shot at us directly with all the fury they were capable of, and especially as they had killed my poor Friday, whom I so entirely loved and valued, and who, indeed, so well deserved it, I thought myself not only justifiable before God and man, but would have been very glad if I could have overset every canoe there, and drowned every one of them.

I can neither tell how many we killed nor how many we wounded at this broadside, but sure such a fright and hurry never were seen among such a multitude; there were thirteen or fourteen of their canoes split and overset in all, and the men all set a-swimming: the rest, frightened out of their wits, scoured away as fast as they could, taking but little care to save those whose boats were split or spoiled with our shot; so I suppose that many of them were lost; and our men took up one poor fellow swimming for his life, above an hour after they were all gone. The small shot from our cannon must needs kill and wound a great many; but, in short, we never knew how it went with them, for they fled so fast, that in three hours or thereabouts we could not see above three or four straggling canoes, nor did we ever see the rest any more; for a breeze of wind springing up the same evening, we weighed and set sail for the Brazils.

We had a prisoner, indeed, but the creature was so sullen that he would neither eat nor speak, and we all fancied he would starve himself to death. But I took a way to cure him: for I had made them take him and turn him into the long-boat, and make him believe they would toss him into the sea again, and so leave him where they found him, if he would not speak; nor would

185

that do, but they really did throw him into the sea, and came away from him. Then he followed them, for he swam like a cork, and called to them in his tongue, though they knew not one word of what he said; however at last they took him in again., and then he began to he more tractable: nor did I ever design they should drown him.

We were now under sail again, but I was the most disconsolate creature alive for want of my man Friday, and would have been very glad to have gone back to the island, to have taken one of the rest from thence for my occasion, but it could not be: so we went on. We had one prisoner, as I have said, and it was a long time before we could make him understand anything; but in time our men taught him some English, and he began to be a little tractable. Afterwards, we inquired what country he came from; but could make nothing of what he said; for his speech was so odd, all gutturals, and he spoke in the throat in such a hollow, odd manner, that we could never form a word after him; and we were all of opinion that they might speak that language as well if they were gagged as otherwise; nor could we perceive that they had any occasion either for teeth, tongue, lips, or palate, but formed their words just as a hunting-horn forms a tune with an open throat. He told us, however, some time after, when we had taught him to speak a little English, that they were going with their kings to fight a great battle. When he said kings, we asked him how many kings? He said they were five nation (we could not make him understand the plural 's), and that they all joined to go against two nation. We asked him what made them come up to us? He said, "To makee te great wonder look." Here it is to be observed that all those natives, as also those of Africa when they learn English, always add two e's at the end of the words where we use one; and they place the accent upon them, as makee, takee, and the like; nay, I could hardly make Friday leave it off, though at last he did.

And now I name the poor fellow once more, I must take my last leave of him. Poor honest Friday! We buried him with all the decency and solemnity possible, by putting him into a coffin, and throwing him into the sea; and I caused them to fire eleven guns for him. So ended the life of the most grateful, faithful, honest, and most affectionate servant that ever man had.

We went now away with a fair wind for Brazil; and in about twelve days' time we made land, in the latitude of five degrees south of the line, being the north-easternmost land of all that part of America. We kept on S. by E., in sight of the shore four days, when we made Cape St. Augustine, and in three days came to an anchor off the bay of All Saints, the old place of my deliverance, from whence came both my good and evil fate. Never ship came to this port that had less business than I had, and yet it was with great difficulty that we were admitted to hold the least correspondence on shore: not my partner himself, who was alive, and made a great figure among them, not my two merchant-trustees, not the fame of my wonderful preservation in the island, could obtain me that favour. My partner, however, remembering that I had given five hundred moidores to the prior of the monastery of the Augustines, and two hundred and seventy-two to the poor, went to the monastery, and obliged the prior that then was to go to the governor, and get leave for me personally, with the captain and one more, besides eight seamen, to come on shore, and no more; and this upon condition, absolutely capitulated for, that we should not offer to land any goods out of the ship, or to carry any person away without licence. They were so strict with us as to landing any goods, that it was with extreme difficulty that I got on shore three bales of English goods, such as fine broadcloths, stuffs, and some linen, which I had brought for a present to my partner.

He was a very generous, open-hearted man, although he began, like me, with little at first. Though he knew not that I had the least design of giving him anything, he sent me on board a present of fresh provisions, wine, and sweetmeats, worth about thirty moidores, including some tobacco, and three or four fine medals of gold: but I was even with him in my present, which, as I have said, consisted of fine broadcloth, English stuffs, lace, and fine holland; also, I delivered him about the value of one hundred pounds sterling in the same goods, for other uses; and I obliged him to set up the sloop, which I had brought with me from England, as I have said, for the use of my colony, in order to send the refreshments I intended to my plantation.

Accordingly, he got hands, and finished the sloop in a very few days, for she was already framed; and I gave the master of her such instructions that he could not miss the place; nor did he, as I had an account from my partner afterwards. I got him soon loaded with the small cargo I sent them; and one of our seamen, that had been on shore with me there, offered to go with the sloop and settle there, upon my letter to the governor Spaniard to allot him a sufficient quantity of land for a plantation, and on my giving him some clothes and tools for his planting work, which he said he understood, having been an old planter at Maryland, and a buccaneer into the bargain. I encouraged the fellow by granting all he desired; and, as an addition, I gave him the savage whom we had taken prisoner of war to be his slave, and ordered the governor Spaniard to give him his share of everything he wanted with the rest.

When we came to fit this man out, my old partner told me there was a certain very honest fellow, a Brazil planter of his acquaintance, who had fallen into the displeasure of the Church. "I know not what the matter is with him," says he, "but, on my conscience, I think he is a heretic in his heart, and he has been obliged to conceal himself for fear of the Inquisition." He then told me that he would be very glad of such an opportunity to make his escape, with his wife and two daughters; and if I would let them go to my island, and allot them a plantation, he would give them a small stock to begin with—for the officers of the Inquisition had seized all his effects and estate, and he had nothing left but a little household stuff and two slaves; "and," adds he, "though I hate his principles, yet I would not have him fall into their hands, for he will be assuredly burned alive if he does." I granted this presently, and joined my Englishman with them: and we concealed the man, and his wife and daughters, on board our ship, till the sloop put out to go to sea; and then having put all their goods on board some time before, we put them on board the sloop after she was got out of the bay. Our seaman was mightily pleased with this new partner; and their stocks, indeed, were much alike, rich in tools, in preparations, and a farm—but nothing to begin with, except as above: however, they carried over with them what was worth all the rest, some materials for planting sugar-canes, with some plants of canes, which he, I mean the Brazil planter, understood very well.

Among the rest of the supplies sent to my tenants in the island, I sent them by the sloop three milch cows and five calves; about twenty-two hogs, among them three sows; two mares, and a stone- horse. For my Spaniards, according to my promise, I engaged three Brazil women to go, and recommended it to them to marry them, and use them kindly. I could have procured more women, but I remembered that the poor persecuted man had two daughters, and that there were but five of the Spaniards that wanted partners; the rest had wives of their own, though in another country. All this cargo arrived safe, and, as you may easily suppose, was very welcome to my old inhabitants, who were now, with this addition, between sixty and seventy people, besides little children, of which there were a great many. I found letters at London from them all, by way of Lisbon, when I came back to England.

I have now done with the island, and all manner of discourse about it: and whoever reads the rest of my memorandums would do well to turn his thoughts entirely from it, and expect to read of the follies of an old man, not warned by his own harms, much less by those of other men, to beware; not cooled by almost forty years' miseries and disappointments—not satisfied with prosperity beyond expectation, nor made cautious by afflictions and distress beyond example.

Chapter 9

Dreadful Occurrences in Madagascar

I had no more business to go to the East Indies than a man at full liberty has to go to the turnkey at Newgate, and desire him to lock him up among the prisoners there, and starve him. Had I taken a small vessel from England and gone directly to the island; had I loaded her, as I did the other vessel, with all the necessaries for the plantation and for my people; taken a patent from the government here to have secured my property, in subjection only to that of England; had I carried over cannon and ammunition, servants and people to plant, and taken possession of the place, fortified and strengthened it in the name of England, and increased it with people, as I might easily have done; had I then settled myself there, and sent the ship back laden with good rice, as I might also have done in six months' time, and ordered my friends to have fitted her out again for our supply—had I done this, and stayed there myself, I had at least acted like a man of common sense. But I was possessed of a wandering spirit, and scorned all advantages: I pleased myself with being the patron of the people I placed there, and doing for them in a kind of haughty, majestic way, like an old patriarchal monarch, providing for them as if I had been father of the whole family, as well as of the plantation. But I never so much as pretended to plant in the name of any government or nation, or to acknowledge any prince, or to call my people subjects to any one nation more than another; nay, I never so much as gave the place a name, but left it as I found it, belonging to nobody, and the people under no discipline or government but my own, who, though I had influence over them as a father and benefactor, had no authority or power to act or command one way or other, further than voluntary consent moved them to comply. Yet even this, had I stayed there, would have done well enough; but as I rambled from them, and came there no more, the last letters I had from any of them were by my partner's means, who afterwards sent another sloop to the place, and who sent me word, though I had not the letter till I got to London, several years after it was written, that they went on but poorly; were discontented with their long stay there; that Will Atkins was dead; that five of the Spaniards were come away; and though they had not been much molested by the savages, yet they had had some skirmishes with them; and that they begged of him to write to me to think of the promise I had made to fetch them away, that they might see their country again before they died.

But I was gone a wildgoose chase indeed, and they that will have any more of me must be content to follow me into a new variety of follies, hardships, and wild adventures, wherein the justice of Providence may be duly observed; and we may see how easily Heaven can gorge us with our own desires, make the strongest of our wishes be our affliction, and punish us most severely with those very things which we think it would be our utmost happiness to be allowed to possess. Whether I had business or no business, away I went: it is no time now to enlarge upon the reason or absurdity of my own conduct, but to come to the history—I was embarked for the voyage, and the voyage I went.

I shall only add a word or two concerning my honest Popish clergyman, for let their opinion of us, and all other heretics in general, as they call us, be as uncharitable as it may, I verily believe this man was very sincere, and wished the good of all men: yet I believe he used reserve in many of his expressions, to prevent giving me offence; for I scarce heard him once call on the Blessed Virgin, or mention St. Jago, or his guardian angel, though so common with the rest of them. However, I say I had not the least doubt of his sincerity and pious intentions; and I am firmly of opinion, if the rest of the Popish missionaries were like him, they would strive to visit even the poor Tartars and Laplanders, where they have nothing to give them, as well as covet to flock to India, Persia, China, &c., the most wealthy of the heathen countries; for if they expected to bring no gains to their Church by it, it may well be admired how they came to admit the Chinese Confucius into the calendar of the Christian saints.

A ship being ready to sail for Lisbon, my pious priest asked me leave to go thither; being still, as he observed, bound never to finish any voyage he began. How happy it had been for me if I had gone with him. But it was too late now; all things Heaven appoints for the best: had I gone with him I had never had so many things to be thankful for, and the reader had never heard of the second part of the travels and adventures of Robinson Crusoe: so I must here leave exclaiming at myself, and go on with my voyage. From the Brazils we made directly over the Atlantic Sea to the Cape of Good Hope, and had a tolerably good voyage, our course generally south-east, now and then a storm, and some contrary winds; but my disasters at sea were at an end— my future rubs and cross events were to befall me on shore, that it might appear the land was as well prepared to be our scourge as the sea.

Our ship was on a trading voyage, and had a supercargo on board, who was to direct all her motions after she arrived at the Cape, only being limited to a certain number of days for stay, by charter-party, at the several ports she was to go to. This was none of my business, neither did I meddle with it; my nephew, the captain, and the supercargo adjusting all those things between them as they thought fit. We stayed at the Cape no longer than was needful to take in-fresh water, but made the best of our way for the coast of Coromandel. We were, indeed, informed that a French man-of-war, of fifty guns, and two large merchant ships, were gone for the Indies; and as I knew we were at war with France, I had some apprehensions of them; but they went their own way, and we heard no more of them.

I shall not pester the reader with a tedious description of places, journals of our voyage, variations of the compass, latitudes, trade-winds, &c.; it is enough to name the ports and places which we touched at, and what occurred to us upon our passages from one to another. We touched first at the island of Madagascar, where, though the people are fierce and treacherous, and very well armed with lances and bows, which they use with inconceivable dexterity, yet we fared very well with them a while. They treated us very civilly; and for some trifles which we gave them, such as knives, scissors, &c., they brought us eleven good fat bullocks, of a middling size, which we took in, partly for fresh provisions for our present spending, and the rest to salt for the ship's use.

We were obliged to stay here some time after we had furnished ourselves with provisions; and I, who was always too curious to look into every nook of the world wherever I came, went on shore as often as I could. It was on the east side of the island that we went on shore one evening: and the people, who, by the way, are very numerous, came thronging about us, and stood gazing at us at a distance. As we had traded freely with them, and had been kindly used, we thought ourselves in no danger; but when we saw the people, we cut three boughs out of a tree, and stuck them up at a distance from us; which, it seems, is a mark in that country not only of a truce and friendship, but when it is accepted the other side set up three poles or boughs, which is a signal that they accept the truce too; but then this is a known condition of the truce, that you are not to pass beyond their three poles towards them, nor they to come past your three poles or boughs towards you; so that you are perfectly secure within the three poles, and all the space between your poles and theirs is allowed like a market for free converse, traffic, and commerce. When you go there you must not carry your weapons with you; and if they come into that space they stick up their javelins and lances all at the first poles, and come on unarmed; but if any violence is offered them, and the truce thereby broken, away they run to the poles, and lay hold of their weapons, and the truce is at an end.

It happened one evening, when we went on shore, that a greater number of their people came down than usual, but all very friendly and civil; and they brought several kinds of provisions, for which we satisfied them with such toys as we had; the women also brought us milk and roots, and several things very acceptable to us, and all was quiet; and we made us a little tent or hut of some boughs or trees, and lay on shore all night. I know not what was the occasion, but I was not so well satisfied to lie on shore as the rest; and the boat riding at an anchor at about a stone's cast from the land, with two men in her to take care of her, I made one of them come on shore; and getting some boughs of trees to cover us also in the boat, I spread the sail on the bottom of the boat, and lay under the cover of the branches of the trees all night in the boat.

About two o'clock in the morning we heard one of our men making a terrible noise on the shore, calling out, for God's sake, to bring the boat in and come and help them, for they were all like to be murdered; and at the same time I heard the fire of five muskets, which was the number of guns they had, and that three times over; for it seems the natives here were not so easily frightened with guns as the savages were in America, where I had to do with them. All this while, I knew not what was the matter, but rousing immediately from sleep with the noise, I caused the boat to be thrust in, and resolved with three fusees we had on board to land and assist our men. We got the boat soon to the shore, but our men were in too much haste; for being come to the shore, they plunged into the water, to get to the boat with all the expedition they could, being pursued by between three and four hundred men. Our men were but nine in all, and only five of them had fusees with them; the rest had pistols and swords, indeed, but they were of small use to them.

We took up seven of our men, and with difficulty enough too, three of them being very ill wounded; and that which was still worse was, that while we stood in the boat to take our men in, we were in as much danger as they were in on shore; for they poured their arrows in upon us so thick that we were glad to barricade the side of the boat up with the benches, and two or three loose boards which, to our great satisfaction, we had by mere accident in the boat. And yet, had it been daylight, they are, it seems, such exact marksmen, that if they could have seen but the least part of any of us, they would have been sure of us. We had, by the light of the moon, a little sight of them, as they stood pelting us from the shore with darts and arrows; and having got ready our firearms, we gave them a volley that we could hear, by the cries of some of them, had wounded several; however, they stood thus in battle array on the shore till break of day, which we supposed was that they might see the better to take their aim at us.

In this condition we lay, and could not tell how to weigh our anchor, or set up our sail, because we must needs stand up in the boat, and they were as sure to hit us as we were to hit a bird in a tree with small shot. We made signals of distress to the ship, and though she rode a league off, yet my nephew, the captain, hearing our firing, and by glasses perceiving the posture we lay in, and that we fired towards the shore, pretty well understood us; and weighing anchor with all speed, he stood as near the shore as he durst with the ship, and then sent another boat with ten hands in her, to assist us. We called to them not to come too near, telling them what condition we were in; however, they stood in near to us, and one of the men taking the end of a tow-line in his hand, and keeping our boat between him and the enemy, so that they could not perfectly see him, swam on board us, and made fast the line to the boat: upon which we slipped out a little cable, and leaving our anchor behind, they towed us out of reach of the arrows; we all the while lying close behind the barricade we had made. As soon as we were got from between the ship and the shore, that we could lay her side to the shore, she ran along just by them, and poured in a broadside among them, loaded with pieces of iron and lead, small bullets, and such stuff, besides the great shot, which made a terrible havoc among them.

When we were got on board and out of danger, we had time to examine into the occasion of this fray; and indeed our supercargo, who had been often in those parts, put me upon it; for he said he was sure the inhabitants would not have touched us after we had

197

made a truce, if we had not done something to provoke them to it. At length it came out that an old woman, who had come to sell us some milk, had brought it within our poles, and a young woman with her, who also brought us some roots or herbs; and while the old woman (whether she was mother to the young woman or no they could not tell) was selling us the milk, one of our men offered some rudeness to the girl that was with her, at which the old woman made a great noise: however, the seaman would not quit his prize, but carried her out of the old woman's sight among the trees, it being almost dark; the old woman went away without her, and, as we may suppose, made an outcry among the people she came from; who, upon notice, raised that great army upon us in three or four hours, and it was great odds but we had all been destroyed.

One of our men was killed with a lance thrown at him just at the beginning of the attack, as he sallied out of the tent they had made; the rest came off free, all but the fellow who was the occasion of all the mischief, who paid dear enough for his brutality, for we could not hear what became of him for a great while. We lay upon the shore two days after, though the wind presented, and made signals for him, and made our boat sail up shore and down shore several leagues, but in vain; so we were obliged to give him over; and if he alone had suffered for it, the loss had been less. I could not satisfy myself, however, without venturing on shore once more, to try if I could learn anything of him or them; it was the third night after the action that I had a great mind to learn, if I could by any means, what mischief we had done, and how the game stood on the Indians' side. I was careful to do it in the dark, lest we should be attacked again: but I ought indeed to have been sure that the men I went with had been under my command, before I engaged in a thing so hazardous and mischievous as I was brought into by it, without design.

We took twenty as stout fellows with us as any in the ship, besides the supercargo and myself, and we landed two hours before midnight, at the same place where the Indians stood drawn up in the evening before. I landed here, because my design, as I have said, was chiefly to see if they had quitted the field, and if they had left any marks behind them of the mischief we had done them, and I thought if we could surprise one or two of them, perhaps we might get our man again, by way of exchange.

We landed without any noise, and divided our men into two bodies, whereof the boatswain commanded one and I the other. We neither saw nor heard anybody stir when we landed: and we marched up, one body at a distance from another, to the place. At first we could see nothing, it being very dark; till by-and-by our boatswain, who led the first party, stumbled and fell over a dead body. This made them halt a while; for knowing by the circumstances that they were at the place where the Indians had stood, they waited for my coming up there. We concluded to halt till the moon began to rise, which we knew would be in less than an hour, when we could easily discern the havoc we had made among them. We told thirty-two bodies upon the ground, whereof two were not quite dead; some had an arm and some a leg shot off, and one his head; those that were wounded, we supposed, they had carried away. When we had made, as I thought, a full discovery of all we could come to the knowledge of, I resolved on going on board; but the boatswain and his party sent me word that they were resolved to make a visit to the Indian town, where these dogs, as they called them, dwelt, and asked me to go along with them; and if they could find them, as they still fancied they should, they did not doubt of getting a good booty; and it might be they might find Tom Jeffry there: that was the man's name we had lost.

Had they sent to ask my leave to go, I knew well enough what answer to have given them; for I should have commanded them instantly on board, knowing it was not a hazard fit for us to run, who had a ship and ship-loading in our charge, and a voyage to make which depended very much upon the lives of the men; but as they sent me word they were resolved to go, and only asked me and my company to go along with them, I positively refused it, and rose up, for I was sitting on the ground, in order to go to the boat. One or two of the men began to importune me to go; and when I refused, began to grumble, and say they were not under my command, and they would go. "Come, Jack," says one of the men, "will you go with me? I'll go for one." Jack said he would—and then another—and, in a word, they all left me but one, whom I persuaded to stay, and a boy left in the boat. So the supercargo and I, with the third man, went back to the boat, where we told them we would stay for them, and take care to take in as many of them as should be left; for I told them it was a mad thing they were going about, and supposed most of them would have the fate of Tom Jeffry.

They told me, like seamen, they would warrant it they would come off again, and they would take care, &c.; so away they went. I entreated them to consider the ship and the voyage, that their lives were not their own, and that they were entrusted with the voyage, in some measure; that if they miscarried, the ship might be lost for want of their help, and that they could not answer for it to God or man. But I might as well have talked to the mainmast of the ship: they were mad upon their journey; only they gave me good words, and begged I would not be angry; that they did not doubt but they would be back again in about an hour at furthest; for the Indian town, they said, was not above half-a mile off, though they found it above two miles before they got to it.

Well, they all went away, and though the attempt was desperate, and such as none but madmen would have gone about, yet, to give them their due, they went about it as warily as boldly; they were gallantly armed, for they had every man a fusee or musket, a bayonet, and a pistol; some of them had broad cutlasses, some of them had hangers, and the boatswain and two more had poleaxes; besides all which they had among them thirteen hand grenadoes. Bolder fellows, and better provided, never went about any wicked work in the world. When they went out their chief design was plunder, and they were in mighty hopes of finding gold there; but a circumstance which none of them were aware of set them on fire with revenge, and made devils of them all.

When they came to the few Indian houses which they thought had been the town, which was not above half a mile off, they were under great disappointment, for there were not above twelve or thirteen houses, and where the town was, or how big, they knew not. They consulted, therefore, what to do, and were some time before they could resolve; for if they fell upon these, they must cut all their throats; and it was ten to one but some of them might escape, it being in the night, though the moon was up; and if one escaped, he would run and raise all the town, so they should have a whole army upon them; on the other hand, if they went away and left those untouched, for the people were all asleep, they could not tell which way to look for the town; however, the last was the best advice, so they resolved to leave them, and look for the town as well as they could. They went on a little way, and found a cow tied to a tree; this, they presently concluded, would be a good guide to them;

for, they said, the cow certainly belonged to the town before them, or the town behind them, and if they untied her, they should see which way she went: if she went back, they had nothing to say to her; but if she went forward, they would follow her. So they cut the cord, which was made of twisted flags, and the cow went on before them, directly to the town; which, as they reported, consisted of above two hundred houses or huts, and in some of these they found several families living together.

Here they found all in silence, as profoundly secure as sleep could make them: and first, they called another council, to consider what they had to do; and presently resolved to divide themselves into three bodies, and so set three houses on fire in three parts of the town; and as the men came out, to seize them and bind them (if any resisted, they need not be asked what to do then), and so to search the rest of the houses for plunder: but they resolved to march silently first through the town, and see what dimensions it was of, and if they might venture upon it or no.

They did so, and desperately resolved that they would venture upon them: but while they were animating one another to the work, three of them, who were a little before the rest, called out aloud to them, and told them that they had found—Tom Jeffry: they all ran up to the place, where they found the poor fellow hanging up naked by one arm, and his throat cut. There was an Indian house just by the tree, where they found sixteen or seventeen of the principal Indians, who had been concerned in the fray with us before, and two or three of them wounded with our shot; and our men found they were awake, and talking one to another in that house, but knew not their number.

The sight of their poor mangled comrade so enraged them, as before, that they swore to one another that they would be revenged, and that not an Indian that came into their hands should have any quarter; and to work they went immediately, and yet not so madly as might be expected from the rage and fury they were in. Their first care was to get something that would soon take fire, but, after a little search, they found that would be to no purpose; for most of the houses were low, and thatched with flags and rushes, of which the country is full; so they presently made some wildfire, as we call it, by wetting a little powder in the palm of their hands, and in a quarter of an hour they set the town on fire in four or five places, and particularly that house where the Indians were not gone to bed.

As soon as the fire begun to blaze, the poor frightened creatures began to rush out to save their lives, but met with their fate in the attempt; and especially at the door, where they drove them back, the boatswain himself killing one or two with his poleaxe. The house being large, and many in it, he did not care to go in, but called for a hand grenado, and threw it among them, which at first frightened them, but, when it burst, made such havoc among them that they cried out in a hideous manner. In short, most of the Indians who were in the open part of the house were killed or hurt with the grenado, except two or three more who pressed to the door, which the boatswain and two more kept, with their bayonets on the muzzles of their pieces, and despatched all that came in their way; but there was another apartment in the house, where the prince or king, or whatever he was, and several others were; and these were kept in till the house, which was by this time all in a light flame, fell in upon them, and they were smothered together.

All this while they fired not a gun, because they would not waken the people faster than they could master them; but the fire began to waken them fast enough, and our fellows were glad to keep a little together in bodies; for the fire grew so raging, all the houses being made of light combustible stuff, that they could hardly bear the street between them. Their business was to follow the fire, for the surer execution: as fast as the fire either forced the people out of those houses which were burning, or frightened them out of others, our people were ready at their doors to knock them on the head, still calling and hallooing one to another to remember Tom Jeffry.

While this was doing, I must confess I was very uneasy, and especially when I saw the flames of the town, which, it being night, seemed to be close by me. My nephew, the captain, who was roused by his men seeing such a fire, was very uneasy, not knowing what the matter was, or what danger I was in, especially hearing the guns too, for by this time they began to use their firearms; a thousand thoughts oppressed his mind concerning me and the supercargo, what would become of us; and at last, though he could ill spare any more men, yet not knowing what exigence we might be in, he took another boat, and with thirteen men and himself came ashore to me.

He was surprised to see me and the supercargo in the boat with no more than two men; and though he was glad that we were well, yet he was in the same impatience with us to know what was doing; for the noise continued, and the flame increased; in short, it was next to an impossibility for any men in the world to restrain their curiosity to know what had happened, or their concern for the safety of the men: in a word, the captain told me he would go and help his men, let what would come. I argued with him, as I did before with the men, the safety of the ship, the danger of the voyage, the interests of the owners and merchants, &c., and told him I and the two men would go, and only see if we could at a distance learn what was likely to be the event, and come back and tell him. It was in vain to talk to my nephew, as it was to talk to the rest before; he would go, he said; and he only wished he had left but ten men in the ship, for he could not think of having his men lost for want of help: he had rather lose the ship, the voyage, and his life, and all; and away he went.

I was no more able to stay behind now than I was to persuade them not to go; so the captain ordered two men to row back the pinnace, and fetch twelve men more, leaving the long-boat at an anchor; and that, when they came back, six men should keep the two boats, and six more come after us; so that he left only sixteen men in the ship: for the whole ship's company consisted of sixty-five men, whereof two were lost in the late quarrel which brought this mischief on.

Being now on the march, we felt little of the ground we trod on; and being guided by the fire, we kept no path, but went directly to the place of the flame. If the noise of the guns was surprising to us before, the cries of the poor people were now quite of another nature, and filled us with horror. I must confess I was never at the sacking a city, or at the taking a town by storm. I had heard of Oliver Cromwell taking Drogheda, in Ireland, and killing man, woman, and child; and I had read of Count Tilly sacking the city of Magdeburg and cutting the throats of twenty-two thousand of all sexes; but I never had an idea of the thing itself before, nor is it possible to describe it, or the horror that was upon our minds at hearing it. However, we went on, and at length came to the town, though there was no entering the streets of it for the fire. The first object we met with was the ruins of a hut or house, or rather the ashes of it, for the house was consumed; and just before it, plainly now to be seen by the light of the fire, lay four men and three women, killed, and, as we thought, one or two more lay in the heap among the fire; in short, there were such instances of rage, altogether barbarous, and of a fury something beyond what was human, that we thought it impossible our men could be guilty of it; or, if they were the authors of it, we thought they ought to be every one of them put to the worst of deaths. But this was not all: we saw the fire increase forward, and the cry went on just as the fire went on; so that we were in the utmost confusion. We advanced a little way farther, and behold, to our astonishment, three naked women, and crying in a most dreadful manner, came flying as if they had wings, and after them sixteen or seventeen men, natives, in the same terror and consternation, with three of our English butchers in the rear, who, when they could not overtake them, fired in among them, and one that was killed by their shot fell down in our sight. When the rest saw us, believing us to be their enemies, and that we would murder them as well as those that pursued them, they set up a most dreadful shriek, especially the women; and two of them fell down, as if already dead, with the fright.

My very soul shrunk within me, and my blood ran chill in my veins, when I saw this; and, I believe, had the three English sailors that pursued them come on, I had made our men kill them all; however, we took some means to let the poor flying creatures know that we would not hurt them; and immediately they came up to us, and kneeling down, with their hands lifted up, made piteous lamentation to us to save them, which we let them know we would: whereupon they crept all together in a huddle close behind us, as for protection. I left my men drawn up together, and, charging them to hurt nobody, but, if possible, to get at some of our people, and see what devil it was possessed them, and what they intended to do, and to command them off; assuring them that if they stayed till daylight they would have a hundred thousand men about their ears: I say I left them, and went among those flying people, taking only two of our men with me; and there was, indeed, a piteous spectacle among them. Some of them had their feet terribly burned with trampling and running through the fire; others their hands burned; one of the women had fallen down in the fire, and was very much burned before she could get out again; and two or three of the men had cuts in their backs and thighs, from our men pursuing; and another was shot through the body and died while I was there.

I would fain have learned what the occasion of all this was; but I could not understand one word they said; though, by signs, I perceived some of them knew not what was the occasion themselves. I was so terrified in my thoughts at this outrageous attempt that I could not stay there, but went back to my own men, and resolved to go into the middle of the town, through the fire, or whatever might be in the way, and put an end to it, cost what it would; accordingly, as I came back to my men, I told them my resolution, and commanded them to follow me, when, at the very moment, came four of our men, with the boatswain at their head, roving over heaps of bodies they had killed, all covered with blood and dust, as if they wanted more people to massacre, when our men hallooed to them as loud as they could halloo; and with much ado one of them made them hear, so that they knew who we were, and came up to us.

As soon as the boatswain saw us, he set up a halloo like a shout of triumph, for having, as he thought, more help come; and without waiting to hear me, "Captain," says he, "noble captain! I am glad you are come; we have not half done yet. Villainous hell-hound dogs! I'll kill as many of them as poor Tom has hairs upon his head: we have sworn to spare none of them; we'll root out the very nation of them from the earth;" and thus he ran on, out of breath, too, with action, and would not give us leave to speak a word. At last, raising my voice that I might silence him a little, "Barbarous dog!" said I, "what are you doing! I won't have one creature touched more, upon pain of death; I charge you, upon your life, to stop your hands, and stand still here, or you are a dead man this minute."—"Why, sir," says he, "do you know what you do, or what they have done? If you want a reason for what we have done, come hither;" and with that he showed me the poor fellow hanging, with his throat cut.

I confess I was urged then myself, and at another time would have been forward enough; but I thought they had carried their rage too far, and remembered Jacob's words to his sons Simeon and Levi: "Cursed be their anger, for it was fierce; and their wrath, for it was cruel." But I had now a new task upon my hands; for when the men I had carried with me saw the sight, as I had done, I had as much to do to restrain them as I should have had with the others; nay, my nephew himself fell in with them, and told me, in their hearing, that he was only concerned for fear of the men being overpowered; and as to the people, he thought not one of them ought to live; for they had all glutted themselves with the murder of the poor man, and that they ought to be used like murderers. Upon these words, away ran eight of my men, with the boatswain and his crew, to complete their bloody work; and I, seeing it quite out of my power to restrain them, came away pensive and sad; for I could not bear the sight, much less the horrible noise and cries of the poor wretches that fell into their hands.

I got nobody to come back with me but the supercargo and two men, and with these walked back to the boat. It was a very great piece of folly in me, I confess, to venture back, as it were, alone; for as it began now to be almost day, and the alarm had run over the country, there stood about forty men armed with lances and boughs at the little place where the twelve or thirteen houses stood, mentioned before: but by accident I missed the place, and came directly to the seaside, and by the time I got to the seaside it was broad day: immediately I took the pinnace and went on board, and sent her back to assist the men in what might happen. I observed, about the time that I came to the boat-side, that the fire was pretty well out, and the noise abated; but in about half- an-hour after I got on board, I heard a volley of our men's firearms, and saw a great smoke. This, as I understood afterwards, was our men falling upon the men, who, as I said, stood at the few houses on the way, of whom they killed sixteen or seventeen, and set all the houses on fire, but did not meddle with the women or children.

By the time the men got to the shore again with the pinnace our men began to appear; they came dropping in, not in two bodies as they went, but straggling here and there in such a manner, that a small force of resolute men might have cut them all off. But the dread of them was upon the whole country; and the men were surprised, and so frightened, that I believe a hundred of them would have fled at the sight of but five of our men. Nor in all this terrible action was there a man that made any considerable defence: they were so surprised between the terror of the fire and the sudden attack of our men in the dark, that they knew not which way to turn themselves; for if they fled one way they were met by one party, if back again by another, so that they were everywhere knocked down; nor did any of our men receive the least hurt, except one that sprained his foot, and another that had one of his hands burned.

Chapter 10

He is Left on Shore

I was very angry with my nephew, the captain, and indeed with all the men, but with him in particular, as well for his acting so out of his duty as a commander of the ship, and having the charge of the voyage upon him, as in his prompting, rather than cooling, the rage of his blind men in so bloody and cruel an enterprise. My nephew answered me very respectfully, but told me that when he saw the body of the poor seaman whom they had murdered in so cruel and barbarous a manner, he was not master of himself, neither could he govern his passion; he owned he should not have done so, as he was commander of the ship; but as he was a man, and nature moved him, he could not bear it. As for the rest of the men, they were not subject to me at all, and they knew it well enough; so they took no notice of my dislike. The next day we set sail, so we never heard any more of it. Our men differed in the account of the number they had killed; but according to the best of their accounts, put all together, they killed or destroyed about one hundred and fifty people, men, women, and children, and left not a house standing in the town. As for the poor fellow Tom Jeffry, as he was quite dead (for his throat was so cut that his head was half off), it would do him no service to bring him away; so they only took him down from the tree, where he was hanging by one hand.

However just our men thought this action, I was against them in it, and I always, after that time, told them God would blast the voyage; for I looked upon all the blood they shed that night to be murder in them. For though it is true that they had killed Tom Jeffry, yet Jeffry was the aggressor, had broken the truce, and had ill-used a young woman of theirs, who came down to them innocently, and on the faith of the public capitulation.

The boatswain defended this quarrel when we were afterwards on board. He said it was true that we seemed to break the truce, but really had not; and that the war was begun the night before by the natives themselves, who had shot at us, and killed one of our men without any just provocation; so that as we were in a capacity to fight them now, we might also be in a capacity to do ourselves justice upon them in an extraordinary manner; that though the poor man had taken a little liberty with the girl, he ought not to have been murdered, and that in such a villainous manner: and that they did nothing but what was just and what the laws of God allowed to be done to murderers. One would think this should have been enough to have warned us against going on shore amongst the heathens and barbarians; but it is impossible to make mankind wise but at their own expense, and their experience seems to be always of most use to them when it is dearest bought.

We were now bound to the Gulf of Persia, and from thence to the coast of Coromandel, only to touch at Surat; but the chief of the supercargo's design lay at the Bay of Bengal, where, if he missed his business outward-bound, he was to go out to China, and return to the coast as he came home. The first disaster that befell us was in the Gulf of Persia, where five of our men, venturing on shore on the Arabian side of the gulf, were surrounded by the Arabians, and either all killed or carried away into slavery; the rest of the boat's crew were not able to rescue them, and had but just time to get off their boat. I began to upbraid them with the just retribution of Heaven in this case; but the boatswain very warmly told me, he thought I went further in my censures than I could show any warrant for in Scripture; and referred to Luke xiii. 4, where our Saviour intimates that those men on whom the Tower of Siloam fell were not sinners above all the Galileans; but that which put me to silence in the case was, that not one of these five men who were now lost were of those who went on shore to the massacre of Madagascar, so I always called it, though our men could not bear to hear the word MASSACRE with any patience.

But my frequent preaching to them on this subject had worse consequences than I expected; and the boatswain, who had been the head of the attempt, came up boldly to me one time, and told me he found that I brought that affair continually upon the stage; that I made unjust reflections upon it, and had used the men very ill on that account, and himself in particular; that as I was but a passenger, and had no command in the ship, or concern in the voyage, they were not obliged to bear it; that they did not know but I might have some ill-design in my head, and perhaps to call them to an account for it when they came to England; and that, therefore, unless I would resolve to have done with it, and also not to concern myself any further with him, or any of his affairs, he would leave the ship; for he did not think it safe to sail with me among them.

I heard him patiently enough till he had done, and then told him that I confessed I had all along opposed the massacre of Madagascar, and that I had, on all occasions, spoken my mind freely about it, though not more upon him than any of the rest; that as to having no command in the ship, that was true; nor did I exercise any authority, only took the liberty of speaking my mind in things which publicly concerned us all; and what concern I had in the voyage was none of his business; that I was a considerable owner in the ship. In that claim I conceived I had a right to speak even further than I had done, and would not be accountable to him or any one else, and began to be a little warm with him. He made but little reply to me at that time, and I thought the affair had been over. We were at this time in the road at Bengal; and being willing to see the place, I went on shore with the supercargo in the ship's boat to divert myself; and towards evening was preparing to go on board, when one of the men came to me, and told me he would not have me trouble myself to come down to the boat, for they had orders not to carry me on board any more. Any one may guess what a surprise I was in at so insolent a message; and I asked the man who bade him deliver that message to me? He told me the coxswain.

I immediately found out the supercargo, and told him the story, adding that I foresaw there would be a mutiny in the ship; and entreated him to go immediately on board and acquaint the captain of it. But I might have spared this intelligence, for before I had spoken to him on shore the matter was effected on board. The boatswain, the gunner, the carpenter, and all the inferior officers, as soon as I was gone off in the boat, came up, and desired to speak with the captain; and then the boatswain, making a long harangue, and repeating all he had said to me, told the captain that as I was now gone peaceably on shore, they were loath to use any violence with me, which, if I had not gone on shore, they would otherwise have done, to oblige me to have gone. They therefore thought fit to tell him that as they shipped themselves to serve in the ship under his command, they would perform it well and faithfully; but if I would not quit the ship, or the captain oblige me to quit it, they would all leave the ship, and sail no further with him; and at that word ALL he turned his face towards the main-mast, which was, it seems, a signal agreed on, when the seamen, being got together there, cried out, "ONE AND ALL! ONE AND ALL!"

My nephew, the captain, was a man of spirit, and of great presence of mind; and though he was surprised, yet he told them calmly that he would consider of the matter, but that he could do nothing in it till he had spoken to me about it. He used some arguments with them, to show them the unreasonableness and injustice of the thing, but it was all in vain; they swore, and shook hands round before his face, that they would all go on shore unless he would engage to them not to suffer me to come any more on board the ship.

This was a hard article upon him, who knew his obligation to me, and did not know how I might take it. So he began to talk smartly to them; told them that I was a very considerable owner of the ship, and that if ever they came to England again it would cost them very dear; that the ship was mine, and that he could not put me out of it; and that he would rather lose the ship, and the voyage too, than disoblige me so much: so they might do as they pleased. However, he would go on shore and talk with me, and invited the boatswain to go with him, and perhaps they might accommodate the matter with me. But they all rejected the proposal, and said they would have nothing to do with me any more; and if I came on board they would all go on shore. "Well," said the captain, "if you are all of this mind, let me go on shore and talk with him." So away he came to me with this account, a little after the message had been brought to me from the coxswain.

I was very glad to see my nephew, I must confess; for I was not without apprehensions that they would confine him by violence, set sail, and run away with the ship;

and then I had been stripped naked in a remote country, having nothing to help myself; in short, I had been in a worse case than when I was alone in the island. But they had not come to that length, it seems, to my satisfaction; and when my nephew told me what they had said to him, and how they had sworn and shook hands that they would, one and all, leave the ship if I was suffered to come on board, I told him he should not be concerned at it at all, for I would stay on shore. I only desired he would take care and send me all my necessary things on shore, and leave me a sufficient sum of money, and I would find my way to England as well as I could. This was a heavy piece of news to my nephew, but there was no way to help it but to comply; so, in short, he went on board the ship again, and satisfied the men that his uncle had yielded to their importunity, and had sent for his goods from on board the ship; so that the matter was over in a few hours, the men returned to their duty, and I began to consider what course I should steer.

I was now alone in a most remote part of the world, for I was near three thousand leagues by sea farther off from England than I was at my island; only, it is true, I might travel here by land over the Great Mogul's country to Surat, might go from thence to Bassora by sea, up the Gulf of Persia, and take the way of the caravans, over the desert of Arabia, to Aleppo and Scanderoon; from thence by sea again to Italy, and so overland into France. I had another way before me, which was to wait for some English ships, which were coming to Bengal from Achin, on the island of Sumatra, and get passage on board them from England. But as I came hither without any concern with the East Indian Company, so it would be difficult to go from hence without their licence, unless with great favour of the captains of the ships, or the company's factors: and to both I was an utter stranger.

Here I had the mortification to see the ship set sail without me; however, my nephew left me two servants, or rather one companion and one servant; the first was clerk to the purser, whom he engaged to go with me, and the other was his own servant. I then took a good lodging in the house of an Englishwoman, where several merchants lodged, some French, two Italians, or rather Jews, and one Englishman. Here I stayed above nine months, considering what course to take. I had some English goods with me of value, and a considerable sum of money; my nephew furnishing me with a thousand pieces of eight, and a letter of credit for more if I had occasion, that I might not be straitened, whatever might happen. I quickly disposed of my goods to advantage; and, as I originally intended, I bought here some very good diamonds, which, of all other things, were the most proper for me in my present circumstances, because I could always carry my whole estate about me.

During my stay here many proposals were made for my return to England, but none falling out to my mind, the English merchant who lodged with me, and whom I had contracted an intimate acquaintance with, came to me one morning, saying: "Countryman, I have a project to communicate, which, as it suits with my thoughts, may, for aught I know, suit with yours also, when you shall have thoroughly considered it. Here we are posted, you by accident and I by my own choice, in a part of the world very remote from our own country; but it is in a country where, by us who understand trade and business, a great deal of money is to be got. If you will put one thousand pounds to my one thousand pounds, we will hire a ship here, the first we can get to our minds. You shall be captain, I'll be merchant, and we'll go a trading voyage to China; for what should we stand still for? The whole world is in motion; why should we be idle?"

I liked this proposal very well; and the more so because it seemed to be expressed with so much goodwill. In my loose, unhinged circumstances, I was the fitter to embrace a proposal for trade, or indeed anything else. I might perhaps say with some truth, that if trade was not my element, rambling was; and no proposal for seeing any part of the world which I had never seen before could possibly come amiss to me. It was, however, some time before we could get a ship to our minds, and when we had got a vessel, it was not easy to get English sailors—that is to say, so many as were necessary to govern the voyage and manage the sailors which we should pick up there. After some time we got a mate, a boatswain, and a gunner, English; a Dutch carpenter, and three foremast men. With these we found we could do well enough, having Indian seamen, such as they were, to make up.

When all was ready we set sail for Achin, in the island of Sumatra, and from thence to Siam, where we exchanged some of our wares for opium and some arrack; the first a commodity which bears a great price among the Chinese, and which at that time was much wanted there. Then we went up to Saskan, were eight months out, and on our return to Bengal I was very well satisfied with my adventure. Our people in England often admire how officers, which the company send into India, and the merchants which generally stay there, get such very great estates as they do, and sometimes come home worth sixty or seventy thousand pounds at a time; but it is little matter for wonder, when we consider the innumerable ports and places where they have a free commerce; indeed, at the ports where the English ships come there is such great and constant demands for the growth of all other countries, that there is a certain vent for the returns, as well as a market abroad for the goods carried out.

I got so much money by my first adventure, and such an insight into the method of getting more, that had I been twenty years younger, I should have been tempted to have stayed here, and sought no farther for making my fortune; but what was all this to a man upwards of threescore, that was rich enough, and came abroad more in obedience to a restless desire of seeing the world than a covetous desire of gaining by it? A restless desire it really was, for when I was at home I was restless to go abroad; and when I was abroad I was restless to be at home. I say, what was this gain to me? I was rich enough already, nor had I any uneasy desires about getting more money; therefore the profit of the voyage to me was of no great force for the prompting me forward to further undertakings. Hence, I thought that by this voyage I had made no progress at all, because I was come back, as I might call it, to the place from whence I came, as to a home: whereas, my eye, like that which Solomon speaks of, was never satisfied with seeing. I was come into a part of the world which I was never in before, and that part, in particular, which I heard much of, and was resolved to see as much of it as I could: and then I thought I might say I had seen all the world that was worth seeing.

But my fellow-traveller and I had different notions: I acknowledge his were the more suited to the end of a merchant's life: who, when he is abroad upon adventures, is wise to stick to that, as the best thing for him, which he is likely to get the most money by. On the other hand, mine was the notion of a mad, rambling boy, that never cares to see a thing twice over. But this was not all: I had a kind of impatience upon me to be nearer home, and yet an unsettled resolution which way to go. In the interval of these consultations, my friend, who was always upon the search for business, proposed another voyage among the Spice Islands, to bring home a loading of cloves from the Manillas, or thereabouts.

We were not long in preparing for this voyage; the chief difficulty was in bringing me to come into it. However, at last, nothing else offering, and as sitting still, to me especially, was the unhappiest part of life, I resolved on this voyage too, which we made very successfully, touching at Borneo and several other islands, and came home in about five months, when we sold our spices, with very great profit, to the Persian merchants, who carried them away to the Gulf. My friend, when we made up this account, smiled at me: "Well, now," said he, with a sort of friendly rebuke on my indolent temper, "is not this better than walking about here, like a man with nothing to do, and spending our time in staring at the nonsense and ignorance of the Pagans?"— "Why, truly," said I, "my friend, I think it is, and I begin to be a convert to the principles of merchandising; but I must tell you, by the way, you do not know what I am doing; for if I once conquer my backwardness, and embark heartily, old as I am, I shall harass you up and down the world till I tire you; for I shall pursue it so eagerly, I shall never let you lie still."

Chapter 11

Warned of Danger by a Countryman

A little while after this there came in a Dutch ship from Batavia; she was a coaster, not an European trader, of about two hundred tons burden; the men, as they pretended, having been so sickly that the captain had not hands enough to go to sea with, so he lay by at Bengal; and having, it seems, got money enough, or being willing, for other reasons, to go for Europe, he gave public notice he would sell his ship. This came to my ears before my new partner heard of it, and I had a great mind to buy it; so I went to him and told him of it. He considered a while, for he was no rash man neither; and at last replied, "She is a little too big—however, we will have her." Accordingly, we bought the ship, and agreeing with the master, we paid for her, and took possession. When we had done so we resolved to engage the men, if we could, to join with those we had, for the pursuing our business; but, on a sudden, they having received not their wages, but their share of the money, as we afterwards learned, not one of them was to be found; we inquired much about them, and at length were told that they were all gone together by land to Agra, the great city of the Mogul's residence, to proceed from thence to Surat, and then go by sea to the Gulf of Persia.

Nothing had so much troubled me a good while as that I should miss the opportunity of going with them; for such a ramble, I thought, and in such company as would both have guarded and diverted me, would have suited mightily with my great design; and I should have both seen the world and gone homeward too. But I was much better satisfied a few days after, when I came to know what sort of fellows they were; for, in short, their history was, that this man they called captain was the gunner only, not the commander; that they had been a trading voyage, in which they had been attacked on shore by some of the Malays, who had killed the captain and three of his men; and that after the captain was killed, these men, eleven in number, having resolved to run away with the ship, brought her to Bengal, leaving the mate and five men more on shore.

Well, let them get the ship how they would, we came honestly by her, as we thought, though we did not, I confess, examine into things so exactly as we ought; for we never inquired anything of the seamen, who would certainly have faltered in their account, and contradicted one another. Somehow or other we should have had reason to have suspected, them; but the man showed us a bill of sale for the ship, to one Emanuel Clostershoven, or some such name, for I suppose it was all a forgery, and called himself by that name, and we could not contradict him: and withal, having no suspicion of the thing, we went through with our bargain. We picked up some more English sailors here after this, and some Dutch, and now we resolved on a second voyage to the south-east for cloves, &c.—that is to say, among the Philippine and Malacca isles. In short, not to fill up this part of my story with trifles when what is to come is so remarkable, I spent, from first to last, six years in this country, trading from port to port, backward and forward, and with very good success, and was now the last year with my new partner, going in the ship above mentioned, on a voyage to China, but designing first to go to Siam to buy rice.

In this voyage, being by contrary winds obliged to beat up and down a great while in the Straits of Malacca and among the islands, we were no sooner got clear of those difficult seas than we found our ship had sprung a leak, but could not discover where it was. This forced us to make some port; and my partner, who knew the country better than I did, directed the captain to put into the river of Cambodia; for I had made the English mate, one Mr. Thompson, captain, not being willing to take the charge of the ship upon myself. This river lies on the north side of the great bay or gulf which goes up to Siam. While we were here, and going often on shore for refreshment, there comes to me one day an Englishman, a gunner's mate on board an English East India ship, then riding in the same river. "Sir," says he, addressing me, "you are a stranger to me, and I to you; but I have something to tell you that very nearly concerns you. I am moved by the imminent danger you are in, and, for aught I see, you have no knowledge of it."—"I know no danger I am in," said I, "but that my ship is leaky, and I cannot find it out; but I intend to lay her aground to-morrow, to see if I can find it."—"But, sir," says he, "leaky or not leaky, you will be wiser than to lay your ship on shore to-morrow when you hear what I have to say to you. Do you know, sir," said he, "the town of Cambodia lies about fifteen leagues up the river; and there are two large English ships about five leagues on this side, and three Dutch?"—"Well," said I, "and what is that to me?"—"Why, sir," said be, "is it for a man that is upon such adventures as you are to come into a port, and not examine first what ships there are there, and whether he is able to deal with them? I suppose you do not think you are a match for them?" I could not conceive what he meant; and I turned short upon him, and said: "I wish you would explain yourself; I cannot imagine what reason I have to be afraid of any of the company's ships, or Dutch ships. I am no interloper. What can they have to say to me?"—"Well, sir," says he, with a smile, "if you think yourself secure you must take your chance; but take my advice, if you do not put to sea immediately, you will the very next tide be attacked by five longboats full of men, and perhaps if you are taken you will be hanged for a pirate, and the particulars be examined afterwards. I thought, sir," added he, "I should have met with a better reception than this for doing you a piece of service of such importance."—"I can never be ungrateful," said I, "for any service, or to any man that offers me any kindness; but it is past my comprehension what they should have such a design upon me for: however, since you say there is no time to be lost, and that there is some villainous design on hand against me, I will go on board this minute, and put to sea immediately, if my men can stop the leak; but, sir," said I, "shall I go away ignorant of the cause of all this? Can you give me no further light into it?"

"I can tell you but part of the story, sir," says he; "but I have a Dutch seaman here with me, and I believe I could persuade him to tell you the rest; but there is scarce time for it. But the short of the story is this—the first part of which I suppose you know well enough—that you were with this ship at Sumatra; that there your captain was murdered by the Malays, with three of his men; and that you, or some of those that were on board with you, ran away with the ship, and are since turned pirates. This is the sum of the story, and you will all be seized as pirates, I can assure you, and executed with very little ceremony; for you know merchant ships show but little law to pirates if they get them into their power."- -"Now you speak plain English," said I, "and I thank you; and though I know nothing that we have done like what you talk of, for I am sure we came honestly and fairly by the ship; yet seeing such a work is doing, as you say, and that you seem to mean honestly, I will be upon my guard."—"Nay, sir," says he, "do not talk of being upon your guard; the best defence is to be out of danger. If you have any regard for your life and the lives of all your men, put to sea without fail at high-water; and as you have a whole tide before you, you will be gone too far out before they can come down; for they will come away at high-water, and as they have twenty miles to come, you will get near two hours of them by the difference of the tide, not reckoning the length of the way: besides, as they are only boats, and not ships, they will not venture to follow you far out to sea, especially if it blows."—"Well," said I, "you have been very kind in this: what shall I do to make you amends?"— "Sir," says he, "you may not be willing to make me any amends, because you may not be convinced of the truth of it. I will make an offer to you: I have nineteen months' pay due to me on board the ship -, which I came out of England in; and the Dutchman that is with me has seven months' pay due to him. If you will make good our pay to us we will go along with you; if you find nothing more in it we will desire no more; but if we do convince you that we have saved your lives, and the ship, and the lives of all the men in her, we will leave the rest to you."

I consented to this readily, and went immediately on board, and the two men with me. As soon as I came to the ship's side, my partner, who was on board, came out on the quarter-deck, and called to me, with a great deal of joy, "We have stopped the leak—we have stopped the leak!"—"Say you so?" said I; "thank God; but weigh anchor, then, immediately."—"Weigh!" says he; "what do you mean by that? What is the matter?"—"Ask no questions," said I; "but set all hands to work, and weigh without losing a minute." He was surprised; however, he called the captain, and he immediately ordered the anchor to be got up; and though the tide was not quite down, yet a little land-breeze blowing, we stood out to sea. Then I called him into the cabin, and told him the story; and we called in the men, and they told us the rest of it; but as it took up a great deal of time, before we had done a seaman comes to the cabin door, and called out to us that the captain bade him tell us we were chased by five sloops, or boats, full of men. "Very well," said I, "then it is apparent there is something in it." I then ordered all our men to be called up, and told them there was a design to seize the ship, and take us for pirates, and asked them if they would stand by us, and by one another; the men answered cheerfully, one and all, that they would live and die with us. Then I asked the captain what way he thought best for us to manage a fight with them; for resist them I was resolved we would, and that to the last drop. He said readily, that the way was to keep them off with our great shot as long as we could, and then to use our small arms, to keep them from boarding us; but when neither of these would do any longer, we would retire to our close quarters, for perhaps they had not materials to break open our bulkheads, or get in upon us.

The gunner had in the meantime orders to bring two guns, to bear fore and aft, out of the steerage, to clear the deck, and load them with musket-bullets, and small pieces of old iron, and what came next to hand. Thus we made ready for fight; but all this while we kept out to sea, with wind enough, and could see the boats at a distance, being five large longboats, following us with all the sail they could make.

Two of those boats (which by our glasses we could see were English) outsailed the rest, were near two leagues ahead of them, and gained upon us considerably, so that we found they would come up with us; upon which we fired a gun without ball, to intimate that they should bring to: and we put out a flag of truce, as a signal for parley: but they came crowding after us till within shot, when we took in our white flag, they having made no answer to it, and hung out a red flag, and fired at them with a shot. Notwithstanding this, they came on till they were near enough to call to them with a speaking-trumpet, bidding them keep off at their peril.

It was all one; they crowded after us, and endeavoured to come under our stern, so as to board us on our quarter; upon which, seeing they were resolute for mischief, and depended upon the strength that followed them, I ordered to bring the ship to, so that they lay upon our broadside; when immediately we fired five guns at them, one of which had been levelled so true as to carry away the stern of the hindermost boat, and we then forced them to take down their sail, and to run all to the head of the boat, to keep her from sinking; so she lay by, and had enough of it; but seeing the foremost boat crowd on after us, we made ready to fire at her in particular. While this was doing one of the three boats that followed made up to the boat which we had disabled, to relieve her, and we could see her take out the men. We then called again to the foremost boat, and offered a truce, to parley again, and to know what her business was with us; but had no answer, only she crowded close under our stern. Upon this, our gunner who was a very dexterous fellow ran out his two case-guns, and fired again at her, but the shot missing, the men in the boat shouted, waved their caps, and came on. The gunner, getting quickly ready again, fired among them a second time, one shot of which, though it missed the boat itself, yet fell in among the men, and we could easily see did a great deal of mischief among them. We now wore the ship again, and brought our quarter to bear upon them, and firing three guns more, we found the boat was almost split to pieces; in particular, her rudder and a piece of her stern were shot quite away; so they handed her sail immediately, and were in great disorder. To complete their misfortune, our gunner let fly two guns at them again; where he hit them we could not tell, but we found the boat was sinking, and some of the men already in the water: upon this, I immediately manned out our pinnace, with orders to pick up some of the men if they could, and save them from drowning, and immediately come on board ship with them, because we saw the rest of the boats began to come up. Our men in the pinnace followed their orders, and took up three men, one of whom was just drowning, and it was a good while before we could recover him. As soon as they were on board we crowded all the sail we could make, and stood farther out to the sea; and we found that when the other boats came up to the first, they gave over their chase.

Being thus delivered from a danger which, though I knew not the reason of it, yet seemed to be much greater than I apprehended, I resolved that we should change our course, and not let any one know whither we were going; so we stood out to sea eastward, quite out of the course of all European ships, whether they were bound to China or anywhere else, within the commerce of the European nations. When we were at sea we began to consult with the two seamen, and inquire what the meaning of all this should be; and the Dutchman confirmed the gunner's story about the false sale of the ship and of the murder of the captain, and also how that he, this Dutchman, and four more got into the woods, where they wandered about a great while, till at length he made his escape, and swam off to a Dutch ship, which was sailing near the shore in its way from China.

He then told us that he went to Batavia, where two of the seamen belonging to the ship arrived, having deserted the rest in their travels, and gave an account that the fellow who had run away with the ship, sold her at Bengal to a set of pirates, who were gone a-cruising in her, and that they had already taken an English ship and two Dutch ships very richly laden. This latter part we found to concern us directly, though we knew it to be false; yet, as my partner said, very justly, if we had fallen into their hands, and they had had such a prepossession against us beforehand, it had been in vain for us to have defended ourselves, or to hope for any good quarter at their hands; especially considering that our accusers had been our judges, and that we could have expected nothing from them but what rage would have dictated, and an ungoverned passion have executed. Therefore it was his opinion we should go directly back to Bengal, from whence we came, without putting in at any port whatever—because where we could give a good account of ourselves, could prove where we were when the ship put in, of whom we bought her, and the like; and what was more than all the rest, if we were put upon the necessity of bringing it before the proper judges, we should be sure to have some justice, and not to be hanged first and judged afterwards.

I was some time of my partner's opinion; but after a little more serious thinking, I told him I thought it was a very great hazard for us to attempt returning to Bengal, for that we were on the wrong side of the Straits of Malacca, and that if the alarm was given, we should be sure to be waylaid on every side—that if we should be taken, as it were, running away, we should even condemn ourselves, and there would want no more evidence to destroy us. I also asked the English sailor's opinion, who said he was of my mind, and that we certainly should be taken. This danger a little startled my partner and all the ship's company, and we immediately resolved to go away to the coast of Tonquin, and so on to the coast of China—and pursuing the first design as to trade, find some way or other to dispose of the ship, and come back in some of the vessels of the country such as we could get. This was approved of as the best method for our security, and accordingly we steered away NNE., keeping above fifty leagues off from the usual course to the eastward. This, however, put us to some inconvenience: for, first, the winds, when we came that distance from the shore, seemed to be more steadily against us, blowing almost trade, as we call it, from the E. and ENE., so that we were a long while upon our voyage, and we were but ill provided with victuals for so long a run; and what was still worse, there was some danger that those English and Dutch ships whose boats pursued us, whereof some were bound that way, might have got in before us, and if not, some other ship bound to China might have information of us from them, and pursue us with the same vigour.

I must confess I was now very uneasy, and thought myself, including the late escape from the longboats, to have been in the most dangerous condition that ever I was in through my past life; for whatever ill circumstances I had been in, I was never pursued for a thief before; nor had I ever done anything that merited the name of dishonest or fraudulent, much less thievish. I had chiefly been my own enemy, or, as I may rightly say, I had been nobody's enemy but my own; but now I was woefully embarrassed: for though I was perfectly innocent, I was in no condition to make that innocence appear; and if I had been taken, it had been under a supposed guilt of the worst kind. This made me very anxious to make an escape, though which way to do it I knew not, or what port or place we could go to. My partner endeavoured to encourage me by describing the several ports of that coast, and told me he would put in on the coast of Cochin China, or the bay of Tonquin, intending afterwards to go to Macao, where a great many European families resided, and particularly the missionary priests, who usually went thither in order to their going forward to China.

Hither then we resolved to go; and, accordingly, though after a tedious course, and very much straitened for provisions, we came within sight of the coast very early in the morning; and upon reflection on the past circumstances of danger we were in, we resolved to put into a small river, which, however, had depth enough of water for us, and to see if we could, either overland or by the ship's pinnace, come to know what ships were in any port thereabouts. This happy step was, indeed, our deliverance: for though we did not immediately see any European ships in the bay of Tonquin, yet the next morning there came into the bay two Dutch ships; and a third without any colours spread out, but which we believed to be a Dutchman, passed by at about two leagues' distance, steering for the coast of China; and in the afternoon went by two English ships steering the same course; and thus we thought we saw ourselves beset with enemies both one way and the other. The place we were in was wild and barbarous, the people thieves by occupation; and though it is true we had not much to seek of them, and, except getting a few provisions, cared not how little we had to do with them, yet it was with much difficulty that we kept ourselves from being insulted by them several ways. We were in a small river of this country, within a few leagues of its utmost limits northward; and by our boat we coasted north-east to the point of land which opens the great bay of Tonquin; and it was in this beating up along the shore that we discovered we were surrounded with enemies. The people we were among were the most barbarous of all the inhabitants of the coast; and among other customs they have this one: that if any vessel has the misfortune to be shipwrecked upon their coast, they make the men all prisoners or slaves; and it was not long before we found a spice of their kindness this way, on the occasion following.

I have observed above that our ship sprung a leak at sea, and that we could not find it out; and it happened that, as I have said, it was stopped unexpectedly, on the eve of our being pursued by the Dutch and English ships in the bay of Siam; yet, as we did not find the ship so perfectly tight and sound as we desired, we resolved while we were at this place to lay her on shore, and clean her bottom, and, if possible, to find out where the leaks were. Accordingly, having lightened the ship, and brought all our guns and other movables to one side, we tried to bring her down, that we might come at her bottom; but, on second thoughts, we did not care to lay her on dry ground, neither could we find out a proper place for it.

Chapter 12

The Carpenter's Whimsical Contrivance

The inhabitants came wondering down the shore to look at us; and seeing the ship lie down on one side in such a manner, and heeling in towards the shore, and not seeing our men, who were at work on her bottom with stages, and with their boats on the off-side, they presently concluded that the ship was cast away, and lay fast on the ground. On this supposition they came about us in two or three hours' time with ten or twelve large boats, having some of them eight, some ten men in a boat, intending, no doubt, to have come on board and plundered the ship, and if they found us there, to have carried us away for slaves.

When they came up to the ship, and began to row round her, they discovered us all hard at work on the outside of the ship's bottom and side, washing, and graving, and stopping, as every seafaring man knows how. They stood for a while gazing at us, and we, who were a little surprised, could not imagine what their design was; but being willing to be sure, we took this opportunity to get some of us into the ship, and others to hand down arms and ammunition to those that were at work, to defend themselves with if there should be occasion. And it was no more than need: for in less than a quarter of an hour's consultation, they agreed, it seems, that the ship was really a wreck, and that we were all at work endeavouring to save her, or to save our lives by the help of our boats; and when we handed our arms into the boat, they concluded, by that act, that we were endeavouring to save some of our goods. Upon this, they took it for granted we all belonged to them, and away they came directly upon our men, as if it had been in a line-of-battle.

Our men, seeing so many of them, began to be frightened, for we lay but in an ill posture to fight, and cried out to us to know what they should do. I immediately called to the men that worked upon the stages to slip them down, and get up the side into the ship, and bade those in the boat to row round and come on board. The few who were on board worked with all the strength and hands we had to bring the ship to rights; however, neither the men upon the stages nor those in the boats could do as they were ordered before the Cochin Chinese were upon them, when two of their boats boarded our longboat, and began to lay hold of the men as their prisoners.

The first man they laid hold of was an English seaman, a stout, strong fellow, who having a musket in his hand, never offered to fire it, but laid it down in the boat, like a fool, as I thought; but he understood his business better than I could teach him, for he grappled the Pagan, and dragged him by main force out of their boat into ours, where, taking him by the ears, he beat his head so against the boat's gunnel that the fellow died in his hands. In the meantime, a Dutchman, who stood next, took up the musket, and with the butt-end of it so laid about him, that he knocked down five of them who attempted to enter the boat. But this was doing little towards resisting thirty or forty men, who, fearless because ignorant of their danger, began to throw themselves into the longboat, where we had but five men in all to defend it; but the following accident, which deserved our laughter, gave our men a complete victory.

Our carpenter being prepared to grave the outside of the ship, as well as to pay the seams where he had caulked her to stop the leaks, had got two kettles just let down into the boat, one filled with boiling pitch, and the other with rosin, tallow, and oil, and such stuff as the shipwrights use for that work; and the man that attended the carpenter had a great iron ladle in his hand, with which he supplied the men that were at work with the hot stuff. Two of the enemy's men entered the boat just where this fellow stood in the foresheets; he immediately saluted them with a ladle full of the stuff, boiling hot which so burned and scalded them, being half-naked that they roared out like bulls, and, enraged with the fire, leaped both into the sea. The carpenter saw it, and cried out, "Well done, Jack! give them some more of it!" and stepping forward himself, takes one of the mops, and dipping it in the pitch-pot, he and his man threw it among them so plentifully that, in short, of all the men in the three boats, there was not one that escaped being scalded in a most frightful manner, and made such a howling and crying that I never heard a worse noise.

I was never better pleased with a victory in my life; not only as it was a perfect surprise to me, and that our danger was imminent before, but as we got this victory without any bloodshed, except of that man the seaman killed with his naked hands, and which I was very much concerned at. Although it maybe a just thing, because necessary (for there is no necessary wickedness in nature), yet I thought it was a sad sort of life, when we must be always obliged to be killing our fellow-creatures to preserve ourselves; and, indeed, I think so still; and I would even now suffer a great deal rather than I would take away the life even of the worst person injuring me; and I believe all considering people, who know the value of life, would be of my opinion, if they entered seriously into the consideration of it.

All the while this was doing, my partner and I, who managed the rest of the men on board, had with great dexterity brought the ship almost to rights, and having got the guns into their places again, the gunner called to me to bid our boat get out of the way, for he would let fly among them. I called back again to him, and bid him not offer to fire, for the carpenter would do the work without him; but bid him heat another pitch-kettle, which our cook, who was on broad, took care of. However, the enemy was so terrified with what they had met with in their first attack, that they would not come on again; and some of them who were farthest off, seeing the ship swim, as it were, upright, began, as we suppose, to see their mistake, and gave over the enterprise, finding it was not as they expected. Thus we got clear of this merry fight; and having got some rice and some roots and bread, with about sixteen hogs, on board two days before, we resolved to stay here no longer, but go forward, whatever came of it; for we made no doubt but we should be surrounded the next day with rogues enough, perhaps more than our pitch-kettle would dispose of for us. We therefore got all our things on board the same evening, and the next morning were ready to sail: in the meantime, lying at anchor at some distance from the shore, we were not so much concerned, being now in a fighting posture, as well as in a sailing posture, if any enemy had presented. The next day, having finished our work within board, and finding our ship was perfectly healed of all her leaks, we set sail. We would have gone into the bay of Tonquin, for we wanted to inform ourselves of what was to be known concerning the Dutch ships that had been there; but we durst not stand in there, because we had seen several ships go in, as we supposed, but a little before; so we kept on NE. towards the island of Formosa, as much afraid of being seen by a Dutch or English merchant ship as a Dutch or English merchant ship in the Mediterranean is of an Algerine man- of-war.

When we were thus got to sea, we kept on NE., as if we would go to the Manillas or the Philippine Islands; and this we did that we might not fall into the way of any of the European ships; and then we steered north, till we came to the latitude of 22 degrees 30 seconds, by which means we made the island of Formosa directly, where we came to an anchor, in order to get water and fresh provisions, which the people there, who are very courteous in their manners, supplied us with willingly, and dealt very fairly and punctually with us in all their agreements and bargains. This is what we did not find among other people, and may be owing to the remains of Christianity which was once planted here by a Dutch missionary of Protestants, and it is a testimony of what I have often observed, viz. that the Christian religion always civilises the people, and reforms their manners, where it is received, whether it works saving effects upon them or no.

From thence we sailed still north, keeping the coast of China at an equal distance, till we knew we were beyond all the ports of China where our European ships usually come; being resolved, if possible, not to fall into any of their hands, especially in this country, where, as our circumstances were, we could not fail of being entirely ruined. Being now come to the latitude of 30 degrees, we resolved to put into the first trading port we should come at; and standing in for the shore, a boat came of two leagues to us with an old Portuguese pilot on board, who, knowing us to be an European ship, came to offer his service, which, indeed, we were glad of and took him on board; upon which, without asking us whither we would go, he dismissed the boat he came in, and sent it back. I thought it was now so much in our choice to make the old man carry us whither we would, that I began to talk to him about carrying us to the Gulf of Nankin, which is the most northern part of the coast of China. The old man said he knew the Gulf of Nankin very well; but smiling, asked us what we would do there? I told him we would sell our cargo and purchase China wares, calicoes, raw silks, tea, wrought silks, &c.; and so we would return by the same course we came. He told us our best port would have been to put in at Macao, where we could not have failed of a market for our opium to our satisfaction, and might for our money have purchased all sorts of China goods as cheap as we could at Nankin.

Not being able to put the old man out of his talk, of which he was very opinionated or conceited, I told him we were gentlemen as well as merchants, and that we had a mind to go and see the great city of Pekin, and the famous court of the monarch of China. "Why, then," says the old man, "you should go to Ningpo, where, by the river which runs into the sea there, you may go up within five leagues of the great canal. This canal is a navigable stream, which goes through the heart of that vast empire of China, crosses all the rivers, passes some considerable hills by the help of sluices and gates, and goes up to the city of Pekin, being in length near two hundred and seventy leagues."—"Well," said I, "Seignior Portuguese, but that is not our business now; the great question is, if you can carry us up to the city of Nankin, from whence we can travel to Pekin afterwards?" He said he could do so very well, and that there was a great Dutch ship gone up that way just before. This gave me a little shock, for a Dutch ship was now our terror, and we had much rather have met the devil, at least if he had not come in too frightful a figure; and we depended upon it that a Dutch ship would be our destruction, for we were in no condition to fight them; all the ships they trade with into those parts being of great burden, and of much greater force than we were.

The old man found me a little confused, and under some concern when he named a Dutch ship, and said to me, "Sir, you need be under no apprehensions of the Dutch; I suppose they are not now at war with your nation?"—"No," said I, "that's true; but I know not what liberties men may take when they are out of the reach of the laws of their own country."—"Why," says he, "you are no pirates; what need you fear? They will not meddle with peaceable merchants, sure." These words put me into the greatest disorder and confusion imaginable; nor was it possible for me to conceal it so, but the old man easily perceived it.

"Sir," says he, "I find you are in some disorder in your thoughts at my talk: pray be pleased to go which way you think fit, and depend upon it, I'll do you all the service I can." Upon this we fell into further discourse, in which, to my alarm and amazement, he spoke of the villainous doings of a certain pirate ship that had long been the talk of mariners in those seas; no other, in a word, than the very ship he was now on board of, and which we had so unluckily purchased. I presently saw there was no help for it but to tell him the plain truth, and explain all the danger and trouble we had suffered through this misadventure, and, in particular, our earnest wish to be speedily quit of the ship altogether; for which reason we had resolved to carry her up to Nankin.

The old man was amazed at this relation, and told us we were in the right to go away to the north; and that, if he might advise us, it should be to sell the ship in China, which we might well do, and buy, or build another in the country; adding that I should meet with customers enough for the ship at Nankin, that a Chinese junk would serve me very well to go back again, and that he would procure me people both to buy one and sell the other. "Well, but, seignior," said I, "as you say they know the ship so well, I may, perhaps, if I follow your measures, be instrumental to bring some honest, innocent men into a terrible broil; for wherever they find the ship they will prove the guilt upon the men, by proving this was the ship."—"Why," says the old man, "I'll find out a way to prevent that; for as I know all those commanders you speak of very well, and shall see them all as they pass by, I will be sure to set them to rights in the thing, and let them know that they had been so much in the wrong; that though the people who were on board at first might run away with the ship, yet it was not true that they had turned pirates; and that, in particular, these were not the men that first went off with the ship, but innocently bought her for their trade; and I am persuaded they will so far believe me as at least to act more cautiously for the time to come."

In about thirteen days' sail we came to an anchor, at the south- west point of the great Gulf of Nankin; where I learned by accident that two Dutch ships were gone the length before me, and that I should certainly fall into their hands. I consulted my partner again in this exigency, and he was as much at a loss as I was. I then asked the old pilot if there was no creek or harbour which I might put into and pursue my business with the Chinese privately, and be in no danger of the enemy. He told me if I would sail to the southward about forty-two leagues, there was a little port called Quinchang, where the fathers of the mission usually landed from Macao, on their progress to teach the Christian religion to the Chinese, and where no European ships ever put in; and if I thought to put in there, I might consider what further course to take when I was on shore. He confessed, he said, it was not a place for merchants, except that at some certain times they had a kind of a fair there, when the merchants from Japan came over thither to buy Chinese merchandises. The name of the port I may perhaps spell wrong, having lost this, together with the names of many other places set down in a little pocket-book, which was spoiled by the water by an accident; but this I remember, that the Chinese merchants we corresponded with called it by a different name from that which our Portuguese pilot gave it, who pronounced it Quinchang. As we were unanimous in our resolution to go to this place, we weighed the next day, having only gone twice on shore where we were, to get fresh water; on both which occasions the people of the country were very civil, and brought abundance of provisions to sell to us; but nothing without money.

We did not come to the other port (the wind being contrary) for five days; but it was very much to our satisfaction, and I was thankful when I set my foot on shore, resolving, and my partner too, that if it was possible to dispose of ourselves and effects any other way, though not profitably, we would never more set foot on board that unhappy vessel. Indeed, I must acknowledge, that of all the circumstances of life that ever I had any experience of, nothing makes mankind so completely miserable as that of being in constant fear. Well does the Scripture say, "The fear of man brings a snare"; it is a life of death, and the mind is so entirely oppressed by it, that it is capable of no relief.

Nor did it fail of its usual operations upon the fancy, by heightening every danger; representing the English and Dutch captains to be men incapable of hearing reason, or of distinguishing between honest men and rogues; or between a story calculated for our own turn, made out of nothing, on purpose to deceive, and a true, genuine account of our whole voyage, progress, and design; for we might many ways have convinced any reasonable creatures that we were not pirates; the goods we had on board, the course we steered, our frankly showing ourselves, and entering into such and such ports; and even our very manner, the force we had, the number of men, the few arms, the little ammunition, short provisions; all these would have served to convince any men that we were no pirates. The opium and other goods we had on board would make it appear the ship had been at Bengal. The Dutchmen, who, it was said, had the names of all the men that were in the ship, might easily see that we were a mixture of English, Portuguese, and Indians, and but two Dutchmen on board. These, and many other particular circumstances, might have made it evident to the understanding of any commander, whose hands we might fall into, that we were no pirates.

But fear, that blind, useless passion, worked another way, and threw us into the vapours; it bewildered our understandings, and set the imagination at work to form a thousand terrible things that perhaps might never happen. We first supposed, as indeed everybody had related to us, that the seamen on board the English and Dutch ships, but especially the Dutch, were so enraged at the name of a pirate, and especially at our beating off their boats and escaping, that they would not give themselves leave to inquire whether we were pirates or no, but would execute us off-hand, without giving us any room for a defence. We reflected that there really was so much apparent evidence before them, that they would scarce inquire after any more; as, first, that the ship was certainly the same, and that some of the seamen among them knew her, and had been on board her; and, secondly, that when we had intelligence at the river of Cambodia that they were coming down to examine us, we fought their boats and fled. Therefore we made no doubt but they were as fully satisfied of our being pirates as we were satisfied of the contrary; and, as I often said, I know not but I should have been apt to have taken those circumstances for evidence, if the tables were turned, and my case was theirs; and have made no scruple of cutting all the crew to pieces, without believing, or perhaps considering, what they might have to offer in their defence.

But let that be how it will, these were our apprehensions; and both my partner and I scarce slept a night without dreaming of halters and yard-arms; of fighting, and being taken; of killing, and being killed: and one night I was in such a fury in my dream, fancying the Dutchmen had boarded us, and I was knocking one of their seamen down, that I struck my doubled fist against the side of the cabin I lay in with such a force as wounded my hand grievously, broke my knuckles, and cut and bruised the flesh, so that it awaked me out of my sleep. Another apprehension I had was, the cruel usage we might meet with from them if we fell into their hands; then the story of Amboyna came into my head, and how the Dutch might perhaps torture us, as they did our countrymen there, and make some of our men, by extremity of torture, confess to crimes they never were guilty of, or own themselves and all of us to be pirates, and so they would put us to death with a formal appearance of justice; and that they might be tempted to do this for the gain of our ship and cargo, worth altogether four or five thousand pounds. We did not consider that the captains of ships have no authority to act thus; and if we had surrendered prisoners to them, they could not answer the destroying us, or torturing us, but would be accountable for it when they came to their country. However, if they were to act thus with us, what advantage would it be to us that they should be called to an account for it?—or if we were first to be murdered, what satisfaction would it be to us to have them punished when they came home?

I cannot refrain taking notice here what reflections I now had upon the vast variety of my particular circumstances; how hard I thought it that I, who had spent forty years in a life of continual difficulties, and was at last come, as it were, to the port or haven which all men drive at, viz. to have rest and plenty, should be a volunteer in new sorrows by my own unhappy choice, and that I, who had escaped so many dangers in my youth, should now come to be hanged in my old age, and in so remote a place, for a crime which I was not in the least inclined to, much less guilty of. After these thoughts something of religion would come in; and I would be considering that this seemed to me to be a disposition of immediate Providence, and I ought to look upon it and submit to it as such. For, although I was innocent as to men, I was far from being innocent as to my Maker; and I ought to look in and examine what other crimes in my life were most obvious to me, and for which Providence might justly inflict this punishment as a retribution; and thus I ought to submit to this, just as I would to a shipwreck, if it had pleased God to have brought such a disaster upon me.

In its turn natural courage would sometimes take its place, and then I would be talking myself up to vigorous resolutions; that I would not be taken to be barbarously used by a parcel of merciless wretches in cold blood; that it were much better to have fallen into the hands of the savages, though I were sure they would feast upon me when they had taken me, than those who would perhaps glut their rage upon me by inhuman tortures and barbarities; that in the case of the savages, I always resolved to die fighting to the last gasp, and why should I not do so now? Whenever these thoughts prevailed, I was sure to put myself into a kind of fever with the agitation of a supposed fight; my blood would boil, and my eyes sparkle, as if I was engaged, and I always resolved to take no quarter at their hands; but even at last, if I could resist no longer, I would blow up the ship and all that was in her, and leave them but little booty to boast of.

Chapter 13

Arrival in China

The greater weight the anxieties and perplexities of these things were to our thoughts while we were at sea, the greater was our satisfaction when we saw ourselves on shore; and my partner told me he dreamed that he had a very heavy load upon his back, which he was to carry up a hill, and found that he was not able to stand longer under it; but that the Portuguese pilot came and took it off his back, and the hill disappeared, the ground before him appearing all smooth and plain: and truly it was so; they were all like men who had a load taken off their backs. For my part I had a weight taken off from my heart that it was not able any longer to bear; and as I said above we resolved to go no more to sea in that ship. When we came on shore, the old pilot, who was now our friend, got us a lodging, together with a warehouse for our goods; it was a little hut, with a larger house adjoining to it, built and also palisadoed round with canes, to keep out pilferers, of which there were not a few in that country: however, the magistrates allowed us a little guard, and we had a soldier with a kind of half-pike, who stood sentinel at our door, to whom we allowed a pint of rice and a piece of money about the value of three-pence per day, so that our goods were kept very safe.

The fair or mart usually kept at this place had been over some time; however, we found that there were three or four junks in the river, and two ships from Japan, with goods which they had bought in China, and were not gone away, having some Japanese merchants on shore.

The first thing our old Portuguese pilot did for us was to get us acquainted with three missionary Romish priests who were in the town, and who had been there some time converting the people to Christianity; but we thought they made but poor work of it, and made them but sorry Christians when they had done. One of these was a Frenchman, whom they called Father Simon; another was a Portuguese; and a third a Genoese. Father Simon was courteous, and very agreeable company; but the other two were more reserved, seemed rigid and austere, and applied seriously to the work they came about, viz. to talk with and insinuate themselves among the inhabitants wherever they had opportunity. We often ate and drank with those men; and though I must confess the conversion, as they call it, of the Chinese to Christianity is so far from the true conversion required to bring heathen people to the faith of Christ, that it seems to amount to little more than letting them know the name of Christ, and say some prayers to the Virgin Mary and her Son, in a tongue which they understood not, and to cross themselves, and the like; yet it must be confessed that the religionists, whom we call missionaries, have a firm belief that these people will be saved, and that they are the instruments of it; and on this account they undergo not only the fatigue of the voyage, and the hazards of living in such places, but oftentimes death itself, and the most violent tortures, for the sake of this work.

Father Simon was appointed, it seems, by order of the chief of the mission, to go up to Pekin, and waited only for another priest, who was ordered to come to him from Macao, to go along with him. We scarce ever met together but he was inviting me to go that journey; telling me how he would show me all the glorious things of that mighty empire, and, among the rest, Pekin, the greatest city in the world: "A city," said he, "that your London and our Paris put together cannot be equal to." But as I looked on those things with different eyes from other men, so I shall give my opinion of them in a few words, when I come in the course of my travels to speak more particularly of them.

Dining with Father Simon one day, and being very merry together, I showed some little inclination to go with him; and he pressed me and my partner very hard to consent. "Why, father," says my partner, "should you desire our company so much? you know we are heretics, and you do not love us, nor cannot keep us company with any pleasure."—"Oh," says he, "you may perhaps be good Catholics in time; my business here is to convert heathens, and who knows but I may convert you too?"—"Very well, father," said I, "so you will preach to us all the way?"—"I will not be troublesome to you," says he; "our religion does not divest us of good manners; besides, we are here like countrymen; and so we are, compared to the place we are in; and if you are Huguenots, and I a Catholic, we may all be Christians at last; at least, we are all gentlemen, and we may converse so, without being uneasy to one another." I liked this part of his discourse very well, and it began to put me in mind of my priest that I had left in the Brazils; but Father Simon did not come up to his character by a great deal; for though this friar had no appearance of a criminal levity in him, yet he had not that fund of Christian zeal, strict piety, and sincere affection to religion that my other good ecclesiastic had.

But to leave him a little, though he never left us, nor solicited us to go with him; we had something else before us at first, for we had all this while our ship and our merchandise to dispose of, and we began to be very doubtful what we should do, for we were now in a place of very little business. Once I was about to venture to sail for the river of Kilam, and the city of Nankin; but Providence seemed now more visibly, as I thought, than ever to concern itself in our affairs; and I was encouraged, from this very time, to think I should, one way or other, get out of this entangled circumstance, and be brought home to my own country again, though I had not the least view of the manner. Providence, I say, began here to clear up our way a little; and the first thing that offered was, that our old Portuguese pilot brought a Japan merchant to us, who inquired what goods we had: and, in the first place, he bought all our opium, and gave us a very good price for it, paying us in gold by weight, some in small pieces of their own coin, and some in small wedges, of about ten or twelves ounces each. While we were dealing with him for our opium, it came into my head that he might perhaps deal for the ship too, and I ordered the interpreter to propose it to him. He shrunk up his shoulders at it when it was first proposed to him; but in a few days after he came to me, with one of the missionary priests for his interpreter, and told me he had a proposal to make to me, which was this: he had bought a great quantity of our goods, when he had no thoughts of proposals made to him of buying the ship; and that, therefore, he had not money to pay for the ship: but if I would let the same men who were in the ship navigate her, he would hire the ship to go to Japan; and would send them from thence to the Philippine Islands with another loading, which he would pay the freight of before they went from Japan: and that at their return he would buy the ship. I began to listen to his proposal, and so eager did my head still run upon rambling, that I could not but begin to entertain a notion of going myself with him, and so to set sail from the

Philippine Islands away to the South Seas; accordingly, I asked the Japanese merchant if he would not hire us to the Philippine Islands and discharge us there. He said No, he could not do that, for then he could not have the return of his cargo; but he would discharge us in Japan, at the ship's return. Well, still I was for taking him at that proposal, and going myself; but my partner, wiser than myself, persuaded me from it, representing the dangers, as well of the seas as of the Japanese, who are a false, cruel, and treacherous people; likewise those of the Spaniards at the Philippines, more false, cruel, and treacherous than they.

But to bring this long turn of our affairs to a conclusion; the first thing we had to do was to consult with the captain of the ship, and with his men, and know if they were willing to go to Japan. While I was doing this, the young man whom my nephew had left with me as my companion came up, and told me that he thought that voyage promised very fair, and that there was a great prospect of advantage, and he would be very glad if I undertook it; but that if I would not, and would give him leave, he would go as a merchant, or as I pleased to order him; that if ever he came to England, and I was there and alive, he would render me a faithful account of his success, which should be as much mine as I pleased. I was loath to part with him; but considering the prospect of advantage, which really was considerable, and that he was a young fellow likely to do well in it, I inclined to let him go; but I told him I would consult my partner, and give him an answer the next day. I discoursed about it with my partner, who thereupon made a most generous offer: "You know it has been an unlucky ship," said he, "and we both resolve not to go to sea in it again; if your steward" (so he called my man) "will venture the voyage, I will leave my share of the vessel to him, and let him make the best of it; and if we live to meet in England, and he meets with success abroad, he shall account for one half of the profits of the ship's freight to us; the other shall be his own."

If my partner, who was no way concerned with my young man, made him such an offer, I could not do less than offer him the same; and all the ship's company being willing to go with him, we made over half the ship to him in property, and took a writing from him, obliging him to account for the other, and away he went to Japan. The Japan merchant proved a very punctual, honest man to him: protected him at Japan, and got him a licence to come on shore, which the Europeans in general have not lately obtained. He paid him his freight very punctually; sent him to the Philippines loaded with Japan and China wares, and a supercargo of their own, who, trafficking with the Spaniards, brought back European goods again, and a great quantity of spices; and there he was not only paid his freight very well, and at a very good price, but not being willing to sell the ship, then the merchant furnished him goods on his own account; and with some money, and some spices of his own which he brought with him, he went back to the Manillas, where he sold his cargo very well. Here, having made a good acquaintance at Manilla, he got his ship made a free ship, and the governor of Manilla hired him to go to Acapulco, on the coast of America, and gave him a licence to land there, and to travel to Mexico, and to pass in any Spanish ship to Europe with all his men. He made the voyage to Acapulco very happily, and there he sold his ship: and having there also obtained allowance to travel by land to Porto Bello, he found means to get to Jamaica, with all his treasure, and about eight years after came to England exceeding rich.

But to return to our particular affairs, being now to part with the ship and ship's company, it came before us, of course, to consider what recompense we should give to the two men that gave us such timely notice of the design against us in the river Cambodia. The truth was, they had done us a very considerable service, and deserved well at our hands; though, by the way, they were a couple of rogues, too; for, as they believed the story of our being pirates, and that we had really run away with the ship, they came down to us, not only to betray the design that was formed against us, but to go to sea with us as pirates. One of them confessed afterwards that nothing else but the hopes of going a-roguing brought him to do it: however, the service they did us was not the less, and therefore, as I had promised to be grateful to them, I first ordered the money to be paid them which they said was due to them on board their respective ships: over and above that, I gave each of them a small sum of money in gold, which contented them very well. I then made the Englishman gunner in the ship, the gunner being now made second mate and purser; the Dutchman I made boatswain; so they were both very well pleased, and proved very serviceable, being both able seamen, and very stout fellows.

We were now on shore in China; if I thought myself banished, and remote from my own country at Bengal, where I had many ways to get home for my money, what could I think of myself now, when I was about a thousand leagues farther off from home, and destitute of all manner of prospect of return? All we had for it was this: that in about four months' time there was to be another fair at the place where we were, and then we might be able to purchase various manufactures of the country, and withal might possibly find some Chinese junks from Tonquin for sail, that would carry us and our goods whither we pleased. This I liked very well, and resolved to wait; besides, as our particular persons were not obnoxious, so if any English or Dutch ships came thither, perhaps we might have an opportunity to load our goods, and get passage to some other place in India nearer home. Upon these hopes we resolved to continue here; but, to divert ourselves, we took two or three journeys into the country.

First, we went ten days' journey to Nankin, a city well worth seeing; they say it has a million of people in it: it is regularly built, and the streets are all straight, and cross one another in direct lines. But when I come to compare the miserable people of these countries with ours, their fabrics, their manner of living, their government, their religion, their wealth, and their glory, as some call it, I must confess that I scarcely think it worth my while to mention them here. We wonder at the grandeur, the riches, the pomp, the ceremonies, the government, the manufactures, the commerce, and conduct of these people; not that there is really any matter for wonder, but because, having a true notion of the barbarity of those countries, the rudeness and the ignorance that prevail there, we do not expect to find any such thing so far off. Otherwise, what are their buildings to the palaces and royal buildings of Europe? What their trade to the universal commerce of England, Holland, France, and Spain? What are their cities to ours, for wealth, strength, gaiety of apparel, rich furniture, and infinite variety? What are their ports, supplied with a few junks and barks, to our navigation, our merchant fleets, our large and powerful navies? Our city of London has more trade than half their mighty empire: one English, Dutch, or French man-of-war of eighty guns would be able to fight almost all the shipping belonging to China: but the greatness of their wealth, their trade, the power of their government, and the strength of their armies, may be a little surprising to us, because, as I have said, considering them as a barbarous nation of pagans, little better than savages, we did not expect such things among them. But all the forces of their empire, though they were to bring two millions of men into the field together, would be able to do nothing but ruin the country and starve themselves; a million of their foot could not stand before one embattled body of our infantry, posted so as not to be surrounded, though they were not to be one to twenty in number; nay, I do not boast if I say that thirty thousand German or English foot, and ten thousand horse, well managed, could defeat all the forces of China. Nor is there a fortified town in China that could hold out one month against the batteries and attacks of an European army. They have firearms, it is true, but they are awkward and uncertain in their going off; and their powder has but little strength. Their armies are badly disciplined, and want skill to attack, or temper to retreat; and therefore, I must confess, it seemed strange to me, when I came home, and heard our people say such fine things of the power, glory, magnificence, and trade of the Chinese; because, as far as I saw, they appeared to be a contemptible herd or crowd of ignorant, sordid slaves, subjected to a government qualified only to rule such a people; and were not its distance inconceivably, great from Muscovy, and that empire in a manner as rude, impotent, and ill governed as they, the Czar of Muscovy might with ease drive them all out of their country, and conquer them in one campaign; and had the Czar (who is now a growing prince) fallen this way, instead of attacking the warlike Swedes, and equally improved himself in the art of war, as they say he has done; and if none of the powers of Europe had envied or interrupted him, he might by this time have been Emperor of China, instead of being beaten by the King of Sweden at Narva, when the latter was not one to six in number.

As their strength and their grandeur, so their navigation, commerce, and husbandry are very imperfect, compared to the same things in Europe; also, in their knowledge, their learning, and in their skill in the sciences, they are either very awkward or defective, though they have globes or spheres, and a smattering of the mathematics, and think they know more than all the world besides. But they know little of the motions of the heavenly bodies; and so grossly and absurdly ignorant are their common people, that when the sun is eclipsed, they think a great dragon has assaulted it, and is going to run away with it; and they fall a clattering with all the drums and kettles in the country, to fright the monster away, just as we do to hive a swarm of bees!

As this is the only excursion of the kind which I have made in all the accounts I have given of my travels, so I shall make no more such. It is none of my business, nor any part of my design; but to give an account of my own adventures through a life of inimitable wanderings, and a long variety of changes, which, perhaps, few that come after me will have heard the like of: I shall, therefore, say very little of all the mighty places, desert countries, and numerous people I have yet to pass through, more than relates to my own story, and which my concern among them will make necessary.

I was now, as near as I can compute, in the heart of China, about thirty degrees north of the line, for we were returned from Nankin. I had indeed a mind to see the city of Pekin, which I had heard so much of, and Father Simon importuned me daily to do it. At length his time of going away being set, and the other missionary who was to go with him being arrived from Macao, it was necessary that we should resolve either to go or not; so I referred it to my partner, and left it wholly to his choice, who at length resolved it in the affirmative, and we prepared for our journey. We set out with very good advantage as to finding the way; for we got leave to travel in the retinue of one of their mandarins, a kind of viceroy or principal magistrate in the province where they reside, and who take great state upon them, travelling with great attendance, and great homage from the people, who are sometimes greatly impoverished by them, being obliged to furnish provisions for them and all their attendants in their journeys. I particularly observed in our travelling with his baggage, that though we received sufficient provisions both for ourselves and our horses from the country, as belonging to the mandarin, yet we were obliged to pay for everything we had, after the market price of the country, and the mandarin's steward collected it duly from us. Thus our travelling in the retinue of the mandarin, though it was a great act of kindness, was not such a mighty favour to us, but was a great advantage to him, considering there were above thirty other people travelled in the same manner besides us, under the protection of his retinue; for the country furnished all the provisions for nothing to him, and yet he took our money for them.

We were twenty-five days travelling to Pekin, through a country exceeding populous, but I think badly cultivated; the husbandry, the economy, and the way of living miserable, though they boast so much of the industry of the people: I say miserable, if compared with our own, but not so to these poor wretches, who know no other. The pride of the poor people is infinitely great, and exceeded by nothing but their poverty, in some parts, which adds to that which I call their misery; and I must needs think the savages of America live much more happy than the poorer sort of these, because as they have nothing, so they desire nothing; whereas these are proud and insolent and in the main are in many parts mere beggars and drudges. Their ostentation is inexpressible; and, if they can, they love to keep multitudes of servants or slaves, which is to the last

258

degree ridiculous, as well as their contempt of all the world but themselves.

I must confess I travelled more pleasantly afterwards in the deserts and vast wildernesses of Grand Tartary than here, and yet the roads here are well paved and well kept, and very convenient for travellers; but nothing was more awkward to me than to see such a haughty, imperious, insolent people, in the midst of the grossest simplicity and ignorance; and my friend Father Simon and I used to be very merry upon these occasions, to see their beggarly pride. For example, coming by the house of a country gentleman, as Father Simon called him, about ten leagues off the city of Nankin, we had first of all the honour to ride with the master of the house about two miles; the state he rode in was a perfect Don Quixotism, being a mixture of pomp and poverty. His habit was very proper for a merry-andrew, being a dirty calico, with hanging sleeves, tassels, and cuts and slashes almost on every side: it covered a taffety vest, so greasy as to testify that his honour must be a most exquisite sloven. His horse was a poor, starved, hobbling creature, and two slaves followed him on foot to drive the poor creature along; he had a whip in his hand, and he belaboured the beast as fast about the head as his slaves did about the tail; and thus he rode by us, with about ten or twelve servants, going from the city to his country seat, about half a league before us. We travelled on gently, but this figure of a gentleman rode away before us; and as we stopped at a village about an hour to refresh us, when we came by the country seat of this great man, we saw him in a little place before his door, eating a repast. It was a kind of garden, but he was easy to be seen; and we were given to understand that the more we looked at him the better he would be pleased. He sat under a tree, something like the palmetto, which effectually shaded him over the head, and on the south side; but under the tree was placed a large umbrella, which made that part look well enough. He sat lolling back in a great elbow-chair, being a heavy corpulent man, and had his meat brought him by two women slaves. He had two more, one of whom fed the squire with a spoon, and the other held the dish with one hand, and scraped off what he let fall upon his worship's beard and taffety vest.

Leaving the poor wretch to please himself with our looking at him, as if we admired his idle pomp, we pursued our journey. Father Simon had the curiosity to stay to inform himself what dainties the country justice had to feed on in all his state, which he had the honour to taste of, and which was, I think, a mess of boiled rice, with a great piece of garlic in it, and a little bag filled with green pepper, and another plant which they have there, something like our ginger, but smelling like musk, and tasting like mustard; all this was put together, and a small piece of lean mutton boiled in it, and this was his worship's repast. Four or five servants more attended at a distance, who we supposed were to eat of the same after their master. As for our mandarin with whom we travelled, he was respected as a king, surrounded always with his gentlemen, and attended in all his appearances with such pomp, that I saw little of him but at a distance. I observed that there was not a horse in his retinue but that our carrier's packhorses in England seemed to me to look much better; though it was hard to judge rightly, for they were so covered with equipage, mantles, trappings, &c., that we could scarce see anything but their feet and their heads as they went along.

I was now light-hearted, and all my late trouble and perplexity being over, I had no anxious thoughts about me, which made this journey the pleasanter to me; in which no ill accident attended me, only in passing or fording a small river, my horse fell and made me free of the country, as they call it—that is to say, threw me in. The place was not deep, but it wetted me all over. I mention it because it spoiled my pocket-book, wherein I had set down the names of several people and places which I had occasion to remember, and which not taking due care of, the leaves rotted, and the words were never after to be read.

At length we arrived at Pekin. I had nobody with me but the youth whom my nephew had given me to attend me as a servant and who proved very trusty and diligent; and my partner had nobody with him but one servant, who was a kinsman. As for the Portuguese pilot, he being desirous to see the court, we bore his charges for his company, and for our use of him as an interpreter, for he understood the language of the country, and spoke good French and a little English. Indeed, this old man was most useful to us everywhere; for we had not been above a week at Pekin, when he came laughing. "Ah, Seignior Inglese," says he, "I have something to tell will make your heart glad."—"My heart glad," says I; "what can that be? I don't know anything in this country can either give me joy or grief to any great degree."—"Yes, yes," said the old man, in broken English, "make you glad, me sorry."—"Why," said I, "will it make you sorry?"—"Because," said he, "you have brought me here twenty-five days' journey, and will leave me to go back alone; and which way shall I get to my port afterwards, without a ship, without a horse, without pecune?" so he called money, being his broken Latin, of which he had abundance to make us merry with. In short, he told us there was a great caravan of Muscovite and Polish merchants in the city, preparing to set out on their journey by land to Muscovy, within four or five weeks; and he was sure we would take the opportunity to go with them, and leave him behind, to go back alone.

I confess I was greatly surprised with this good news, and had scarce power to speak to him for some time; but at last I said to him, "How do you know this? are you sure it is true?"—"Yes," says he; "I met this morning in the street an old acquaintance of mine, an Armenian, who is among them. He came last from Astrakhan, and was designed to go to Tonquin, where I formerly knew him, but has altered his mind, and is now resolved to go with the caravan to Moscow, and so down the river Volga to Astrakhan."—"Well, Seignior," says I, "do not be uneasy about being left to go back alone; if this be a method for my return to England, it shall be your fault if you go back to Macao at all." We then went to consult together what was to be done; and I asked my partner what he thought of the pilot's news, and whether it would suit with his affairs? He told me he would do just as I would; for he had settled all his affairs so well at Bengal, and left his effects in such good hands, that as we had made a good voyage, if he could invest it in China silks, wrought and raw, he would be content to go to England, and then make a voyage back to Bengal by the Company's ships.

Having resolved upon this, we agreed that if our Portuguese pilot would go with us, we would bear his charges to Moscow, or to England, if he pleased; nor, indeed, were we to be esteemed over- generous in that either, if we had not rewarded him further, the service he had done us being really worth more than that; for he had not only been a pilot to us at sea, but he had been like a broker for us on shore; and his procuring for us a Japan merchant was some hundreds of pounds in our pockets. So, being willing to gratify him, which was but doing him justice, and very willing also to have him with us besides, for he was a most necessary man on all occasions, we agreed to give him a quantity of coined gold, which, as I computed it, was worth one hundred and seventy-five pounds sterling, between us, and to bear all his charges, both for himself and horse, except only a horse to carry his goods. Having settled this between ourselves, we called him to let him know what we had resolved. I told him he had complained of our being willing to let him go back alone, and I was now about to tell him we designed he should not go back at all. That as we had resolved to go to Europe with the caravan, we were very willing he should go with us; and that we called him to know his mind. He shook his head and said it was a long journey, and that he had no pecune to carry him thither, or to subsist himself when he came there. We told him we believed it was so, and therefore we had resolved to do something for him that should let him see how sensible we were of the service he had done us, and also how agreeable he was to us: and then I told him what we had resolved to give him here, which he might lay out as we would do our own; and that as for his charges, if he would go with us we would set him safe on shore (life and casualties excepted), either in Muscovy or England, as he would choose, at our own charge, except only the carriage of his goods. He received the proposal like a man transported, and told us he would go with us over all the whole world; and so we all prepared for our journey. However, as it was with us, so it was with the other merchants: they had many things to do, and instead of being ready in five weeks, it was four months and some days before all things were got together.

Chapter 14

Attacked by Tartars

It was the beginning of February, new style, when we set out from Pekin. My partner and the old pilot had gone express back to the port where we had first put in, to dispose of some goods which we had left there; and I, with a Chinese merchant whom I had some knowledge of at Nankin, and who came to Pekin on his own affairs, went to Nankin, where I bought ninety pieces of fine damasks, with about two hundred pieces of other very fine silk of several sorts, some mixed with gold, and had all these brought to Pekin against my partner's return. Besides this, we bought a large quantity of raw silk, and some other goods, our cargo amounting, in these goods only, to about three thousand five hundred pounds sterling; which, together with tea and some fine calicoes, and three camels' loads of nutmegs and cloves, loaded in all eighteen camels for our share, besides those we rode upon; these, with two or three spare horses, and two horses loaded with provisions, made together twenty-six camels and horses in our retinue.

The company was very great, and, as near as I can remember, made between three and four hundred horses, and upwards of one hundred and twenty men, very well armed and provided for all events; for as the Eastern caravans are subject to be attacked by the Arabs, so are these by the Tartars. The company consisted of people of several nations, but there were above sixty of them merchants or inhabitants of Moscow, though of them some were Livonians; and to our particular satisfaction, five of them were Scots, who appeared also to be men of great experience in business, and of very good substance.

When we had travelled one day's journey, the guides, who were five in number, called all the passengers, except the servants, to a great council, as they called it. At this council every one deposited a certain quantity of money to a common stock, for the necessary expense of buying forage on the way, where it was not otherwise to be had, and for satisfying the guides, getting horses, and the like. Here, too, they constituted the journey, as they call it, viz. they named captains and officers to draw us all up, and give the word of command, in case of an attack, and give every one their turn of command; nor was this forming us into order any more than what we afterwards found needful on the way.

The road all on this side of the country is very populous, and is full of potters and earth-makers—that is to say, people, that temper the earth for the China ware. As I was coming along, our Portuguese pilot, who had always something or other to say to make us merry, told me he would show me the greatest rarity in all the country, and that I should have this to say of China, after all the ill-humoured things that I had said of it, that I had seen one thing which was not to be seen in all the world beside. I was very importunate to know what it was; at last he told me it was a gentleman's house built with China ware. "Well," says I, "are not the materials of their buildings the products of their own country, and so it is all China ware, is it not?"—"No, no," says he, "I mean it is a house all made of China ware, such as you call it in England, or as it is called in our country, porcelain."—"Well," says I, "such a thing may be; how big is it? Can we carry it in a box upon a camel? If we can we will buy it."—"Upon a camel!" says the old pilot, holding up both his hands; "why, there is a family of thirty people lives in it."

I was then curious, indeed, to see it; and when I came to it, it was nothing but this: it was a timber house, or a house built, as we call it in England, with lath and plaster, but all this plastering was really China ware— that is to say, it was plastered with the earth that makes China ware. The outside, which the sun shone hot upon, was glazed, and looked very well, perfectly white, and painted with blue figures, as the large China ware in England is painted, and hard as if it had been burnt. As to the inside, all the walls, instead of wainscot, were lined with hardened and painted tiles, like the little square tiles we call galley-tiles in England, all made of the finest china, and the figures exceeding fine indeed, with extraordinary variety of colours, mixed with gold, many tiles making but one figure, but joined so artificially, the mortar being made of the same earth, that it was very hard to see where the tiles met. The floors of the rooms were of the same composition, and as hard as the earthen floors we have in use in several parts of England; as hard as stone, and smooth, but not burnt and painted, except some smaller rooms, like closets, which were all, as it were, paved with the same tile; the ceiling and all the plastering work in the whole house were of the same earth; and, after all, the roof was covered with tiles of the same, but of a deep shining black. This was a China warehouse indeed, truly and literally to be called so, and had I not been upon the journey, I could have stayed some days to see and examine the particulars of it. They told me there were fountains and fishponds in the garden, all paved on the bottom and sides with the same; and fine statues set up in rows on the walks, entirely formed of the porcelain earth, burnt whole.

As this is one of the singularities of China, so they may be allowed to excel in it; but I am very sure they excel in their accounts of it; for they told me such incredible things of their performance in crockery-ware, for such it is, that I care not to relate, as knowing it could not be true. They told me, in particular, of one workman that made a ship with all its tackle and masts and sails in earthenware, big enough to carry fifty men. If they had told me he launched it, and made a voyage to Japan in it, I might have said something to it indeed; but as it was, I knew the whole of the story, which was, in short, that the fellow lied: so I smiled, and said nothing to it. This odd sight kept me two hours behind the caravan, for which the leader of it for the day fined me about the value of three shillings; and told me if it had been three days' journey without the wall, as it was three days' within, he must have fined me four times as much, and made me ask pardon the next council-day. I promised to be more orderly; and, indeed, I found afterwards the orders made for keeping all together were absolutely necessary for our common safety.

In two days more we passed the great China wall, made for a fortification against the Tartars: and a very great work it is, going over hills and mountains in an endless track, where the rocks are impassable, and the precipices such as no enemy could possibly enter, or indeed climb up, or where, if they did, no wall could hinder them. They tell us its length is near a thousand English miles, but that the country is five hundred in a straight measured line, which the wall bounds without measuring the windings and turnings it takes; it is about four fathoms high, and as many thick in some places.

I stood still an hour or thereabouts without trespassing on our orders (for so long the caravan was in passing the gate), to look at it on every side, near and far off; I mean what was within my view: and the guide, who had been extolling it for the wonder of the world, was mighty eager to hear my opinion of it. I told him it was a most excellent thing to keep out the Tartars; which he happened not to understand as I meant it and so took it for a compliment; but the old pilot laughed! "Oh, Seignior Inglese," says he, "you speak in colours."—"In colours!" said I; "what do you mean by that?"—"Why, you speak what looks white this way and black that way—gay one way and dull another. You tell him it is a good wall to keep out Tartars; you tell me by that it is good for nothing but to keep out Tartars. I understand you, Seignior Inglese, I understand you; but Seignior Chinese understood you his own way."—"Well," says I, "do you think it would stand out an army of our country people, with a good train of artillery; or our engineers, with two companies of miners? Would not they batter it down in ten days, that an army might enter in battalia; or blow it up in the air, foundation and all, that there should be no sign of it left?"—"Ay, ay," says he, "I know that." The Chinese wanted mightily to know what I said to the pilot, and I gave him leave to tell him a few days after, for we were then almost out of their country, and he was to leave us a little time after this; but when he knew what I said, he was dumb all the rest of the way, and we heard no more of his fine story of the Chinese power and greatness while he stayed.

After we passed this mighty nothing, called a wall, something like the Picts' walls so famous in Northumberland, built by the Romans, we began to find the country thinly inhabited, and the people rather confined to live in fortified towns, as being subject to the inroads and depredations of the Tartars, who rob in great armies, and therefore are not to be resisted by the naked inhabitants of an open country. And here I began to find the necessity of keeping together in a caravan as we travelled, for we saw several troops of Tartars roving about; but when I came to see them distinctly, I wondered more that the Chinese empire could be conquered by such contemptible fellows; for they are a mere horde of wild fellows, keeping no order and understanding no discipline or manner of it. Their horses are poor lean creatures, taught nothing, and fit for nothing; and this we found the first day we saw them, which was after we entered the wilder part of the country. Our leader for the day gave leave for about sixteen of us to go a hunting as they call it; and what was this but a hunting of sheep!—however, it may be called hunting too, for these creatures are the wildest and swiftest of foot that ever I saw of their kind! only they will not run a great way, and you are sure of sport when you begin the chase, for they appear generally thirty or forty in a flock, and, like true sheep, always keep together when they fly.

In pursuit of this odd sort of game it was our hap to meet with about forty Tartars: whether they were hunting mutton, as we were, or whether they looked for another kind of prey, we know not; but as soon as they saw us, one of them blew a hideous blast on a kind of horn. This was to call their friends about them, and in less than ten minutes a troop of forty or fifty more appeared, at about a mile distance; but our work was over first, as it happened.

One of the Scots merchants of Moscow happened to be amongst us; and as soon as he heard the horn, he told us that we had nothing to do but to charge them without loss of time; and drawing us up in a line, he asked if we were resolved. We told him we were ready to follow him; so he rode directly towards them. They stood gazing at us like a mere crowd, drawn up in no sort of order at all; but as soon as they saw us advance, they let fly their arrows, which missed us, very happily. Not that they mistook their aim, but their distance; for their arrows all fell a little short of us, but with so true an aim, that had we been about twenty yards nearer we must have had several men wounded, if not killed.

Immediately we halted, and though it was at a great distance, we fired, and sent them leaden bullets for wooden arrows, following our shot full gallop, to fall in among them sword in hand—for so our bold Scot that led us directed. He was, indeed, but a merchant, but he behaved with such vigour and bravery on this occasion, and yet with such cool courage too, that I never saw any man in action fitter for command. As soon as we came up to them we fired our pistols in their faces and then drew; but they fled in the greatest confusion imaginable. The only stand any of them made was on our right, where three of them stood, and, by signs, called the rest to come back to them, having a kind of scimitar in their hands, and their bows hanging to their backs. Our brave commander, without asking anybody to follow him, gallops up close to them, and with his fusee knocks one of them off his horse, killed the second with his pistol, and the third ran away. Thus ended our fight; but we had this misfortune attending it, that all our mutton we had in chase got away. We had not a man killed or hurt; as for the Tartars, there were about five of them killed—how many were wounded we knew not; but this we knew, that the other party were so frightened with the noise of our guns that they fled, and never made any attempt upon us.

We were all this while in the Chinese dominions, and therefore the Tartars were not so bold as afterwards; but in about five days we entered a vast wild desert, which held us three days' and nights' march; and we were obliged to carry our water with us in great leathern bottles, and to encamp all night, just as I have heard they do in the desert of Arabia. I asked our guides whose dominion this was in, and they told me this was a kind of border that might be called no man's land, being a part of Great Karakathy, or Grand Tartary: that, however, it was all reckoned as belonging to China, but that there was no care taken here to preserve it from the inroads of thieves, and therefore it was reckoned the worst desert in the whole march, though we were to go over some much larger.

In passing this frightful wilderness we saw, two or three times, little parties of the Tartars, but they seemed to be upon their own affairs, and to have no design upon us; and so, like the man who met the devil, if they had nothing to say to us, we had nothing to say to them: we let them go. Once, however, a party of them came so near as to stand and gaze at us. Whether it was to consider if they should attack us or not, we knew not; but when we had passed at some distance by them, we made a rear-guard of forty men, and stood ready for them, letting the caravan pass half a mile or thereabouts before us. After a while they marched off, but they saluted us with five arrows at their parting, which wounded a horse so that it disabled him, and we left him the next day, poor creature, in great need of a good farrier. We saw no more arrows or Tartars that time.

We travelled near a month after this, the ways not being so good as at first, though still in the dominions of the Emperor of China, but lay for the most part in the villages, some of which were fortified, because of the incursions of the Tartars. When we were come to one of these towns (about two days and a half's journey before we came to the city of Naum), I wanted to buy a camel, of which there are plenty to be sold all the way upon that road, and horses also, such as they are, because, so many caravans coming that way, they are often wanted. The person that I spoke to to get me a camel would have gone and fetched one for me; but I, like a fool, must be officious, and go myself along with him; the place was about two miles out of the village, where it seems they kept the camels and horses feeding under a guard.

I walked it on foot, with my old pilot and a Chinese, being very desirous of a little variety. When we came to the place it was a low, marshy ground, walled round with stones, piled up dry, without mortar or earth among them, like a park, with a little guard of Chinese soldiers at the door. Having bought a camel, and agreed for the price, I came away, and the Chinese that went with me led the camel, when on a sudden came up five Tartars on horseback. Two of them seized the fellow and took the camel from him, while the other three stepped up to me and my old pilot, seeing us, as it were, unarmed, for I had no weapon about me but my sword, which could but ill defend me against three horsemen. The first that came up stopped short upon my drawing my sword, for they are arrant cowards; but a second, coming upon my left, gave me a blow on the head, which I never felt till afterwards, and wondered, when I came to myself, what was the matter, and where I was, for he laid me flat on the ground; but my never-failing old pilot, the Portuguese, had a pistol in his pocket, which I knew nothing of, nor the Tartars either: if they had, I suppose they would not have attacked us, for cowards are always boldest when there is no danger. The old man seeing me down, with a bold heart stepped up to the fellow that had struck me, and laying hold of his arm with one hand, and pulling him down by main force a little towards him, with the other shot him into the head, and laid him dead upon the spot. He then immediately stepped up to him who had stopped us, as I said, and before he could come forward again, made a blow at him with a scimitar, which he always wore, but missing the man, struck his horse in the side of his head, cut one of the ears off by the root, and a great slice down by the side of his face. The poor beast, enraged with the wound, was no more to be governed by his rider, though the fellow sat well enough too, but away he flew, and carried him quite out of the pilot's reach; and at some distance, rising upon his hind legs, threw down the Tartar, and fell upon him.

In this interval the poor Chinese came in who had lost the camel, but he had no weapon; however, seeing the Tartar down, and his horse fallen upon him, away he runs to him, and seizing upon an ugly weapon he had by his side, something like a pole-axe, he wrenched it from him, and made shift to knock his Tartarian brains out with it. But my old man had the third Tartar to deal with still; and seeing he did not fly, as he expected, nor come on to fight him, as he apprehended, but stood stock still, the old man stood still too, and fell to work with his tackle to charge his pistol again: but as soon as the Tartar saw the pistol away he scoured, and left my pilot, my champion I called him afterwards, a complete victory.

By this time I was a little recovered. I thought, when I first began to wake, that I had been in a sweet sleep; but, as I said above, I wondered where I was, how I came upon the ground, and what was the matter. A few moments after, as sense returned, I felt pain, though I did not know where; so I clapped my hand to my head, and took it away bloody; then I felt my head ache: and in a moment memory returned, and everything was present to me again. I jumped upon my feet instantly, and got hold of my sword, but no enemies were in view: I found a Tartar lying dead, and his horse standing very quietly by him; and, looking further, I saw my deliverer, who had been to see what the Chinese had done, coming back with his hanger in his hand. The old man, seeing me on my feet, came running to me, and joyfully embraced me, being afraid before that I had been killed. Seeing me bloody, he would see how I was hurt; but it was not much, only what we call a broken head; neither did I afterwards find any great inconvenience from the blow, for it was well again in two or three days.

We made no great gain, however, by this victory, for we lost a camel and gained a horse. I paid for the lost camel, and sent for another; but I did not go to fetch it myself: I had had enough of that.

The city of Naum, which we were approaching, is a frontier of the Chinese empire, and is fortified in their fashion. We wanted, as I have said, above two days' journey of this city when messengers were sent express to every part of the road to tell all travellers and caravans to halt till they had a guard sent for them; for that an unusual body of Tartars, making ten thousand in all, had appeared in the way, about thirty miles beyond the city.

This was very bad news to travellers: however, it was carefully done of the governor, and we were very glad to hear we should have a guard. Accordingly, two days after, we had two hundred soldiers sent us from a garrison of the Chinese on our left, and three hundred more from the city of Naum, and with these we advanced boldly. The three hundred soldiers from Naum marched in our front, the two hundred in our rear, and our men on each side of our camels, with our baggage and the whole caravan in the centre; in this order, and well prepared for battle, we thought ourselves a match for the whole ten thousand Mogul Tartars, if they had appeared; but the next day, when they did appear, it was quite another thing.

Chapter 15

Description of an Idol, Which They Destroy

Early in the morning, when marching from a little town called Changu, we had a river to pass, which we were obliged to ferry; and, had the Tartars had any intelligence, then had been the time to have attacked us, when the caravan being over, the rear-guard was behind; but they did not appear there. About three hours after, when we were entered upon a desert of about fifteen or sixteen miles over, we knew by a cloud of dust they raised, that the enemy was at hand, and presently they came on upon the spur.

Our Chinese guards in the front, who had talked so big the day before, began to stagger; and the soldiers frequently looked behind them, a certain sign in a soldier that he is just ready to run away. My old pilot was of my mind; and being near me, called out, "Seignior Inglese, these fellows must be encouraged, or they will ruin us all; for if the Tartars come on they will never stand it."- -"If am of your mind," said I; "but what must be done?"—"Done?" says he, "let fifty of our men advance, and flank them on each wing, and encourage them. They will fight like brave fellows in brave company; but without this they will every man turn his back." Immediately I rode up to our leader and told him, who was exactly of our mind; accordingly, fifty of us marched to the right wing, and fifty to the left, and the rest made a line of rescue; and so we marched, leaving the last two hundred men to make a body of themselves, and to guard the camels; only that, if need were, they should send a hundred men to assist the last fifty.

At last the Tartars came on, and an innumerable company they were; how many we could not tell, but ten thousand, we thought, at the least. A party of them came on first, and viewed our posture, traversing the ground in the front of our line; and, as we found them within gunshot, our leader ordered the two wings to advance swiftly, and give them a salvo on each wing with their shot, which was done. They then went off, I suppose to give an account of the reception they were like to meet with; indeed, that salute cloyed their stomachs, for they immediately halted, stood a while to consider of it, and wheeling off to the left, they gave over their design for that time, which was very agreeable to our circumstances.

Two days after we came to the city of Naun, or Naum; we thanked the governor for his care of us, and collected to the value of a hundred crowns, or thereabouts, which we gave to the soldiers sent to guard us; and here we rested one day. This is a garrison indeed, and there were nine hundred soldiers kept here; but the reason of it was, that formerly the Muscovite frontiers lay nearer to them than they now do, the Muscovites having abandoned that part of the country, which lies from this city west for about two hundred miles, as desolate and unfit for use; and more especially being so very remote, and so difficult to send troops thither for its defence; for we were yet above two thousand miles from Muscovy properly so called. After this we passed several great rivers, and two dreadful deserts; one of which we were sixteen days passing over; and on the 13th of April we came to the frontiers of the Muscovite dominions. I think the first town or fortress, whichever it may he called, that belonged to the Czar, was called Arguna, being on the west side of the river Arguna.

I could not but feel great satisfaction that I was arrived in a country governed by Christians; for though the Muscovites do, in my opinion, but just deserve the name of Christians, yet such they pretend to be, and are very devout in their way. It would certainly occur to any reflecting man who travels the world as I have done, what a blessing it is to be brought into the world where the name of God and a Redeemer is known, adored, and worshipped; and not where the people, given up to strong delusions, worship the devil, and prostrate themselves to monsters, elements, horrid- shaped animals, and monstrous images. Not a town or city we passed through but had their pagodas, their idols, and their temples, and ignorant people worshipping even the works of their own hands. Now we came where, at least, a face of the Christian worship appeared; where the knee was bowed to Jesus: and whether ignorantly or not, yet the Christian religion was owned, and the name of the true God was called upon and adored; and it made my soul rejoice to see it. I saluted the brave Scots merchant with my first acknowledgment of this; and taking him by the hand, I said to him, "Blessed be God, we are once again amongst Christians." He smiled, and answered, "Do not rejoice too soon, countryman; these Muscovites are but an odd sort of Christians; and but for the name of it you may see very little of the substance for some months further of our journey."— "Well," says I, "but still it is better than paganism, and worshipping of devils."—"Why, I will tell you," says he; "except the Russian soldiers in the garrisons, and a few of the inhabitants of the cities upon the road, all the rest of this country, for above a thousand miles farther, is inhabited by the worst and most ignorant of pagans." And so, indeed, we found it.

We now launched into the greatest piece of solid earth that is to be found in any part of the world; we had, at least, twelve thousand miles to the sea eastward; two thousand to the bottom of the Baltic Sea westward; and above three thousand, if we left that sea, and went on west, to the British and French channels: we had full five thousand miles to the Indian or Persian Sea south; and about eight hundred to the Frozen Sea north.

We advanced from the river Arguna by easy and moderate journeys, and were very visibly obliged to the care the Czar has taken to have cities and towns built in as many places as it is possible to place them, where his soldiers keep garrison, something like the stationary soldiers placed by the Romans in the remotest countries of their empire; some of which I had read of were placed in Britain, for the security of commerce, and for the lodging of travellers. Thus it was here; for wherever we came, though at these towns and stations the garrisons and governors were Russians, and professed Christians, yet the inhabitants were mere pagans, sacrificing to idols, and worshipping the sun, moon, and stars, or all the host of heaven; and not only so, but were, of all the heathens and pagans that ever I met with, the most barbarous, except only that they did not eat men's flesh.

Some instances of this we met with in the country between Arguna, where we enter the Muscovite dominions, and a city of Tartars and Russians together, called Nortziousky, in which is a continued desert or forest, which cost us twenty days to travel over. In a village near the last of these places I had the curiosity to go and see their way of living, which is most brutish and unsufferable. They had, I suppose, a great sacrifice that day; for there stood out, upon an old stump of a tree, a diabolical kind of idol made of wood; it was dressed up, too, in the most filthy manner; its upper garment was of sheepskins, with the wool outward; a great Tartar bonnet on the head, with two horns growing through it; it was about eight feet high, yet had no feet or legs, nor any other proportion of parts.

This scarecrow was set up at the outer side of the village; and when I came near to it there were sixteen or seventeen creatures all lying flat upon the ground round this hideous block of wood; I saw no motion among them, any more than if they had been all logs, like the idol, and at first I really thought they had been so; but, when I came a little nearer, they started up upon their feet, and raised a howl, as if it had been so many deep-mouthed hounds, and walked away, as if they were displeased at our disturbing them. A little way off from the idol, and at the door of a hut, made of sheep and cow skins dried, stood three men with long knives in their hands; and in the middle of the tent appeared three sheep killed, and one young bullock. These, it seems, were sacrifices to that senseless log of an idol; the three men were priests belonging to it, and the seventeen prostrated wretches were the people who brought the offering, and were offering their prayers to that stock.

I confess I was more moved at their stupidity and brutish worship of a hobgoblin than ever I was at anything in my life, and, overcome with rage, I rode up to the hideous idol, and with my sword made a stroke at the bonnet that was on its head, and cut it in two; and one of our men that was with me, taking hold of the sheepskin that covered it, pulled at it, when, behold, a most hideous outcry ran through the village, and two or three hundred people came about my ears, so that I was glad to scour for it, for some had bows and arrows; but I resolved from that moment to visit them again. Our caravan rested three nights at the town, which was about four miles off, in order to provide some horses which they wanted, several of the horses having been lamed and jaded with the long march over the last desert; so we had some leisure here to put my design in execution. I communicated it to the Scots merchant, of whose courage I had sufficient testimony; I told him what I had seen, and with what indignation I had since thought that human nature could be so degenerate; I told him if I could get but four or five men well armed to go with me, I was resolved to go and destroy that vile, abominable idol, and let them see that it had no power to help itself, and consequently could not be an object of worship, or to be prayed to, much less help them that offered sacrifices to it.

He at first objected to my plan as useless, seeing that, owing to the gross ignorance of the people, they could not be brought to profit by the lesson I meant to teach them; and added that, from his knowledge of the country and its customs, he feared we should fall into great peril by giving offence to these brutal idol worshippers. This somewhat stayed my purpose, but I was still uneasy all that day to put my project in execution; and that evening, meeting the Scots merchant in our walk about the town, I again called upon him to aid me in it. When he found me resolute he said that, on further thoughts, he could not but applaud the design, and told me I should not go alone, but he would go with me; but he would go first and bring a stout fellow, one of his countrymen, to go also with us; "and one," said he, "as famous for his zeal as you can desire any one to be against such devilish things as these." So we agreed to go, only we three and my man-servant, and resolved to put it in execution the following night about midnight, with all possible secrecy.

We thought it better to delay it till the next night, because the caravan being to set forward in the morning, we suppose the governor could not pretend to give them any satisfaction upon us when we were out of his power. The Scots merchant, as steady in his resolution for the enterprise as bold in executing, brought me a Tartar's robe or gown of sheepskins, and a bonnet, with a bow and arrows, and had provided the same for himself and his countryman, that the people, if they saw us, should not determine who we were. All the first night we spent in mixing up some combustible matter, with aqua vitae, gunpowder, and such other materials as we could get; and having a good quantity of tar in a little pot, about an hour after night we set out upon our expedition.

We came to the place about eleven o'clock at night, and found that the people had not the least suspicion of danger attending their idol. The night was cloudy: yet the moon gave us light enough to see that the idol stood just in the same posture and place that it did before. The people seemed to be all at their rest; only that in the great hut, where we saw the three priests, we saw a light, and going up close to the door, we heard people talking as if there were five or six of them; we concluded, therefore, that if we set wildfire to the idol, those men would come out immediately, and run up to the place to rescue it from destruction; and what to do with them we knew not. Once we thought of carrying it away, and setting fire to it at a distance; but when we came to handle it, we found it too bulky for our carriage, so we were at a loss again. The second Scotsman was for setting fire to the hut, and knocking the creatures that were there on the head when they came out; but I could not join with that; I was against killing them, if it were possible to avoid it. "Well, then," said the Scots merchant, "I will tell you what we will do: we will try to make them prisoners, tie their hands, and make them stand and see their idol destroyed."

As it happened, we had twine or packthread enough about us, which we used to tie our firelocks together with; so we resolved to attack these people first, and with as little noise as we could. The first thing we did, we knocked at the door, when one of the priests coming to it, we immediately seized upon him, stopped his mouth, and tied his hands behind him, and led him to the idol, where we gagged him that he might not make a noise, tied his feet also together, and left him on the ground.

Two of us then waited at the door, expecting that another would come out to see what the matter was; but we waited so long till the third man came back to us; and then nobody coming out, we knocked again gently, and immediately out came two more, and we served them just in the same manner, but were obliged to go all with them, and lay them down by the idol some distance from one another; when, going back, we found two more were come out of the door, and a third stood behind them within the door. We seized the two, and immediately tied them, when the third, stepping back and crying out, my Scots merchant went in after them, and taking out a composition we had made that would only smoke and stink, he set fire to it, and threw it in among them. By that time the other Scotsman and my man, taking charge of the two men already bound, and tied together also by the arm, led them away to the idol, and left them there, to see if their idol would relieve them, making haste back to us.

When the fuze we had thrown in had filled the hut with so much smoke that they were almost suffocated, we threw in a small leather bag of another kind, which flamed like a candle, and, following it in, we found there were but four people, who, as we supposed, had been about some of their diabolical sacrifices. They appeared, in short, frightened to death, at least so as to sit trembling and stupid, and not able to speak either, for the smoke.

We quickly took them from the hut, where the smoke soon drove us out, bound them as we had done the other, and all without any noise. Then we carried them all together to the idol; when we came there, we fell to work with him. First, we daubed him all over, and his robes also, with tar, and tallow mixed with brimstone; then we stopped his eyes and ears and mouth full of gunpowder, and wrapped up a great piece of wildfire in his bonnet; then sticking all the combustibles we had brought with us upon him, we looked about to see if we could find anything else to help to burn him; when my Scotsman remembered that by the hut, where the men were, there lay a heap of dry forage; away he and the other Scotsman ran and fetched their arms full of that. When we had done this, we took all our prisoners, and brought them, having untied their feet and ungagged their mouths, and made them stand up, and set them before their monstrous idol, and then set fire to the whole.

We stayed by it a quarter of an hour or thereabouts, till the powder in the eyes and mouth and ears of the idol blew up, and, as we could perceive, had split altogether; and in a word, till we saw it burned so that it would soon be quite consumed. We then began to think of going away; but the Scotsman said, "No, we must not go, for these poor deluded wretches will all throw themselves into the fire, and burn themselves with the idol." So we resolved to stay till the forage has burned down too, and then came away and left them. After the feat was performed, we appeared in the morning among our fellow-travellers, exceedingly busy in getting ready for our journey; nor could any man suppose that we had been anywhere but in our beds.

But the affair did not end so; the next day came a great number of the country people to the town gates, and in a most outrageous manner demanded satisfaction of the Russian governor for the insulting their priests and burning their great Cham Chi-Thaungu. The people of Nertsinkay were at first in a great consternation, for they said the Tartars were already no less than thirty thousand strong. The Russian governor sent out messengers to appease them, assuring them that he knew nothing of it, and that there had not a soul in his garrison been abroad, so that it could not be from anybody there: but if they could let him know who did it, they should be exemplarily punished. They returned haughtily, that all the country reverenced the great Cham Chi-Thaungu, who dwelt in the sun, and no mortal would have dared to offer violence to his image but some Christian miscreant; and they therefore resolved to denounce war against him and all the Russians, who, they said, were miscreants and Christians.

The governor, unwilling to make a breach, or to have any cause of war alleged to be given by him, the Czar having strictly charged him to treat the conquered country with gentleness, gave them all the good words he could. At last he told them there was a caravan gone towards Russia that morning, and perhaps it was some of them who had done them this injury; and that if they would be satisfied with that, he would send after them to inquire into it. This seemed to appease them a little; and accordingly the governor sent after us, and gave us a particular account how the thing was; intimating withal, that if any in our caravan had done it they should make their escape; but that whether we had done it or no, we should make all the haste forward that was possible: and that, in the meantime, he would keep them in play as long as he could.

This was very friendly in the governor; however, when it came to the caravan, there was nobody knew anything of the matter; and as for us that were guilty, we were least of all suspected. However, the captain of the caravan for the time took the hint that the governor gave us, and we travelled two days and two nights without any considerable stop, and then we lay at a village called Plothus: nor did we make any long stop here, but hastened on towards Jarawena, another Muscovite colony, and where we expected we should be safe. But upon the second day's march from Plothus, by the clouds of dust behind us at a great distance, it was plain we were pursued. We had entered a vast desert, and had passed by a great lake called Schanks Oser, when we perceived a large body of horse appear on the other side of the lake, to the north, we travelling west. We observed they went away west, as we did, but had supposed we would have taken that side of the lake, whereas we very happily took the south side; and in two days more they disappeared again: for they, believing we were still before them, pushed on till they came to the Udda, a very great river when it passes farther north, but when we came to it we found it narrow and fordable.

The third day they had either found their mistake, or had intelligence of us, and came pouring in upon us towards dusk. We had, to our great satisfaction, just pitched upon a convenient place for our camp; for as we had just entered upon a desert above five hundred miles over, where we had no towns to lodge at, and, indeed, expected none but the city Jarawena, which we had yet two days' march to; the desert, however, had some few woods in it on this side, and little rivers, which ran all into the great river Udda; it was in a narrow strait, between little but very thick woods, that we pitched our camp that night, expecting to be attacked before morning. As it was usual for the Mogul Tartars to go

287

about in troops in that desert, so the caravans always fortify themselves every night against them, as against armies of robbers; and it was, therefore, no new thing to be pursued. But we had this night a most advantageous camp: for as we lay between two woods, with a little rivulet running just before our front, we could not be surrounded, or attacked any way but in our front or rear. We took care also to make our front as strong as we could, by placing our packs, with the camels and horses, all in a line, on the inside of the river, and felling some trees in our rear.

In this posture we encamped for the night; but the enemy was upon us before we had finished. They did not come on like thieves, as we expected, but sent three messengers to us, to demand the men to be delivered to them that had abused their priests and burned their idol, that they might burn them with fire; and upon this, they said, they would go away, and do us no further harm, otherwise they would destroy us all. Our men looked very blank at this message, and began to stare at one another to see who looked with the most guilt in their faces; but nobody was the word—nobody did it. The leader of the caravan sent word he was well assured that it was not done by any of our camp; that we were peaceful merchants, travelling on our business; that we had done no harm to them or to any one else; and that, therefore, they must look further for the enemies who had injured them, for we were not the people; so they desired them not to disturb us, for if they did we should defend ourselves.

They were far from being satisfied with this for an answer: and a great crowd of them came running down in the morning, by break of day, to our camp; but seeing us so well posted, they durst come no farther than the brook in our front, where they stood in such number as to terrify us very much; indeed, some spoke of ten thousand. Here they stood and looked at us a while, and then, setting up a great howl, let fly a crowd of arrows among us; but we were well enough sheltered under our baggage, and I do not remember that one of us was hurt.

Some time after this we saw them move a little to our right, and expected them on the rear: when a cunning fellow, a Cossack of Jarawena, calling to the leader of the caravan, said to him, "I will send all these people away to Sibeilka." This was a city four or five days' journey at least to the right, and rather behind us. So he takes his bow and arrows, and getting on horseback, he rides away from our rear directly, as it were back to Nertsinskay; after this he takes a great circuit about, and comes directly on the army of the Tartars as if he had been sent express to tell them a long story that the people who had burned the Cham Chi-Thaungu were gone to Sibeilka, with a caravan of miscreants, as he called them—that is to say, Christians; and that they had resolved to burn the god Scal-Isar, belonging to the Tonguses. As this fellow was himself a Tartar, and perfectly spoke their language, he counterfeited so well that they all believed him, and away they drove in a violent hurry to Sibeilka. In less than three hours they were entirely out of our sight, and we never heard any more of them, nor whether they went to Sibeilka or no. So we passed away safely on to Jarawena, where there was a Russian garrison, and there we rested five days.

From this city we had a frightful desert, which held us twenty- three days' march. We furnished ourselves with some tents here, for the better accommodating ourselves in the night; and the leader of the caravan procured sixteen waggons of the country, for carrying our water or provisions, and these carriages were our defence every night round our little camp; so that had the Tartars appeared, unless they had been very numerous indeed, they would not have been able to hurt us. We may well be supposed to have wanted rest again after this long journey; for in this desert we neither saw house nor tree, and scarce a bush; though we saw abundance of the sable-hunters, who are all Tartars of Mogul Tartary; of which this country is a part; and they frequently attack small caravans, but we saw no numbers of them together.

After we had passed this desert we came into a country pretty well inhabited—that is to say, we found towns and castles, settled by the Czar with garrisons of stationary soldiers, to protect the caravans and defend the country against the Tartars, who would otherwise make it very dangerous travelling; and his czarish majesty has given such strict orders for the well guarding the caravans, that, if there are any Tartars heard of in the country, detachments of the garrison are always sent to see the travellers safe from station to station. Thus the governor of Adinskoy, whom I had an opportunity to make a visit to, by means of the Scots merchant, who was acquainted with him, offered us a guard of fifty men, if we thought there was any danger, to the next station.

I thought, long before this, that as we came nearer to Europe we should find the country better inhabited, and the people more civilised; but I found myself mistaken in both: for we had yet the nation of the Tonguses to pass through, where we saw the same tokens of paganism and barbarity as before; only, as they were conquered by the Muscovites, they were not so dangerous, but for rudeness of manners and idolatry no people in the world ever went beyond them. They are all clothed in skins of beasts, and their houses are built of the same; you know not a man from a woman, neither by the ruggedness of their countenances nor their clothes; and in the winter, when the ground is covered with snow, they live underground in vaults, which have

290

cavities going from one to another. If the Tartars had their Cham Chi-Thaungu for a whole village or country, these had idols in every hut and every cave. This country, I reckon, was, from the desert I spoke of last, at least four hundred miles, half of it being another desert, which took us up twelve days' severe travelling, without house or tree; and we were obliged again to carry our own provisions, as well water as bread. After we were out of this desert and had travelled two days, we came to Janezay, a Muscovite city or station, on the great river Janezay, which, they told us there, parted Europe from Asia.

All the country between the river Oby and the river Janezay is as entirely pagan, and the people as barbarous, as the remotest of the Tartars. I also found, which I observed to the Muscovite governors whom I had an opportunity to converse with, that the poor pagans are not much wiser, or nearer Christianity, for being under the Muscovite government, which they acknowledged was true enough—but that, as they said, was none of their business; that if the Czar expected to convert his Siberian, Tonguse, or Tartar subjects, it should be done by sending clergymen among them, not soldiers; and they added, with more sincerity than I expected, that it was not so much the concern of their monarch to make the people Christians as to make them subjects.

From this river to the Oby we crossed a wild uncultivated country, barren of people and good management, otherwise it is in itself a pleasant, fruitful, and agreeable country. What inhabitants we found in it are all pagans, except such as are sent among them from Russia; for this is the country—I mean on both sides the river Oby—whither the Muscovite criminals that are not put to death are banished, and from whence it is next to impossible they should ever get away. I have nothing material to say of my particular affairs till I came to Tobolski, the capital city of Siberia, where I continued some time on the following account.

We had now been almost seven months on our journey, and winter began to come on apace; whereupon my partner and I called a council about our particular affairs, in which we found it proper, as we were bound for England, to consider how to dispose of ourselves. They told us of sledges and reindeer to carry us over the snow in the winter time, by which means, indeed, the Russians travel more in winter than they can in summer, as in these sledges they are able to run night and day: the snow, being frozen, is one universal covering to nature, by which the hills, vales, rivers, and lakes are all smooth and hard is a stone, and they run upon the surface, without any regard to what is underneath.

But I had no occasion to urge a winter journey of this kind. I was bound to England, not to Moscow, and my route lay two ways: either I must go on as the caravan went, till I came to Jarislaw, and then go off west for Narva and the Gulf of Finland, and so on to Dantzic, where I might possibly sell my China cargo to good advantage; or I must leave the caravan at a little town on the Dwina, from whence I had but six days by water to Archangel, and from thence might be sure of shipping either to England, Holland, or Hamburg.

Now, to go any one of these journeys in the winter would have been preposterous; for as to Dantzic, the Baltic would have been frozen up and I could not get passage; and to go by land in those countries was far less safe than among the Mogul Tartars; likewise, as to Archangel in October, all the ships would be gone from thence, and even the merchants who dwell there in summer retire south to Moscow in the winter, when the ships are gone; so that I could have nothing but extremity of cold to encounter, with a scarcity of provisions, and must lie in an empty town all the winter. Therefore, upon the whole, I thought it much my better way to let the caravan go, and make provision to winter where I was, at Tobolski, in Siberia, in the latitude of about sixty degrees, where I was sure of three things to wear out a cold winter with, viz. plenty of provisions, such as the country afforded, a warm house, with fuel enough, and excellent company.

I was now in quite a different climate from my beloved island, where I never felt cold, except when I had my ague; on the contrary, I had much to do to bear any clothes on my back, and never made any fire but without doors, which was necessary for dressing my food, &c. Now I had three good vests, with large robes or gowns over them, to hang down to the feet, and button close to the wrists; and all these lined with furs, to make them sufficiently warm. As to a warm house, I must confess I greatly dislike our way in England of making fires in every room of the house in open chimneys, which, when the fire is out, always keeps the air in the room cold as the climate. So I took an apartment in a good house in the town, and ordered a chimney to be built like a furnace, in the centre of six several rooms, like a stove; the funnel to carry the smoke went up one way, the door to come at the fire went in another, and all the rooms were kept equally warm, but no fire seen, just as they heat baths in England. By this means we had always the same climate in all the rooms, and an equal heat was preserved, and yet we saw no fire, nor were ever incommoded with smoke.

The most wonderful thing of all was, that it should be possible to meet with good company here, in a country so barbarous as this—one of the most northerly parts of Europe. But this being the country where the state criminals of Muscovy, as I observed before, are all banished, the city was full of Russian noblemen, gentlemen, soldiers, and courtiers. Here was the famous Prince Galitzin, the old German Robostiski, and several other persons of note, and some ladies. By means of my Scotch merchant, whom, nevertheless, I parted with here, I made an acquaintance with several of these gentlemen; and from these, in the long winter nights in which I stayed here, I received several very agreeable visits.

Chapter 16

Safe Arrival in England

It was talking one night with a certain prince, one of the banished ministers of state belonging to the Czar, that the discourse of my particular case began. He had been telling me abundance of fine things of the greatness, the magnificence, the dominions, and the absolute power of the Emperor of the Russians: I interrupted him, and told him I was a greater and more powerful prince than ever the Czar was, though my dominion were not so large, or my people so many. The Russian grandee looked a little surprised, and, fixing his eyes steadily upon me, began to wonder what I meant. I said his wonder would cease when I had explained myself, and told him the story at large of my living in the island; and then how I managed both myself and the people that were under me, just as I have since minuted it down. They were exceedingly taken with the story, and especially the prince, who told me, with a sigh, that the true greatness of life was to be masters of ourselves; that he would not have exchanged such a state of life as mine to be Czar of Muscovy; and that he found more felicity in the retirement he seemed to be banished to there, than ever he found in the highest authority he enjoyed in the court of his master the Czar; that the height of human wisdom was to bring our tempers down to our circumstances, and to make a calm within, under the weight of the greatest storms without. When he came first hither, he said, he used to tear the hair from his head, and the clothes from his back, as others had done before him; but a little time and consideration had made him look into himself, as well as round him to things without; that he found the mind of man, if it was but once brought to reflect upon the state of universal life, and how little this world was concerned in its true felicity, was perfectly capable of making a felicity for itself, fully satisfying to itself, and suitable to its own best ends and desires, with but very little assistance from the world. That being now deprived of all the fancied felicity which he enjoyed in the full exercise of worldly pleasures, he said he was at leisure to look upon the dark side of them, where he found all manner of deformity; and was now convinced that virtue only makes a man truly wise, rich, and great, and preserves him in the way to a superior happiness in a future state; and in this, he said, they were more happy in their banishment than all their enemies were, who had the full possession of all the wealth and power they had left behind them. "Nor, sir," says he, "do I bring my mind to this politically, from the necessity of my circumstances, which some call miserable; but, if I know anything of myself, I would not now go back, though the Czar my master should call me, and reinstate me in all my former grandeur."

He spoke this with so much warmth in his temper, so much earnestness and motion of his spirits, that it was evident it was the true sense of his soul; there was no room to doubt his sincerity. I told him I once thought myself a kind of monarch in my old station, of which I had given him an account; but that I thought he was not only a monarch, but a great conqueror; for he that had got a victory over his own exorbitant desires, and the absolute dominion over himself, he whose reason entirely governs his will, is certainly greater than he that conquers a city.

I had been here eight months, and a dark, dreadful winter I thought it; the cold so intense that I could not so much as look abroad without being wrapped in furs, and a kind of mask of fur before my face, with only a hole for breath, and two for sight: the little daylight we had was for three months not above five hours a day, and six at most; only that the snow lying on the ground continually, and the weather being clear, it was never quite dark. Our horses were kept, or rather starved, underground; and as for our servants, whom we hired here to look after ourselves and horses, we had, every now and then, their fingers and toes to thaw and take care of, lest they should mortify and fall off.

It is true, within doors we were warm, the houses being close, the walls thick, the windows small, and the glass all double. Our food was chiefly the flesh of deer, dried and cured in the season; bread good enough, but baked as biscuits; dried fish of several sorts, and some flesh of mutton, and of buffaloes, which is pretty good meat. All the stores of provisions for the winter are laid up in the summer, and well cured: our drink was water, mixed with aqua vitae instead of brandy; and for a treat, mead instead of wine, which, however, they have very good. The hunters, who venture abroad all weathers, frequently brought us in fine venison, and sometimes bear's flesh, but we did not much care for the last. We had a good stock of tea, with which we treated our friends, and we lived cheerfully and well, all things considered.

It was now March, the days grown considerably longer, and the weather at least tolerable; so the other travellers began to prepare sledges to carry them over the snow, and to get things ready to be going; but my measures being fixed, as I have said, for Archangel, and not for Muscovy or the Baltic, I made no motion; knowing very well that the ships from the south do not set out for that part of the world till May or June, and that if I was there by the beginning of August, it would be as soon as any ships would be ready to sail. Therefore I made no haste to be gone, as others did: in a word, I saw a great many people, nay, all the travellers, go away before me. It seems every year they go from thence to Muscovy, for trade, to carry furs, and buy necessaries, which they bring back with them to furnish their shops: also others went on the same errand to Archangel.

In the month of May I began to make all ready to pack up; and, as I was doing this, it occurred to me that, seeing all these people were banished by the Czar to Siberia, and yet, when they came there, were left at liberty to go whither they would, why they did not then go away to any part of the world, wherever they thought fit: and I began to examine what should hinder them from making such an attempt. But my wonder was over when I entered upon that subject with the person I have mentioned, who answered me thus: "Consider, first, sir," said he, "the place where we are; and, secondly, the condition we are in; especially the generality of the people who are banished thither. We are surrounded with stronger things than bars or bolts; on the north side, an unnavigable ocean, where ship never sailed, and boat never swam; every other way we have above a thousand miles to pass through the Czar's own dominion, and by ways utterly impassable, except by the roads made by the government, and through the towns garrisoned by his troops; in short, we could neither pass undiscovered by the road, nor subsist any other way, so that it is in vain to attempt it."

I was silenced at once, and found that they were in a prison every jot as secure as if they had been locked up in the castle at Moscow: however, it came into my thoughts that I might certainly be made an instrument to procure the escape of this excellent person; and that, whatever hazard I ran, I would certainly try if I could carry him off. Upon this, I took an occasion one evening to tell him my thoughts. I represented to him that it was very easy for me to carry him away, there being no guard over him in the country; and as I was not going to Moscow, but to Archangel, and that I went in the retinue of a caravan, by which I was not obliged to lie in the stationary towns in the desert, but could encamp every night where I would, we might easily pass uninterrupted to Archangel, where I would immediately secure him on board an English ship, and carry him safe along with me; and as to his subsistence and other particulars, it should be my care till he could better supply himself.

He heard me very attentively, and looked earnestly on me all the while I spoke; nay, I could see in his very face that what I said put his spirits into an exceeding ferment; his colour frequently changed, his eyes looked red, and his heart fluttered, till it might be even perceived in his countenance; nor could he immediately answer me when I had done, and, as it were, hesitated what he would say to it; but after he had paused a little, he embraced me, and said, "How unhappy are we, unguarded creatures as we are, that even our greatest acts of friendship are made snares unto us, and we are made tempters of one another!" He then heartily thanked me for my offers of service, but withstood resolutely the arguments I used to urge him to set himself free. He declared, in earnest terms, that he was fully bent on remaining where he was rather than seek to return to his former miserable greatness, as he called it: where the seeds of pride, ambition, avarice, and luxury might revive, take root, and again overwhelm him. "Let me remain, dear sir," he said, in conclusion—"let me remain in this blessed confinement, banished from the crimes of life, rather than purchase a show of freedom at the expense of the liberty of my reason, and at the future happiness which I now have in my view, but should then, I fear, quickly lose sight of; for I am but flesh; a man, a mere man; and have passions and affections as likely to possess and overthrow me as any man: Oh, be not my friend and tempter both together!"

If I was surprised before, I was quite dumb now, and stood silent, looking at him, and, indeed, admiring what I saw. The struggle in his soul was so great that, though the weather was extremely cold, it put him into a most violent heat; so I said a word or two, that I would leave him to consider of it, and wait on him again, and then I withdrew to my own apartment.

About two hours after I heard somebody at or near the door of my room, and I was going to open the door, but he had opened it and come in. "My dear friend," says he, "you had almost overset me, but I am recovered. Do not take it ill that I do not close with your offer. I assure you it is not for want of sense of the kindness of it in you; and I came to make the most sincere acknowledgment of it to you; but I hope I have got the victory over myself."—"My lord," said I, "I hope you are fully satisfied that you do not resist the call of Heaven."—"Sir," said he, "if it had been from Heaven, the same power would have influenced me to have accepted it; but I hope, and am fully satisfied, that it is from Heaven that I decline it, and I have infinite satisfaction in the parting, that you shall leave me an honest man still, though not a free man."

I had nothing to do but to acquiesce, and make professions to him of my having no end in it but a sincere desire to serve him. He embraced me very passionately, and assured me he was sensible of that, and should always acknowledge it; and with that he offered me a very fine present of sables—too much, indeed, for me to accept from a man in his circumstances, and I would have avoided them, but he would not be refused. The next morning I sent my servant to his lordship with a small present of tea, and two pieces of China damask, and four little wedges of Japan gold, which did not all weigh above six ounces or thereabouts, but were far short of the value of his sables, which, when I came to England, I found worth near two hundred pounds. He accepted the tea, and one piece of the damask, and one of the pieces of gold, which had a fine stamp upon it, of the Japan coinage, which I found he took for the rarity of it, but would not take any more: and he sent word by my servant that he desired to speak with me.

When I came to him he told me I knew what had passed between us, and hoped I would not move him any more in that affair; but that, since I had made such a generous offer to him, he asked me if I had kindness enough to offer the same to another person that he would name to me, in whom he had a great share of concern. In a word, he told me it was his only son; who, though I had not seen him, was in the same condition with himself, and above two hundred miles from him, on the other side of the Oby; but that, if I consented, he would send for him.

I made no hesitation, but told him I would do it. I made some ceremony in letting him understand that it was wholly on his account; and that, seeing I could not prevail on him, I would show my respect to him by my concern for his son. He sent the next day for his son; and in about twenty days he came back with the messenger, bringing six or seven horses, loaded with very rich furs, which, in the whole, amounted to a very great value. His servants brought the horses into the town, but left the young lord at a distance till night, when he came incognito into our apartment, and his father presented him to me; and, in short, we concerted the manner of our travelling, and everything proper for the journey.

I had bought a considerable quantity of sables, black fox-skins, fine ermines, and such other furs as are very rich in that city, in exchange for some of the goods I had brought from China; in particular for the cloves and nutmegs, of which I sold the greatest part here, and the rest afterwards at Archangel, for a much better price than I could have got at London; and my partner, who was sensible of the profit, and whose business, more particularly than mine, was merchandise, was mightily pleased with our stay, on account of the traffic we made here.

It was the beginning of June when I left this remote place. We were now reduced to a very small caravan, having only thirty-two horses and camels in all, which passed for mine, though my new guest was proprietor of eleven of them. It was natural also that I should take more servants with me than I had before; and the young lord passed for my steward; what great man I passed for myself I know not, neither did it concern me to inquire. We had here the worst and the largest desert to pass over that we met with in our whole journey; I call it the worst, because the way was very deep in some places, and very uneven in others; the best we had to say for it was, that we thought we had no troops of Tartars or robbers to fear, as they never came on this side of the river Oby, or at least very seldom; but we found it otherwise.

My young lord had a faithful Siberian servant, who was perfectly acquainted with the country, and led us by private roads, so that we avoided coming into the principal towns and cities upon the great road, such as Tumen, Soloy Kamaskoy, and several others; because the Muscovite garrisons which are kept there are very curious and strict in their observation upon travellers, and searching lest any of the banished persons of note should make their escape that way into Muscovy; but, by this means, as we were kept out of the cities, so our whole journey was a desert, and we were obliged to encamp and lie in our tents, when we might have had very good accommodation in the cities on the way; this the young lord was so sensible of, that he would not allow us to lie abroad when we came to several cities on the way, but lay abroad himself, with his servant, in the woods, and met us always at the appointed places.

We had just entered Europe, having passed the river Kama, which in these parts is the boundary between Europe and Asia, and the first city on the European side was called Soloy Kamaskoy, that is, the great city on the river Kama. And here we thought to see some evident alteration in the people; but we were mistaken, for as we had a vast desert to pass, which is near seven hundred miles long in some places, but not above two hundred miles over where we passed it, so, till we came past that horrible place, we found very little difference between that country and Mogul Tartary. The people are mostly pagans; their houses and towns full of idols; and their way of living wholly barbarous, except in the cities and villages near them, where they are Christians, as they call themselves, of the Greek Church: but have their religion mingled with so many relics of superstition, that it is scarce to be known in some places from mere sorcery and witchcraft.

In passing this forest (after all our dangers were, to our imagination, escaped), I thought, indeed, we must have been plundered and robbed, and perhaps murdered, by a troop of thieves: of what country they were I am yet at a loss to know; but they were all on horseback, carried bows and arrows, and were at first about forty-five in number. They came so near to us as to be within two musket-shot, and, asking no questions, surrounded

303

us with their horses, and looked very earnestly upon us twice; at length, they placed themselves just in our way; upon which we drew up in a little line, before our camels, being not above sixteen men in all. Thus drawn up, we halted, and sent out the Siberian servant, who attended his lord, to see who they were; his master was the more willing to let him go, because he was not a little apprehensive that they were a Siberian troop sent out after him. The man came up near them with a flag of truce, and called to them; but though he spoke several of their languages, or dialects of languages rather, he could not understand a word they said; however, after some signs to him not to come near them at his peril, the fellow came back no wiser than he went; only that by their dress, he said, he believed them to be some Tartars of Kalmuck, or of the Circassian hordes, and that there must be more of them upon the great desert, though he never heard that any of them were seen so far north before.

This was small comfort to us; however, we had no remedy: there was on our left hand, at about a quarter of a mile distance, a little grove, and very near the road. I immediately resolved we should advance to those trees, and fortify ourselves as well as we could there; for, first, I considered that the trees would in a great measure cover us from their arrows; and, in the next place, they could not come to charge us in a body: it was, indeed, my old Portuguese pilot who proposed it, and who had this excellency attending him, that he was always readiest and most apt to direct and encourage us in cases of the most danger. We advanced immediately, with what speed we could, and gained that little wood; the Tartars, or thieves, for we knew not what to call them, keeping their stand, and not attempting to hinder us. When we came thither, we found, to our great satisfaction, that it was a swampy piece of ground, and on the one side a very great spring of water, which, running out in a little brook, was a little farther joined by another of the like size; and was, in short, the source of a considerable river, called afterwards the Wirtska; the trees which grew about this spring were not above two hundred, but very large, and stood pretty thick, so that as soon as we got in, we saw ourselves perfectly safe from the enemy unless they attacked us on foot.

While we stayed here waiting the motion of the enemy some hours, without perceiving that they made any movement, our Portuguese, with some help, cut several arms of trees half off, and laid them hanging across from one tree to another, and in a manner fenced us in. About two hours before night they came down directly upon us; and though we had not perceived it, we found they had been joined by some more, so that they were near fourscore horse; whereof, however, we fancied some were women. They came on till they were within half-shot of our little wood, when we fired one musket without ball, and called to them in the Russian tongue to know what they wanted, and bade them keep off; but they came on with a double fury up to the wood-side, not imagining we were so barricaded that they could not easily break in. Our old pilot was our captain as well as our engineer, and desired us not to fire upon them till they came within pistol-shot, that we might be sure to kill, and that when we did fire we should be sure to take good aim; we bade him give the word of command, which he delayed so long that they were some of them within two pikes' length of us when we let fly. We aimed so true that we killed fourteen of them, and wounded several others, as also several of their horses; for we had all of us loaded our pieces with two or three bullets apiece at least.

They were terribly surprised with our fire, and retreated immediately about one hundred rods from us;

in which time we loaded our pieces again, and seeing them keep that distance, we sallied out, and caught four or five of their horses, whose riders we supposed were killed; and coming up to the dead, we judged they were Tartars, but knew not how they came to make an excursion such an unusual length.

About an hour after they again made a motion to attack us, and rode round our little wood to see where they might break in; but finding us always ready to face them, they went off again; and we resolved not to stir for that night.

We slept little, but spent the most part of the night in strengthening our situation, and barricading the entrances into the wood, and keeping a strict watch. We waited for daylight, and when it came, it gave us a very unwelcome discovery indeed; for the enemy, who we thought were discouraged with the reception they met with, were now greatly increased, and had set up eleven or twelve huts or tents, as if they were resolved to besiege us; and this little camp they had pitched upon the open plain, about three- quarters of a mile from us. I confess I now gave myself over for lost, and all that I had; the loss of my effects did not lie so near me, though very considerable, as the thoughts of falling into the hands of such barbarians at the latter end of my journey, after so many difficulties and hazards as I had gone through, and even in sight of our port, where we expected safety and deliverance. As to my partner, he was raging, and declared that to lose his goods would be his ruin, and that he would rather die than be starved, and he was for fighting to the last drop.

The young lord, a most gallant youth, was for fighting to the last also; and my old pilot was of opinion that we were able to resist them all in the situation we were then in. Thus we spent the day in debates of what we should do; but towards evening we found that the number of our enemies still increased, and we did not know but by the morning they might still be a greater number: so I began to inquire of those people we had brought from Tobolski if there were no private ways by which we might avoid them in the night, and perhaps retreat to some town, or get help to guard us over the desert. The young lord's Siberian servant told us, if we designed to avoid them, and not fight, he would engage to carry us off in the night, to a way that went north, towards the river Petruz, by which he made no question but we might get away, and the Tartars never discover it; but, he said, his lord had told him he would not retreat, but would rather choose to fight. I told him he mistook his lord: for that he was too wise a man to love fighting for the sake of it; that I knew he was brave enough by what he had showed already; but that he knew better than to desire seventeen or eighteen men to fight five hundred, unless an unavoidable necessity forced them to it; and that if he thought it possible for us to escape in the night, we had nothing else to do but to attempt it. He answered, if his lordship gave him such orders, he would lose his life if he did not perform it; we soon brought his lord to give that order, though privately, and we immediately prepared for putting it in practice.

And first, as soon as it began to be dark, we kindled a fire in our little camp, which we kept burning, and prepared so as to make it burn all night, that the Tartars might conclude we were still there; but as soon as it was dark, and we could see the stars (for our guide would not stir before), having all our horses and camels ready loaded, we followed our new guide, who I soon found steered himself by the north star, the country being level for a long way.

After we had travelled two hours very hard, it began to be lighter still; not that it was dark all night, but the moon began to rise, so that, in short, it was rather lighter than we wished it to be; but by six o'clock the next morning we had got above thirty miles, having almost spoiled our horses. Here we found a Russian village, named Kermazinskoy, where we rested, and heard nothing of the Kalmuck Tartars that day. About two hours before night we set out again, and travelled till eight the next morning, though not quite so hard as before; and about seven o'clock we passed a little river, called Kirtza, and came to a good large town inhabited by Russians, called Ozomys; there we heard that several troops of Kalmucks had been abroad upon the desert, but that we were now completely out of danger of them, which was to our great satisfaction. Here we were obliged to get some fresh horses, and having need enough of rest, we stayed five days; and my partner and I agreed to give the honest Siberian who conducted us thither the value of ten pistoles.

In five days more we came to Veussima, upon the river Witzogda, and running into the Dwina: we were there, very happily, near the end of our travels by land, that river being navigable, in seven days' passage, to Archangel. From hence we came to Lawremskoy, the 3rd of July; and providing ourselves with two luggage boats, and a barge for our own convenience, we embarked the 7th, and arrived all safe at Archangel the 18th; having been a year, five months, and three days on the journey, including our stay of about eight months at Tobolski.

We were obliged to stay at this place six weeks for the arrival of the ships, and must have tarried longer, had not a Hamburgher come in above a month sooner than any of the English ships; when, after some consideration that the city of Hamburgh might happen to be as good a market for our goods as London, we all took freight with him; and, having put our goods on board, it was most natural for me to put my steward on board to take care of them; by which means my young lord had a sufficient opportunity to conceal himself, never coming on shore again all the time we stayed there; and this he did that he might not be seen in the city, where some of the Moscow merchants would certainly have seen and discovered him.

We then set sail from Archangel the 20th of August, the same year; and, after no extraordinary bad voyage, arrived safe in the Elbe the 18th of September. Here my partner and I found a very good sale for our goods, as well those of China as the sables, &c., of Siberia: and, dividing the produce, my share amounted to 3475 pounds, 17s 3d., including about six hundred pounds' worth of diamonds, which I purchased at Bengal.

Here the young lord took his leave of us, and went up the Elbe, in order to go to the court of Vienna, where he resolved to seek protection and could correspond with those of his father's friends who were left alive. He did not part without testimonials of gratitude for the service I had done him, and for my kindness to the prince, his father.

To conclude: having stayed near four months in Hamburgh, I came from thence by land to the Hague, where I embarked in the packet, and arrived in London the 10th of January 1705, having been absent from England ten years and nine months. And here, resolving to harass myself no more, I am preparing for a longer journey than all these, having lived seventy-two years a life of infinite variety, and learned sufficiently to know the value of retirement, and the blessing of ending our days in peace.

Printed in Great Britain
by Amazon